Pick
of the
Litter

Pick
of the
Litter

BILL WALLACE

Holiday House / New York

In memory of
J. C.,
who shared so much love with all of us

Library of Congress Cataloging-in-Publication Data
Wallace, Bill, 1947–
Pick of the litter / by Bill Wallace.— 1st ed.
p.   cm.
Summary: Twelve-year-old Tom learns first-hand about honor,
first when he is wrongly accused of lying at school, then when
he faces the risk of losing a puppy he has come to love while
helping his grandfather train hunting dogs, but writing to a
new friend helps him sort his feelings and do the right thing.
ISBN 0-8234-1921-5 (hardcover)
[1. Conduct of life—Fiction.   2. Pointer (Dog breed)—Fiction.
3. Dogs—Training—Fiction.   4. Grandfathers—Fiction.
5. Letters—Fiction].   I. Title.

PZ7.W15473Pi 2005
[Fic]—dc22   2004052321

Chapter 1

My eyes were so tight and hot, the paper in front of me looked red. When I glared at the two columns of gray words, my vision blurred, and the lines squiggled and zigzagged down the page.

I didn't like spelling. No—I take that back.

I *hated* spelling!

What I wanted to do was rip the papers to shreds, storm out the door, and not come back. I could tell Mama I was sick. If that didn't work—what could my teacher do? Send me to the office? Big deal! Mrs. Bowlin never did anything. She probably wouldn't even be there.

Another puff of red clouded my vision when I glanced up from my paper to the window. Kids were still on the playground, but Danny and Mark weren't around—they were headed to the creek to look for frogs and snakes. They were probably already there, finding all sorts of neat stuff.

Not me. I was stuck in the teachers' lounge. All alone. Writing spelling words I missed on the test.

Why would *anyone* have a spelling test on the last Wednesday of school? Nobody had tests the last week of school. It was ridiculous! Stupid.

I hated spelling.

I clutched my pencil in my hand like a dagger.

"I'd like to . . . ," I muttered. Then I turned the pencil back the way it was supposed to be. If I stabbed the paper, I'd just break my lead and have to go sharpen it again. I wrote the word "persuade" at the top of the third column.

"*U*," I snarled to myself. "Not *W*, you dummy!"

Then I wrote it again, right under the first "persuade."

But what I hated even more than spelling was having to write the words—in cursive. I hated *that* more than chicken pox. More than poison ivy.

Mrs. Dunn made us learn cursive in third grade, but when it came to a spelling test we could either write or print. In fourth grade, Mrs. Cooperton made us use cursive. But when we had to write the words we missed, she would accept them either way. With Mrs. Nash . . . we didn't have a choice.

I could remember, back in the old days, when printing was a lot faster. I could do one column of *p*, go back to the top and scamper down with *e*, then back up, and do the *rs*'s. With cursive, I had to write the whole, stinking word. No short-cuts. Just "persuade," "persuade," "persuade," "persuade" . . . until I was so sick of it I could barf.

I ought to go home, I thought. *Why not? The worst that could happen was miss recess tomor-row. I could sneak off and—*

My head snapped up. The sound of the door-knob rattling yanked my eyes from the window, back to the page.

Footsteps.

Probably one of the teachers coming in to get something from the pop machine.

No. The clopping shoes came closer. They stopped right behind me.

"Almost done?" Mrs. Nash's voice made me want to turn and look up at her. I didn't. I just kept writing "persuade," over and over and over again.

She stood there, for a long time, without a word. Finally she moved beside me, turned, and leaned against the edge of the table. She didn't sit on it or my paper, but she was so close, I couldn't get my elbow up there to write. When I realized I couldn't avoid her any longer, I put my pencil down and looked up.

Mrs. Nash's eyebrows arched. "I'm sorry you're mad at me," she began.

All right, I guess I didn't *look up* at her— maybe it was more like a glare.

"But . . . ," she went on, "staying after school to write your spelling words really wasn't my idea. It was *yours*."

My mouth flopped open so wide, my chin almost bumped the table. I snapped my mouth shut and kept it shut.

Mrs. Nash held her school bag in her lap. She reached in, pulled out her grade book, and ran her finger down the page.

"First nine weeks, you struggled a little. Either you didn't know how to study your spelling words, or you didn't take the time to learn them." She flipped the page. "Second nine weeks, you did really well. Only missed two words, right before Christmas vacation"—she turned another page—"and two more right before spring break." She flipped the last page.

"Then you quit!"

I looked up at her, but for only an instant before I turned my eyes away.

"Not only did you quit, but two weeks ago"— she tapped her finger on the page—"you missed five and you didn't turn in your spelling words the next day. I let that one slide. I knew you were worried about your grandfather, and there was a lot going on. But last week you missed two words. I was willing to forget that, too. I know your grandfather was scheduled for surgery on the day after the test. However . . ." She took a breath. "Thursday morning, you told me your paper was in your backpack, but you couldn't find it. You promised you'd keep looking. And?" she asked.

I kept my eyes on the page.

"And?" she repeated.

When I still didn't say anything, she answered herself. "And you spent every spare minute you had, writing the spelling words that you *told me you did* Wednesday. Right?"

"Yes, ma'am."

She sat quietly for a long time. Finally she leaned down, and made me look at her.

"You remember how we've talked about honor?"

"Yes, ma'am."

"Do you remember what honor means?"

"Yes, ma'am. It means doing what's right. Not fighting on the playground, not telling lies, not cheating on a test, and . . . you know . . . stuff like that."

"It means a lot more, Tom. It also means trust. Trust and honor are both forms of respect. You're not on your honor just during school, or when you're taking a test. You're on your honor every day. And Tom . . ."

She made me look at her.

". . . it's not for me, but for *you*. You know what's right—what's honest. You do it, not because someone might catch you, but because it's the right thing to do." She paused. "When you finish, leave your paper right here on the table. I'll pick it up in the morning." She stood and walked across the room. At the door, she hesitated. "Your mom is waiting in the west parking lot. See you to-morrow."

I sat there for a long time. Even though it made me mad to miss going to the creek with my friends, I knew Mrs. Nash was right. I did lie to her. Last week I told her I had done my spelling when I hadn't. This week I figured, since it was the end of school, she wouldn't bother. I'd lied to her. Not just once but . . .

I wrote the word "persuade" again, then again, then again, then . . .

Between "bureau," "tournament," and "per-suade," I ran out of room on the first page. "Quotient" and "variety" took two columns on a second piece of paper.

When I finally finished, I left the papers, hopped up, raced down the hall, out the front door, and around the side of the school. As I came into view of the parking lot, I slowed down and let my shoulders slump. Trudged slowly, almost painfully, toward Mama's car.

Racing to the car wouldn't work. Maybe if I looked sad and remorseful enough, she wouldn't be so tough on me.

Mama never said a word. Not on the way home. Not during supper, not even the next morning when she drove me to school.

In a way, I wish she had. I wish she'd yelled at me, or told Daddy what I did. Or grounded me. Something. Anything!

Not saying one single word made me feel terrible. I didn't think anything could make me feel worse.

At least, that's what I *thought* . . . until Mrs. Nash finished taking attendance and lunch count on Friday morning.

She closed her grade book, stood up, and smoothed down the front of her dress. Then very softly—almost a whisper—she said:

"Thomas. I need to see you in the hall."

Chapter 2

The instant Mrs. Nash closed the door, she wheeled on me. Glaring down with her fists on her hips, she leaned so close that her nose almost touched mine.

"Thomas, until the last three weeks, you have been one of my best students, honest and dependable. I don't have to worry about your getting in trouble on the playground, or cheating on tests.

"But what you did yesterday afternoon was *totally* unacceptable!"

I felt my mouth fall open. I wanted to ask what I did, but she didn't give me the chance.

"You were to finish your spelling words *before* you went home. Not take them with you to work on. You were to stay and then leave them on the table. Go get them—right now!"

Somehow, I managed to force my mouth to work.

"I . . . I . . . but I . . ." Even with my lips moving, I still couldn't talk. All I could do was stammer. Mrs. Nash sighed.

"I never *ever* dreamed I could be so disappointed in you. Even if it *is* the last day of school, I fully intend to call your mother and father in for a conference. I cannot believe you did that."

"Did what?" I gasped, finally.

Mrs. Nash hovered over me. Looking straight up, all I could see was her chin, and her eyes glaring down from beneath her glasses.

"You left without finishing your spelling words."

"I—I finished them, Mrs. Nash."

"Then where are they?"

My arms shook. My legs trembled. My mouth flopped, but no words came out. All I could do was point down the hall toward the teachers' lounge.

Mrs. Nash stomped off. After a few paces, she realized I wasn't following. She turned and crooked her finger. My legs were shaking so hard I didn't know if they'd hold me up. Almost staggering, I followed.

This couldn't be happening. I *did* my words. All five of them. Twenty-five times, each. I even counted them, twice, just to make sure. I left them on the table, like she told me.

It was a dream.

It had to be a bad dream. I was still in my bed, at home. In a second I'd wake up and . . . and . . .

And Mrs. Nash opened the door to the teachers' lounge. Holding it wide open, she made a swooping motion with her arm for me to go in.

Maybe it wasn't a dream.

Come on, I urged. *Wake up. Open your eyes.*

There was the table—TOTALLY EMPTY!

This wasn't a nightmare. I was awake.

"Where are your spelling words, Tom?"

My finger shook when I pointed at the table. Then it curled into a fist, with the rest of my fingers. My arms shook at my side. My knees trembled. Suddenly, I felt dizzy.

"Right there, Mrs. Nash." The words whooshed out of me like a gust of wind. But when I sucked in another breath, I didn't feel dizzy anymore. "I left them right there on the table."

"They're not there now."

I stared at the empty tabletop.

"Did you tell your mother you were done and run off to play with your friends? Are they in your backpack, finished? Or did you simply stop the second I left the building, not write another word, and plan to finish them during class?"

I shook my head.

"Go back to the room and get your spelling words, Tom. Let me see how much you have done."

Don't hold your breath, I told myself, forcing in another gulp of air. *You'll end up flat on your face if you don't keep breathing.* I felt my nostrils clamp together as I struggled to let the air out slowly.

"They were right there," I whispered. "I swear, Mrs. Nash. I finished all . . ." Pausing, I heard a gulping sound when I swallowed. ". . . of them. They were right there. I promise!"

For a long time she stood, looking down at me. I could see the expression on her face, and I could tell she still didn't believe me.

The longer we stood there, the worse I felt. My fists were so tight, my fingernails dug into my palms. My knees locked—muscles straining until I could feel myself shaking all over. And I hurt. Not a hurt like scraping my knee on the sidewalk or getting tackled in football and landing on my shoulder. The hurt was deeper. It was clear down in the pit of my stomach.

A hurt that gnawed on my insides, because I *was* telling her the truth—only she didn't (or couldn't) believe me.

I guess she was waiting for me to "break." Waiting for me to tell her the truth. Waiting for me to go back to the room and get my half-finished list of spelling words out of my backpack.

But I couldn't. I *had* told her the truth. There was nothing more I could do.

"Let's go back to the room," she said, finally.

We were almost out the door when Mrs. Nash stopped. I dodged to get out of her way, but she still bumped into me. "Sorry," she said as she walked to the far side of the teachers' lounge. I stood and watched. In the corner, she leaned over and picked up the trash can. She looked inside, then set it down. Her eyes seemed to scan every part of the room as she turned.

There was a bookshelf on the wall beside the pop machine. She walked to it, looked on each shelf, even felt above the books with her hand. She looked behind the little table where the coffeepot was, and behind the pop machine. Finally her gaze fell on me.

"Go on, Tom. I'll be down there in a second."

"May I stop by the restroom?"

She nodded.

I didn't need to go. I just needed a couple of minutes to quit shaking. Everybody knew something was going on—something was wrong.

She wants to believe me, I thought as I washed my hands at the sink. I glanced at the mirror. The face that looked back at me wasn't a very nice face. It was the face of a liar.

How could Mrs. Nash believe me? I'd lied to her about forgetting my spelling words. She'd trusted me, and I'd lied to her. Even if she wanted to believe me—even though I *was* telling the truth—how could she now?

Why would she even try?

Chapter 3

Friday was the longest day I ever spent in my entire life!

Mrs. Nash didn't say anything when I came back to the room. None of the guys tried to ask what was going on, either. Although I tried my best to look calm and relaxed, everybody could probably tell I was upset.

Mrs. Nash gathered up our social studies, math, and science texts. Then she let people go, one at a time, to return any library books that they had forgotten to bring back.

When Carl Decker went, Mrs. Nash followed him to the door. She had good cause to keep an eye on Carl. He was one of those guys who was always doing stuff he wasn't supposed to.

I couldn't help wondering if I was "one of those guys" now. I didn't *think* I was. But I'd given Mrs. Nash more than enough cause to feel that way about me. From now on, she'd probably watch me like she did Carl. Keep an eye on him until he got where he was headed, then come back to work with us.

Only today, as soon as Carl had time to make it to the library, Mrs. Nash slipped out the door.

The pencil sharpener was on the doorjamb. I found a pencil and went to sharpen it. When I leaned to peek around the corner, Mrs. Nash was no place in sight.

Ms. Lee's room was right across from ours. Her door opened. Mrs. Nash backed out, said "Thank you," then trotted next door to Mr. Marcum's class. I kept sharpening the pencil. Finally she went to Mrs. Meyer's room.

I glanced at my pencil. It was just about down to the nub, so I scampered to my seat. I timed it perfectly, because she came back a second or two after I plopped into my chair.

When Harry Croft went to take his library books, she did the same thing she'd done before.

Harry was always getting into stuff, just like Carl—only worse. Harry was mean. He was always trying to bully people. She waited by the door a moment or two, then slipped out and went in the other direction. My timing was a little off. When she came out of Miss McMaster's room, I was watching under my left elbow. I pretty much knew she saw me, because nobody sticks their elbow in the air and leans under it while they're sharpening a pencil.

Instead of trying to make it to my desk, I just kept grinding.

Mrs. Nash paused at the door and turned like she was watching for Harry.

"That pencil is almost down to the eraser." She whispered so none of the other kids could hear. "Go sit."

Sitting was next to impossible. I wiggled, squirmed, shifted my weight from one cheek to the other. I wondered if she'd already called Mama and Daddy. I wondered if she was waiting for Mrs. Bowlin to come and take me to the office.

I didn't know what was going to happen to me. The not knowing made every breath stick in my throat. It forced all thoughts of summer, and playing with my friends, clear to the back of my head—to a dark, sinister place, where I couldn't even dream about fun. All I could see was trouble. Disaster.

At morning recess, Danny and Mark came tearing up to me. "What happened, Tom?" The two voices sounded together like a yell that echoed across the playground.

I shushed them.

"Nothing," I lied.

Four eyes stared at me.

"Okay," I confessed. "I missed some words on my spelling test, but I didn't write them and turn them in on Thursday morning. Mrs. Nash made me stay after school to finish them."

Mark scratched his nose. "We wondered why you didn't show up at the creek yesterday."

Danny kind of shoved him aside with an elbow. "Yeah, but why were you shaking so hard when you came back to the room? Why were you so upset?"

"She can't find my papers."

Mark tilted his head to the side. "Did you really do them?"

Danny and I both glared at him.

Taking a step back, he gave a little shrug. "Just asking."

Danny looked over his shoulder. "Bet Carl or Harry got them. Sounds like something those two would do. Soon as we get back in the room, I'll check Carl's desk. Mark, you take a peek in Harry's and—"

"No," I said, cutting him off. "I was in the teachers' lounge. I left them on the—"

"The teachers' lounge?" Mark yelped. "You mean you really got to go in there? What's it like? Do they have soft couches? Recliners? A big-screen TV? Do they really have an electric paddle? Daddy always told me they did—you know—back in the old days. Did they have it stored in there? What does it look like? Were there any—"

"Mark!" Danny snarled. "Shut! Up! Tom's in trouble and you're flapping your lips like a complete dork." He turned back to me. "Did you look on the floor? Maybe they fell off and . . ."

I shook my head. "They weren't on the floor."

"How about the trash can? Maybe somebody threw them away and . . ."

I shook my head again. "Mrs. Nash looked there. She looked behind the coffeepot, the pop machine, she even felt around on top of the books on the tall bookshelf. No spelling papers."

"Maybe somebody threw them out in the trash," Mark suggested. "At noon recess, we could dig around in the Dumpsters."

Danny rolled his eyes. "Mark, every teacher in the building dumps paper and trash on the last day of school. It'd be like trying to find a flea on an elephant's butt."

"Well." Mark held his hands up. "We might get lucky."

Danny just stared at him. Finally, Mark shrugged and offered a halfhearted smile. "I'm gonna go play softball. See ya later."

With that he sprinted off across the playground.

Morning recess was a little longer than usual, but I couldn't enjoy it. When we got back in, Mrs.

Nash handed out art paper and we got to draw and visit for a while—"As long as we kept the noise down."

Still nervous and shaky, the two pictures I drew were terrible. I kept glancing at my teacher. She watched the clock on our wall.

What was she going to do to me? And WHEN was she going to do it?

Not finding the papers that I *really* did was bad enough. But what was worse was Mrs. Nash didn't believe me. That hurt. I liked Mrs. Nash. She was the best teacher I'd ever had. She'd never trust me again. Just the thought made me feel like dirt. No, I felt lower than dirt.

All of a sudden, she sort of hopped up from her desk and trotted to the door.

"I'm going to be out of the room for a moment," she announced. "I want you to stay in your seats, and I want all visiting to stop until I get back. And I mean *all*. Samantha, take names at the chalkboard. When I get back, if there is a name up there, that person will be the *last* to leave the room on the *last day* of school." Her gaze seemed to drift to Carl Decker's side of the room. "And if anyone threatens Samantha for putting his name on the board—that person will wait with me, *after school,* until every single person in the entire building has gone home."

This was it. Mama and Daddy were probably waiting for her in the office. I was dead. The whole summer would be shot. I'd be grounded until school started next year.

I began to put a smile on the face I was drawing on my art paper.

I hadn't even finished drawing it, when my own smile vanished and a knot came up in my throat.

It took forever for Mrs. Nash to come back. When I heard the door open, my heart skipped a beat. She stood in the doorway for a second, then . . .

"Thomas Danfield," she called. "I have something to say to you."

My heart stopped.

Slowly. Every eye in the room. Turned. Toward. Me.

This was it! I was dead.

I wanted *not* to be here. I wished I could vanish. Suddenly appear somewhere else.

If I were only small enough to slink under my desk and hide there, never to be seen again. If only . . .

Chapter 4

"Tom," she repeated as she started across the room. "I owe you an apology."

My head snapped up.

"I made you stay after school yesterday to write your spelling words. When I couldn't find them this morning, I accused you of taking them home, or not even doing them.

"I was wrong!"

My eyes flashed.

She walked slowly, speaking each word softly yet loud enough so everyone could hear. She crossed the front of the room and paused at my row.

"When I confronted you and threatened to call your parents, you swore that you had done your work. I didn't believe you. But you were so sincere, I decided to ask the teachers if anyone had seen them."

She was almost to my chair now.

"Not one single teacher, secretary, not even the principal had seen them." She stood, towering above me, leaning forward with her arms behind her.

"Mr. Clark comes in at ten forty-five, to set up the lunch tables. I asked him." She brought her arms from behind her back. In her right hand were two sheets of paper. They were folded, kind of sloppy and crooked, but the instant she opened them . . .

"He cleaned the lounge yesterday afternoon. The papers were in his way, but he couldn't tell if they were important or not, so instead of throwing them in the trash, he folded them and stuck them on top of the bookshelf. They were back from the edge, where neither you nor I could see them." She folded the papers, then dropped to one knee beside my desk.

"I really am sorry," she whispered, so no one

else could hear. Her soft, gentle hands forced the folded papers into my grasp. "You're a good and honest young man. I should have believed you."

As I looked at her eyes, I heard the words—not from her mouth—but straight from her heart.

A little chill shot across my back and shoulders. The kind that races up your neck and around your head to tug at your eyes. For the first time since I was little, I felt like crying. I didn't, but I couldn't say anything, either. All I could do was smile at her, and nod my head.

We got an extra-long lunch recess. That was fun. Once back in our room, Mrs. Nash read the last two chapters of *Stubby and the Puppy Pack: To the Rescue.*

The fact that we kept pestering her to finish the book probably had something to do with it. I was glad she did. There was a part of me that kind of hoped Stubby and the dogs would leave that nasty Kylie stuck in the hole. But they were nice, and that wouldn't be a very nice thing to do. I liked the way it ended.

By the time she was done, we were a lot quieter than we had been when we first came in from the playground. She had us all clean out our desks and put our personal things like pencils, extra notebook paper, and junk into our backpacks.

Terri and Debra volunteered to clean out the big cardboard box where we kept our playground balls, baseballs, and bats. Some people had been using the box like a trash can—there was so much paper in the bottom, we had to dig to find anything to play with.

They dragged the huge box up beside the front door, so it was closer to the trash can. When the can was full, Mrs. Nash picked me to take it out. I chose Danny to help.

"That was totally awesome this morning," Danny said when we opened the Dumpster.

"What was?" I asked, lifting the trash can to the edge and pouring the paper in.

"The way Mrs. Nash apologized to you. I mean, I never heard a teacher apologize to a kid before. What was she doing when she got down on one knee?"

"She gave my papers back to me."

"She said something." Danny arched an eyebrow. "What did she say?"

I didn't answer him. I never told anyone what Mrs. Nash said to me.

When we got back, Terri and Debra had the box tipped over on its side so Terri could crawl in and dig out the paper. About halfway in the box, she kind of looked like a dog digging for a bone. She scraped paper beside herself, between her legs, and even tossed some over her shoulders. Debra grabbed what she raked out and started stuffing it into the trash can that we just set down.

The can was almost full again when Mrs. Bowlin popped in.

She always showed up on the last day of school to give her end-of-the-year speech.

First she would tell everyone what a good year it had been. Then she'd warn us that, just because it was the last day of school, we shouldn't get too excited and forget to watch for cars on our way home. Finally she'd give us a big smile and tell all of us to have a fun summer.

Right as she walked through the doorway, she opened her mouth to start her speech. Then she glanced down. I guess—from where she stood—

all she could see was Terri's bottom sticking out of the big box.

She blinked a couple of times, turned to Mrs. Nash, and grinned.

"Cleaning the room before summer vacation is always appreciated," she said. "But don't you think that throwing away a perfectly good student is a little much?"

Mrs. Nash put both fists on her hips and shot Mrs. Bowlin an irritated look—the same look we got when we were too noisy or someone acted smart-alecky with her. Mrs. Bowlin clamped her lips together, spun, and was out of the room before Terri could back out of the box.

"Who was that?" Terri asked. "What's going on?"

Suddenly Mrs. Bowlin leaned her head back inside. I guess she remembered why she'd come to our room in the first place.

"Hope all of you have a good summer!" she yelled, still grinning.

"Thank you," we called back.

Danny and I hauled another load of trash to the Dumpster. The thing was so full, Danny had to climb in and jump up and down to pack the paper enough so we could close the lid. Bob Evans and Randall Jenkins brought a pile of trash from their room.

"You two gonna be on our baseball team this summer?" Bob asked.

"Don't know." Danny grinned. "I heard you were gonna be the pitcher. I didn't think you could even get the ball across the plate."

He punched Bob on the shoulder. Bob shoved him back, and they both started laughing and scuffling.

I looked at them, then turned and headed for the building.

Chapter 5

Everyone was seated. Hands folded on the desk-tops and sitting up straight, they all watched our teacher. As soon as I put down the trash can, she motioned me to my chair. Keeping her eyes on the door, Mrs. Nash stood for a moment until Danny came in and sat down. Clearing her throat, she smiled. "I am pretty sure most of you already know this, but next year our school system is starting what they call 'tracking.' This means that a teacher will start with a class in third grade and stay with that same class every year until the students finish sixth grade, and move to junior high.

"What it means to you, specifically, is that I will be your teacher again next year."

She had to stop talking, because some of the girls started clapping. All of us joined in.

Well . . . all except Carl and Harry. The rest of us liked Mrs. Nash and were glad that she was going to be our teacher again next year. They didn't. Of course, they didn't like Mrs. Parks from first grade or Mrs. Dunn from third grade, either. That's probably because they didn't like anyone who expected them to mind. So we just ignored them and clapped even harder.

Mrs. Nash glanced at the clock and held up her hands to get us quiet.

"I'm looking forward to having each of you again. There is a lot more reading in sixth grade, so I hope you will find some time to read this summer. We'll also do a lot more work on our writing skills next year. Keeping a journal over the summer or writing letters will help maintain the skills you already have and improve them for next school year."

Better write that down, I thought. I grabbed my spelling papers from my backpack and scribbled: Writing skills. Journal. Letters.

The bell rang!

I couldn't believe it. I had all but given up on ever getting out of school for summer. We all started grabbing stuff and leaping to our feet.

"Stop!"

We stopped.

"Sit down!"

Not too quiet, we shuffled back into our chairs. The bell had stopped ringing by the time we were settled.

"Read some and write some!" Then Mrs. Nash's face softened to a gentle smile. "And have a fun summer. Samantha's row."

My row was next to last. Once we were all waiting in line at the door, Mrs. Nash told us to watch for cars and to play safe. Then she let us go. Some of the girls stopped to give her a quick hug. I acted like I was trying to find something in my backpack. The people behind me went on around. Once everyone was out of the room, I gave Mrs. Nash a hug, too.

"It wasn't your fault," I told her. "If I had done my words, like I was supposed to . . . well . . . it was *my* fault."

Mrs. Nash hugged me back. "I'm glad you're going to be in my room next year." She smiled.

"Me too."

I took off to catch up with my class.

"Don't run in the halls!" she called, loud enough so we could hear her over all the commotion.

Mama always parked near the front of the car line, but I didn't see her when I got outside. Not that I thought much about it. Lots of parents picked up their kids on the last day of school, because they had so much stuff to lug around. She was probably someplace at the back of the line.

I walked down a ways. When I still didn't spot our car, I sat on the benches near the front door.

Checking to make sure no one was watching, I opened my backpack just enough to slip my hand inside and pull out the two sheets of paper with my spelling words on them.

You're not on your honor just during school, or when you're taking a test. Mrs. Nash's words rattled inside my head, when I stared at the words I'd written. *You know what's right—what's honest. You do it, not because someone might catch you, but because it's the right thing to do.*

"Tom."

Mrs. Nash's voice made my head snap up. I stuffed the pages back in my pack.

"Yes, ma'am?"

"Your mother is parked out on the road. Weren't you supposed to go someplace today?"

Suddenly remembering, I hopped to my feet and trotted toward her.

"Yes, ma'am," I said. "My grandfather just got home from the hospital. Mama and I are going to help feed the dogs and clean the kennels until he's feeling better."

She held up a hand, stopping the car that was trying to pull around us. I scurried across the drive.

With all that had happened the last couple of days—mad because I had to write spelling words, guilty because I lied to Mrs. Nash, scared because we couldn't find my papers, humiliated because I couldn't hide how upset it made me, proud when she called me "an honorable young man"—all those feelings mixed up and jumbled together and all flying at me—all at once . . .

I was more than ready for summer. I wanted to tell Mama everything that had happened. I wanted to see how Grandpa was feeling. I could hardly wait to run and play and go fishing. I was dying to kick off my shoes and run around barefoot. I longed for the sweet smell of summer.

Chapter 6

When longing for the sweet smell of summer, a dog kennel isn't exactly the place to hang out.

"Mama. It stinks!"

"What did you expect?" She offered a half-hearted smile. "There are thirty-six dogs and twenty-eight pens. That's not even counting the puppies. Your grandmother's done a fabulous job. Two weeks ago, when your grandfather had his heart attack, she rushed him to the hospital, and stayed with him. Your father took the day off from his job to be here and clean kennels and feed. After they got him stabilized—you know—when your grandfather wasn't in danger, they did two days of testing. She got up before daylight, came out with the flashlight to feed, then rushed to the hospital so she could be there with him. Same thing in the evenings.

"Your dad and I helped cleaned the pens. But since we don't know the names, we couldn't let them out to run or go poop—they could only go to their outside runs."

"Know the names?" I asked.

"Your grandfather trains his dogs to respond to their names—he calls them by name then gives a command, like 'come' or 'sit' . . . you know? How he remembers all of them, I have no idea. But your grandmother only knows some. That's fine, though. Except for these six in the old milk barn, they all have outside runs. They don't have to poop inside, but they still can't go in the pasture. They're not getting the exercise they should, either. Your dad and grandmother wash the runs out two times a day, but it all flows out the end of the barn. Once we get the dogs back on their regular schedule, it won't be so bad."

"Promise?"

"Well . . . not *quite* as bad."

The roar of a jet engine made my muscles

tighten. As it drew closer, the noise—a deafening screaming roar—made my neck kind of scrunch down between my shoulders like a turtle trying to duck inside his shell. The noise grew so loud, the walls of the old barn seemed to shake. I could swear I saw dust falling between the boards.

"Watch the hose, Tom. Try not to get it wet inside the doghouses."

When I glanced down, the water spray was landing two pens away. A little Brittany spaniel flopped her ears, shook, and darted into the safety of her doghouse.

"Sorry."

The rumbling from above finally faded. I concentrated on spraying the doggy poop out of the pens. Most of it rolled. Tumbling with the spray and force of the water, it finally fell over the edge and into the trough. The wet stuff . . . well, it just kind of broke apart. Sometimes it stuck on the chain-link and I had to keep the hose on it a little longer.

I'd only gotten to three more pens when another jet took off. My neck scrunched down between my shoulders and my eyes clamped shut. But only for a second. I didn't want to soak another poor dog, so I forced them to open.

My grandfather's dog kennel was really an old dairy barn. The farm was here long before they built the airport. When the farmer who used to own the place retired, Grandpa bought it. Even though it was real close to the airport, he thought it would be a good place to raise and train his bird dogs. Besides, Grandpa had told me that, after a while, he got used to the noise. I didn't see how that could ever happen.

Then about a year after they came to live here, the airport needed to expand. They built a new runway west of the others. That put the flight path right over their house. It made for a lot of noise, but Grandma and Grandpa didn't mind. The dogs didn't seem bothered by it either.

Grandpa used the old hay barn for storage, a place to keep a couple of horses, and a pigeon coop with about ten birds. He also put part of the dog pens on the south side—protected from the north wind in the winter, and shaded by the long, sloping, roof overhang in the summer. Grandma turned the two brooding houses (where the farmer's wife raised baby chickens) into places for the mother dogs to have their puppies.

The dairy barn worked perfect for the main kennel. Made of concrete, the whole floor sloped a little to the east. It was so slight I couldn't even notice it. And about where the cows' tails would be, when they were being milked, there was a trough in the concrete, on both sides of the barn. Grandpa said that when the farmer poured the floor, he probably just laid down a couple of twelve-inch boards. When the concrete dried, he pulled them up and had his trough. That way he could wash out whatever mess the cows made, and not have to clean the entire barn until he was through milking.

Grandpa built six dog pens on each side of the barn. Each had a doggy door so the dogs could get outside to a concrete run he had built. That still left a wide empty space, in the middle of the barn. So Grandpa built six more pens there.

Those were the ones Mama and I saved for last, because they were the most important to keep clean.

"Want to spray down those last three pens?"

Mama's voice jerked me from my memories. My head snapped up.

"What?"

"Spray down those last three pens," she repeated, more like an order this time instead of a question. "That trough's about as clean as it's going to get. All you're doing is running water."

I glanced down. Sure enough, there wasn't anything left. Just three more pens, then we could go see Grandma and Grandpa—and go home. Trouble was, there were still dogs in the last two.

"Aren't you going to let those two out? Aren't we supposed to let them run for a few minutes?"

"No!"

The way Mama snapped at me made me jerk my hand. I accidentally sprayed the dog in the next to the last pen.

"No," she repeated, softer this time. "Your grandmother said that the female is young and really high-strung. She's not trained to come, so we'd need to put a leash on her. She's also a fraidy-cat. Your grandmother's afraid she might bite someone she doesn't know.

"The other one is Old Gabe. We don't let him out at all."

"That's not fair," I protested.

Mama nodded. "You're right. It's not fair. But only your grandfather can let him out."

"Why?"

"He's Old Gabe." Mama shrugged.

I finished spraying the last pen. The dog there didn't bark or spin around like some of the others had. He just lay in his doghouse and watched me. When I was done, I turned to wash the waste out of the trough.

"Why can't we let him out?" I asked again, looking at Mama instead of him.

A roaring, snapping, slashing growl sent the hair standing straight up on the back of my neck. The chain-link fence rattled. I could swear I heard the gate fly open.

Without even glancing back, I dropped the water hose and took off.

When I finally realized nothing was snapping at my heels, I stopped and turned.

The dog in the last pen stood with his front paws against the fence. Still growling and snarling, he shook the wire and glared at me. I glared back—mad that he'd scared me.

Then I could almost see a grin on his face.

He wagged his tail and trotted back to lie down in his doghouse, just as cool and calm as if he'd intended to make me jump clean out of my socks.

Only after he disappeared inside did I realize how far I'd run. I'd stopped a good ten feet outside the doorway. Right where all the water, and mud, and doggy-doo flowed out and into the pasture.

When I looked down, I felt my nose crinkle and my toes curl. The mud and goo was oozing—clear up over the top of my tennis shoes.

"That's why," Mama called.

Chapter 7

Grandma met us at the back door. She glanced down at my muddy shoes, and sighed.

"You been playing in the mud? Or did you meet Old Gabe?"

Mama giggled. When I glared at her, she clamped a hand over her mouth—only I could still see her eyes twinkling. She helped me hose down my tennis shoes. Then I pulled off my socks, and she ran the water over my feet. Grandma got me a pair of Grandpa's old coaching shorts from his drawer, and she put my tennis shoes, socks, and jeans in the washer. My pants weren't really that muddy, but what with tearing through the slop, I did get splatters on them.

Grandpa's shorts were a little big, so I had

to hold them with one hand when I followed Grandma and Mama to the bedroom.

Grandpa sat on the edge of the bed, clutching a pillow against his chest.

"You're not supposed to get up without someone in here to help," Grandma scolded.

"I'm not *getting* up, I'm just *sitting* up."

When he saw us in the doorway, Grandpa smiled. Instantly the smile disappeared. He took a deep breath and coughed, his face wrinkled to a grimace, teeth gritted, eyes clinched shut, and tendons in his neck bulging out with the strain.

"Oh . . . man, that hurts." He sighed, loosening his grip on the pillow. "Them doctors split me open like a ripe melon." The grimace returned to his face—like he was bracing himself—then he coughed again. Little beads of sweat popped out on his forehead. Grandpa sat for a moment, breathing soft and easy, until he caught his breath.

"Sorry about that. Doctors told me to cough a lot. Keeps the fluid from collecting in my lungs, so I don't get pneumonia. Sure do hurt, though."

He slipped a hand between himself and the pillow and patted his chest, very gently.

"How you doing, Tom? Glad school's out for the summer?"

"Yes, sir." I smiled. "I sure am."

Holding his breath a moment, as if fighting back another cough, he nodded at Mama.

"How about you, Jillian? Any problems at work? Your boss give you any static about leaving the office early?"

Mama leaned forward and kissed him on the cheek.

"No. I offered to come in at seven, so I could make up the time I missed. That way Tom and I could get here around four or so to help Mama. Johnny said not to worry about it. Said family's more important, and that's what I needed to be taking care of right now."

"How about the dogs? Any problems out there?"

Mama shook her head. "Everything went just fine." She paused a moment, her eyes cut toward me. "Well . . ."

I felt my mouth twist up on one side when I saw the twinkle in her eye.

"Old Gabe pulled a sneak attack on Tom."

Grandpa shot her a stern look. "You didn't let him out, did you?"

"No. He was still in his pen, but . . ."

"Jumped on the fence and started snarling and barking, right?"

Mama smiled at Grandpa. "Right."

Grandpa only got in one little laugh before his eyes flashed. He clutched the pillow and started coughing again.

Grandma motioned us toward the door. "Got cheese and turkey in the fridge. You and Tom go fix yourselves a sandwich. I'll wait till he's through coughing, and tuck him back in bed. Oh, there's chips in the pantry."

Mama and I went to the kitchen.

"Is Grandpa gonna be okay?" I asked.

"Huh?"

Mama didn't hear me because she had her head in the fridge.

"Is Grandpa gonna be okay?" I repeated. "I mean, with all that coughing and stuff?"

"White or wheat?"

"White."

"Your grandpa's fine, Tom. Triple bypass surgery used to be very dangerous. Nowadays, it's pretty simple. He has to take it easy for a while, though."

"But the way he grabs his chest . . . I mean, his face and . . . and, well . . . it really looks like it hurts."

"I imagine it *does* hurt," she said. "The doctors explained that his heart is working fine now. The pain comes from the muscles in his chest and his ribs trying to mend. It's normal."

Grandma came in, opened the pantry door, and stretched up on her tiptoes. "Barbecue or plain?"

"Plain," Mama answered.

"And barbecue," I added.

She brought both packages of chips and laid them on the bar. They started talking about Grandpa, and the dogs, and a bunch of other stuff while they were making the sandwiches.

After supper, Grandma went with us to feed.

"It's right simple, once you get the hang of it," she explained as we followed her to the big barn.

Just inside the door, on the right, was a box made of concrete blocks. It had a sheet of iron for a top. Grandma twisted the latch and lifted it. It must have been heavier than it looked, judging by the way her muscles strained.

"Don't get your hand in the way when you close the lid," she warned. "Thing's heavy enough to take a finger or two clean off."

Inside the box were a bunch of dog food sacks, all standing on end in neat rows.

"The ones on the left are for the mama dogs. They're higher in protein and have some added nutrients that they need when they're nursing their pups." She picked up a coffee can. "Angie's got a litter of seven. Since she's nursing, I usually give her about a can and a half." She dumped the dog food into a plastic bucket, then dipped the coffee can into the dog food sack again. "Sal is expecting any day now. Till the pups get here, I keep her at one pound." Dumping that into the bucket, she glanced over her shoulder and winked at Mama. "Don't want her to lose her girlish figure."

Next she leaned over and lifted a sack from the rows on the right. She took hold of the little string that stuck out from one corner, and ripped the sack open. She poured that into the plastic bucket.

"Been doing this ever since your grandpa had his heart attack. Gettin' used to it."

Once the first plastic bucket was full, she poured more food in a second bucket.

"This is the regular dog food. Everybody gets a one-pound coffee can." Her eyes cut to the side as she glanced first one way, then the other. "All right, not everybody. There are two Brittany females—one in the center run where Old Gabe is, the other on the south side of this barn. They're kind of small, so I usually just give them three-quarters of a can. Ty is the biggest darned bird dog I ever saw in my life. Sweet as he can be. Just big." She pointed to the south side of the hay barn. "Your grandpa's not training him, he's just board-ing him for a fella down in Dallas. That dog can scarf down two cans without batting an eye. Old Gabe gets a little more, too. But I'll feed him myself. Neither one of you need to mess with him."

"I can't believe he's still so mean and nasty," Mama said. "I figured, when he got up in years, he'd kind of mellow out."

Grandma gave a little laugh. "Old rascal's just like your dad, Jillian. He ain't never gonna mellow out."

It was dark by the time Mama and I got home. The last day of school I usually played with Danny and Mark. We threw a baseball, or played setback with the football, or just horsed around.

But it had been a long day. I mean—*really long*!

I gave Daddy a hug, tossed my backpack in the closet, took a shower, and climbed into bed.

I was asleep before the sheet even settled!

Chapter 8

Daddy didn't have to work on the weekend, so all three of us went to help with the dogs. We also visited with Grandpa, but mostly he slept. Mama and Grandma fixed baked beans and scalloped potatoes. Daddy and I cooked hamburgers on Grandpa's grill.

After dinner Mama and Grandma drove to an office supply store. I don't know what the thing was called, but they brought back this little hand-held machine that you could make plastic labels with. The strips were about a half-inch wide, and the back peeled off so we could stick them to the gate on the dog pens.

Some dog trainers teach their dogs to come by

whistling. Others use a police whistle. Grandpa trains his dogs to come when he calls their name.

Only trouble, Mama and I didn't know their names.

Things had been so hectic since Grandpa got sick that the dogs had hardly had a good run. They really needed some exercise.

Grandma and Mama were cleaning the pens on the south side of the big barn while Daddy and I handled the others. Each time Grandma finished, she'd let a dog run. While the dog was flying around the barn and across the pasture, she'd make a name tag and stick it to the pole beside its gate.

It took a while. Between squeezing the machine so the letters came through on the plastic strip, and having to trot back to the house to ask Grandpa when she forgot a dog's name, Daddy and I were already finished with our side.

So we helped with the name-making thingy. It really was hard to get those letters to come through. I mean, you had to squeeze like mad. I only did about five names before my hand and fingers got numb. Daddy took it for a while.

Tess was the name of the high-strung little pointer bird dog in the pen next to Gabe. I made her name tag. Grandma had me put the word "wild" in parentheses next to it. She was the one who didn't mind very well and didn't come when called. I stood way back from Old Gabe's pen when I made his name. (Not that I really needed to make a nameplate for him.) After scaring me into the doggy poop yesterday, I knew good and well I'd never forget him. As I squeezed the letters onto the plastic strip, I watched him out of the corner of my eye. Any second I expected him to come barking, and roaring, and slamming against the fence. He didn't. He just lay in his doghouse and watched *me* out of the corner of *his* eye.

I held my breath when I stuck the name tag to his gatepost. He still didn't move. *Bet he's waiting till I turn my back on him,* I thought. *That's when he'll launch his sneak attack.*

Still holding the air inside my lungs, I turned my back and braced. When nothing happened, I moved away, still stiff. *Stay ready. Any second now.*

. . .

A whole week went by and Old Gabe never tried to scare me. I was ready for him, but he never once jumped at the fence like he was gonna tear me up.

That first week, I got to sleep late. I was awake enough to hear when Mama and Daddy left for work, but I stayed in bed. Around ten or so I'd get up and fix something for breakfast.

The second week, Little League baseball started. So did a three-week soccer camp. Mr. Storms, our soccer coach, called and said they had two young men from England coming this year. He said they were really good.

It was a hard decision to make. Danny and Mark wanted me to play baseball this summer and I wanted to be with my friends. But I liked soccer a whole lot more than baseball.

Soccer camp lasted from seven-thirty until one, and I sure hated getting up that early. Mama would drop me off on her way to work and Daddy would pick me up on his lunch hour and run me back home. When Mama got home, she and I drove out to the kennel, cleaned dog pens, fed dogs, and visited. Then it was back home, eat supper, and go to sleep so I could get up in time for soccer.

Grandma didn't let Grandpa out of the house until near the end of the second week. Then she only let him as far as the porch.

Whenever we let a dog loose to exercise, Grandpa clutched a pillow over his chest. Every one of those dogs was so glad to see him, they'd race straight for him. Some cowed down, all bashful and shylike. Wiggling and easing close, they'd wait until he leaned over to pet them, then go tearing off. Others would try to jump up so he'd pet them.

That's what the pillow was for.

Grandpa used it kind of like a shield to keep the dogs from jabbing him in the chest with their paws.

Friday of the third week, Grandma let him wander out into the yard. He petted the dogs when they came to greet him, but mostly Grandma wanted him to walk. "Doctor said he needs to start exercising," she told us.

I was almost through feeding my dogs when Grandpa waved me over. "There are some wooden pegs next to the feed box, in the big barn," he said.

"Get that thick cotton rope with a leather collar clipped to it. Tess really needs to run. Make sure the collar's tight. Don't choke her, but get it tight enough so she can't slip it over her head." He turned and started back for the porch. "I'm gonna go get my pillow and sit down. Crazy as that little pup is, she'd probably wrap the rope around my legs and end up dumping me on my nose. Hang on to the rope until I call her. Need to work on getting her to respond to her name."

Grandpa hobbled along. I found the long rope with the collar and was almost back to Tess's pen before he went inside. Keeping my foot and knee in the opening, so she couldn't slip past, I squeezed inside and put the collar on her.

It wasn't easy, what with her wiggling and trying to jump up on me. Once I had it around her neck, I slipped my finger under it. I tightened it another notch and turned to open the gate. Leaning against the chain-link, I reached for the latch.

The snarling, roaring growl sent the hairs at the back of my neck bristling. Goose bumps popped up on my arms and across my shoulders. Something hit the fence where I leaned. I could swear I felt teeth sink into my flesh.

I jumped and tripped over Tess. She yelped.

I remember falling. I remember trying to grab the gate and catch myself. But I didn't remember anything else until I landed on the far side of the pen, with my left ear, cheek, and head in her water bowl.

Sitting up, I wiped the water off my face and out of my eyes. I could have sworn Old Gabe bit me through the fence, but there wasn't a mark on me.

Old Gabe sat in front of his doghouse. Wagging his tail and watching me, I could swear the old dog was smiling from ear to floppy ear.

I crawled to my feet, stomped over, and kicked the chain-link.

Now come and get me! I raged inside my head. *Come bite at the fence again. I'll kick you right in the nose.*

Old Gabe just sat there, smiling.

Something brushed against my ankle. I jerked my foot away from whatever touched me, and glanced down.

The tail end of a cotton rope whipped around the gate. Spinning and flopping, it slid down the concrete floor and disappeared around the corner of the barn.

"Tess," I breathed.

She was gone.

What if Grandpa wasn't sitting down? What if he didn't have his pillow against his chest and she jumped on him?

"Tess!"

I screamed the name this time. I raced out of the pen, running as hard as I could.

Chapter 9

When I rounded the far corner of the barn, my eyes sprang wide open. Grandpa was just coming through the front door. Holding his pillow down at his side, he turned to make sure the screen was shut. He wasn't paying a bit of attention.

"Tess!" I screamed.

If nothing else, maybe he'd hear me and be ready if she jumped on him.

"Tess?" I called the name again. Only this time it wasn't a scream. It was more like a question. Tess wasn't headed for Grandpa, like all the other dogs had done.

Tess was no place in sight.

I glanced left. Right. Behind me. She wasn't there.

Grandpa must have heard me yelling for her. When I looked back at him, he waved his pillow at the big barn.

"She inside with the other dogs?" I asked as I ran past him.

"Far side. Headed out to the horse pasture."

The dogs in the big barn barked when I raced past. At the far side of the barn, there was still no sign of Tess. I climbed up on the big metal gate.

Joe and Ginger were munching grass in the middle of the field. Swishing flies with their tails, their heads suddenly sprang up, their ears perked straight for the sky, and they stampeded across the pasture, racing toward the gate.

That's when I finally spotted Tess.

Grandpa's horses weren't afraid of dogs—they were used to them. But the big cotton rope flopping through the grass behind Tess must have spooked them.

I spotted that rope before I saw her. She was running so hard and fast, the tail end of the rope was flipping and bouncing clear above the tall grass. Floppy ears waving in the wind, Tess was at the other end of it.

Soccer is a pretty good sport. Nathan and Jerome, the guys who were doing our three-week soccer camp, worked with us on ball-handling skills. We'd practice trapping the ball, heading, and using our bodies to bring down a pass. We had to bounce the ball twenty times with our right foot and twenty times with our left without letting it touch the ground. And we practiced dribbling. We'd also sprint from one end of the field and back—running as hard as we could, but still keeping control of the ball. We dribbled around cones—changing pace, sprinting, trapping the ball to a dead stop, dribbling—slow and changing direction, fast and changing direction. Then we ran some more.

Not only is soccer a good sport, it comes in handy sometimes.

If I hadn't spent two weeks doing all that running at soccer camp, I would have probably never caught Tess.

That stupid dog ran me all over the horse pasture. She slipped under the fence and made it halfway across the airport property before she circled back. I finally trapped the rope with my foot, like I trapped a soccer ball. Only the bird dog was running so fast, she just ripped it from under me.

The next time I caught up with the end of that rope, I pounced on it with both feet.

Forget soccer, I'm so out of breath I'm about to drop.

Tess hit the end of the rope at full speed. She flipped herself over backwards, got up, shook herself, and tried to take off again. I had her this time, though.

Looping the rope around my arm and hand like an electrical cord, I pulled her to me. Rope and dog in tow, I dragged her back to the kennels and to Grandpa.

Both of us were still panting by the time we got to the porch. That didn't keep Tess from lunging and pulling at the rope. Her tongue was almost dragging on the ground when I sat on the steps.

"What happened?" Grandpa sighed.

"That darned Gabe," I gasped. "I was watching Tess really close. You know—being careful not to let her out till I had a good hold on the rope. He jumped up and tried to bite my arm through the chain-link." I stopped, sucking in more oxygen.

"Why do you keep that darned old dog anyway, Grandpa?"

He pulled a cigar from the table beside his chair and started chewing on it. He didn't light it, though. Between the heart attack, the surgery, the doctor, and Grandma fussing at him, he finally figured out that smoking wasn't that good an idea.

"Gabe's my honors dog," Grandpa answered.

"Huh?"

"Honors dog. He helps me train the pups to honor point."

I shook my head. "I don't understand, Grandpa. What's an honors dog? What's honor point?"

Grandpa took the cigar out of his mouth, used his tongue to pick a little piece of tobacco from between his teeth, and spit.

"Okay. You've seen a dog point, right?"

I nodded, remembering how they freeze, tail all straight and stiff, and usually a front paw tucked up by their chest.

"If you're hunting with more than one dog, they'll both point singles—one dog will come down on point, another dog will stumble on a different bird and lock up. But when they're working a covey, usually one dog will spot them before the others. Honor means that the dogs point the first dog. They trust his judgment—that he's found birds—and stop, dead in their tracks, to point the dog, instead of trying to find the birds themselves."

My brow wrinkled.

"It's a hard thing for even the smartest bird dog pup to learn. They're *bred* to hunt birds. They want to keep running until they find the covey. End up tearing through the birds and flushing them." He spit another piece of tobacco. Nodded toward the rope wrapped in my hand. "Even tugging on the rope and yelling at them can't make them understand, sometimes.

"But Old Gabe's got a way of communicating with them. It ain't too pretty. But that old dog's taught a hundred and fifty, maybe two hundred pups, about honor."

I guess the look on my face was enough for Grandpa.

"Doctor said I could get back to work next week." He smiled. "I'll take you out with one of the pups who's almost finished, and show you."

"He said you could work, but *just a little.*"

Grandpa and I both jumped. We hadn't seen or heard Grandma come to the screen door. "He also said you weren't to lift anything heavier than a newspaper, remember? That included yanking on a rope with some wild pup pulling on the other end."

Grandpa stuck the cigar back in his mouth. Raised an eyebrow at her.

"You sure?"

"I asked him about that, specifically." Grandma smiled. "Those were his exact words."

Grandpa folded his arms and glared at her. "Well, I won't pull hard. I'll just work with the more experienced dogs and—"

"And," Grandma butted in, "you'll end up busting your incision open and we'll have to rush you back to the hospital—*if* we're lucky."

"Now, Beth," he soothed. "Don't get all worked up."

"I'm not gettin' all worked up. I'm just stating

facts, you old coot. You gotta take care of your-self or—"

"Hey, I got an idea." I don't know whether I really had a good idea, or if I was just trying to keep them from arguing. "Soccer camp is over on Saturday. Indoor soccer doesn't start until September. I could help Grandpa train the pups."

When they both stopped to stare at me, I shrugged.

"Well, there's nothing else to do. I could sit home and watch TV. But after ten, there's nothing on but soap operas and talk shows. Maybe Mama or Daddy could bring me out on their way to work. Or . . . or maybe I could spend a night or two . . . or something."

Grandpa picked a piece of tobacco off his tongue, rolled it between his finger and thumb, then flipped it on the ground.

"I guess I could tell Tom what needs to be done. How to do it. Just might work."

I shrugged again.

"Yeah, Grandma. It might be fun."

Chapter 10

Soccer camp was fun.

Nathan and Jerome were both really good. They showed us a lot of things. It was neat to listen to them talk, too. Their English accents made them a little hard to understand sometimes. Whether they were around or not, almost all of us tried to imitate them. They got as tickled as we did.

Short and kind of stocky, Nathan had muscles like you wouldn't believe. But Jerome was my favorite—especially his legs. Jerome was tall and skinny. I'd never seen legs as long as his. When I first saw him run, he looked kind of clumsy and disconnected. But he could do *unbelievable* things with a soccer ball.

He could sprint down the field, as fast as the

wind, jump and land on the ball—with both feet at the same time, no less. Then spin in midair and race off to the side before we could even get stopped. He was always laughing and telling us jokes, too.

Jerome always waited on his jokes until the girls were off working with Nathan. That's probably because a lot of them were kind of dirty. Some, I didn't even get. But both the guys were fun to be around and fun to listen to.

Six Flags was fun, too.

Mama talked to Grandma on Thursday. She thought Grandpa needed a couple more days before he started working again. She told Mama that if they didn't start bringing me out to help him until Tuesday or Wednesday, it would make it easier on her to keep him inside.

Daddy said we didn't have much money or time for a vacation this year, but driving down to Six Flags would give us a little break. All three of us talked it over and decided we'd go down Saturday night, spend Sunday and Monday at the park, then just lie around the house on Tuesday.

Saturday, after soccer camp, we loaded in the car and headed out. We didn't even try to go to the park on Saturday evening, since it was always too crowded on Saturdays. So we kind of hung around the motel. All three of us swam and played in the pool. I found some guys about my own age to swim and play with, while Mama and Daddy visited and made friends with the grown-ups.

It was late when we got to bed. But it was still hard to get to sleep. It'd been two years since we'd come to the amusement park, and I guess I was excited about checking out some of the new rides. I spent a lot of time flipping and flopping, until I finally settled down and dozed off.

Superman and the Thunderbolt were my two favorites. I take that back. I always loved the log ride and the Roaring Rapids. But of the new rides, the Thunderbolt and Superman were the best!

There was a long line at Superman. Daddy didn't like heights, so he chickened out. Said he'd wait for us. When we finally got to the front of the line, the attendant opened the gate, told us not to run, and stepped aside. Everybody ran.

Nobody ran when we got off.

Mama said it was exciting, but if I wanted to go again she'd wait with Daddy.

A teenage boy—I guess he was about fifteen or sixteen—had to sit next to me, because each bench held three people. The guy acted real cool and calm, but he never said a word.

He screamed a lot, though. I never knew guys could scream that loud and shrill. He was about six feet behind us when we came out the exit gate. Yelling and shouting, a bunch of his friends came rushing up. They surrounded him asking all sorts of questions—"Was it scary? Was it fun? Did you like it?"

He just laughed and told them it was kind of a sissy ride, and he wanted to go on something more exciting.

It was all I could do to keep from turning around and laughing out loud.

The Thunderbolt was a big, wooden roller coaster. The attendant stuck me about three seats behind Mama and Daddy, with a girl about my age. She was kinda cute. She smiled when I sat down, but neither one of us said anything.

The cars clunked and rattled as we chugged to the top. I could swear the first hill was higher than Superman—and that was the tallest ride I'd ever been on.

Then we slowly went over the top.

It was wild! Steep and fast, some of the curves made me feel like I was going to fly out. The way the cars rattled and clunked, I could picture the whole thing jumping off the tracks, and sailing out across the park on the very next turn.

It scared me, but I didn't scream like the teenage boy did. I *did* know that we'd probably never get Daddy on it again.

That's why it surprised me when he and Mama were waiting at the end of the exit ramp. They grabbed my hands and practically dragged me back to the entrance.

The third time they wanted to ride, I told them I needed to go to the bathroom. I'd wait for them at the bench by the ice cream parlor. They rode the thing three more times before they were ready to race on to something else. I was kind of glad they did. It gave my stomach time to settle down.

That night, at the pool, Mama and Daddy went

to the hot tub. The girl who rode the Thunderbolt with me was there with her parents. I went to play in the pool while they visited.

Monday was fantastic!

There was hardly anybody in the park. We could run from one ride to the next. Go straight to the front, and practically hop on without having to wait.

About noon Mama and Daddy pooped out.

We found a place to grab a hamburger, fries, and a fountain drink, then went outside to the seating area.

"John. Jillian," someone called. "Over here."

It was the people from last night, the ones with the girl. I followed Mama and Daddy to the table. Before I even got my leg over the bench, Daddy motioned to me with his tray.

"This is our son, Thomas. Thomas, this is Daniel, Margie, and Angie Sullivan. They're from Minnesota. Angie's going to be in sixth grade next year, too."

I smiled.

"Well," Mama urged. "Say hello."

I smiled again. "Hi."

The girl smiled back, nodded, then stuck another french fry in her mouth. Her mom and dad said hello, then started visiting with Mama and Daddy, again. Every once in a while they'd ask me something like what sports I liked, what sort of things my friends and I did after school. Mama and Daddy asked the girl what her favorite subject was and stuff like that. I guess our parents were just being polite and trying to include both of us in their conversation. But I don't think either one of us was that interested. I didn't know about her, but I just wanted to finish eating so I could hit the rides again.

Besides that, I didn't like sitting across from a girl. Not while I was trying to eat, anyway. I don't know *why* I didn't like it. I just didn't.

While our parents chatted, Angie and I just sat and tried not to look at each other. Finally Mama leaned toward me.

"I don't think Angie is going to bite you," she teased.

"Huh?"

"You and Angie can visit," she encouraged. "I met her last night. She's really nice."

I smiled at Mama. Smiled at Angie. And took another bite of my hamburger.

Mama's look was a bit more stern when she leaned over a few minutes later. "Say something to her, Tom," she whispered. "Angie doesn't have anybody to visit with. No sense in you just sitting there like a lump on a log."

I swallowed the bite of hamburger—hoping it would help me swallow the lump in my throat when it went down. I didn't know what to say. So I went with the first thing that popped into my head.

"My grandpa has a dog named Angie. She's got puppies."

Chapter 11

It took me more than an hour to work up the nerve.

"Okay," I asked finally, right before our raft went under the waterfall, "what was that look about?"

"What look?" Angie's smile was sweet and innocent as could be. "I don't have the slightest idea what you're talking about."

The raft swung around just as we went under the falls. A bunch of high school girls on the opposite side squealed and laughed. Then they batted the water with their hands, trying to get the rest of us as wet as they were.

Our parents had dragged us around on about five or six different rides. I don't know whether it had been on purpose or not, but they kept getting on things that seated two people—together—instead of three or four. That left me stuck with Angie. Then they'd found a place to sit in the shade, and "suggested" that we go ahead and hit the rides while they rested.

After the Roaring Rapids, we went to the swinging ship, then to the log ride. There was absolutely no one in line there. So they stuck us in a log all by ourselves, waited a moment, and when no one else came running down the ramp, they launched us on our way. I sat way in the front. Angie sat way in the back.

After the first drop—when we started floating gently down the trough—I swung my leg over the bench and turned around to face her.

"Look. If I said something wrong—I'm sorry. At least let me know *what* I said."

"You just don't know how to talk to a girl, do you?" She tossed her head to get the long strands of blonde hair out of her eyes.

Straddling the bench, facing her, all I could do was hold out my hands, helplessly, and shrug.

"You're right. I don't. Fact is, I usually try *not* to talk to girls, unless I absolutely have to. Now what did I say that made you so mad?"

She sighed and rolled her eyes.

"Please?"

"Okay. When someone introduces you, you should say something nice—like, 'Hello. It's a pleasure to meet you.' Or you could say, 'Angie. What a lovely name.' You don't just blurt out, 'Duh . . . I got me a dog,'" she drawled, trying to imitate my southern accent. "Her name's the same as yours. She done went and had puppies."

I felt my lip curl.

"That's not what I said. And I don't talk like that. People from Minnesota are the ones who talk funny. And . . . and, well . . . Angie belongs to my grandpa. He raises and trains bird dogs. She's nice, and . . . well . . . okay, I apologize for not saying something polite."

She just sat and stared at me.

I guess I could have done a better job of sounding sincere. I cleared my throat. "I'm sorry. Really. Okay?"

Angie's lips curled toward a smile. But the

corners only got about halfway up when her eyes suddenly flashed wide, and her mouth fell open.

I didn't even have time to glance over my shoulder when something jerked the log and lurched me forward. The cogs beneath us caught on the rail. A quick glance told me we were on the last steep climb before we plunged into the water at the end of the ride.

I let go with one hand and tried to swing my leg over. But the slope was so steep that as soon as I let go, I slid. Now I was in the middle of the log.

Maybe I can get my leg over, then turn—real quick, catch myself, and . . .

That didn't work, either. As soon as I lifted my foot, the other foot slipped on the wet floor.

Pushing with both legs, and holding as tight as I could with both hands, didn't help, either. By the time we neared the top, I'd slid all the way to the back of the car. Our knees were crammed together, and Angie's eyes were so big around, I thought they might pop clean out of her head.

"Hang on," I yelled. "As soon as we start over, I'll spin and try to brace us. Hold on."

We slowed at the peak. I yanked my leg from the floor and spun on my bottom.

I got turned, only . . .

We were going down.

No. We weren't going down—we were *flying* down. Wind pushed the breath back into my throat. It whipped a strand of long blonde hair across my eyes.

I grabbed for the side of the log, but I couldn't get a good grip. My feet weren't planted, either. The harder I shoved on the floor of the log, the more my tennis shoes slipped and slid.

We were almost at the bottom. In a second or two, the front of the log would hit the water and . . .

THIS IS GONNA HURT!

I leaned back. Lifted both feet. Aimed them at the front of the log. Arms bent, just a little, my muscles tensed to help catch us if my legs didn't hold. My teeth clinched tight. I could hear them grinding inside my skull, and . . .

And . . .

The next thing I knew, we were both totally

drenched. Angie's cheek was tight against my left ear. I could hear her laughing. I could hear me laughing.

One of Angie's arms was wrapped around my head, the other around my chest. She was plastered against my back like wallpaper, and the padded bar at the front of the log was shoved so far into my stomach, I could hardly breathe—much less laugh.

But that's exactly what we were doing. Both of us were laughing our fool heads off.

Angie scooted back by the time we got to the attendant. It felt good to get the padded bar out of my stomach, and my thumb knuckles out from under my ribs. The attendant held the log against the side with her foot and reached out a hand to help me. I turned to help Angie, who looked like a drowned rat. Long blonde hair plastered against her face. Water dripping from her shorts plopped in little puddles beside her feet. I guess I was just as wet. When she looked at me, she giggled.

"Let's do it again." Both of us laughed at the exact same moment. Water squishing and sloshing inside our tennis shoes, we sprinted up the ramp and back around to the entrance.

We talked and laughed and . . . I didn't even realize we were still holding hands until we had to let go to get into the log.

"You have fun today?" Mama asked when I finished brushing my teeth and climbed into the roll-away bed next to theirs.

I nodded.

"That Angie's a cute little thing." Daddy raised up from his pillow to peek over the top of his magazine. "Was she fun? Did you like her?"

Angie's GREAT!

That's what I wanted to say. I wanted to tell Mama and Daddy that this was the best trip *ever* to Six Flags. I wanted to tell them that Angie wasn't like the girls at school. She didn't act snooty. She was just fun.

I wanted to tell them that we could talk or hold hands or laugh at dumb stuff. I didn't have to act mean or tough when I was around her. None of the guys were watching. I didn't have to worry about them saying stuff like "Tom's got a girlfriend," or singing "Tom and Angie, sittin' in a tree . . ."

I wanted to tell them that I didn't have to impress her or act cool. We'd never see each other again. They had to go back to Minnesota and we had to get back to help Grandpa with the dogs. So . . . we could both just be ourselves and have fun.

I wanted to tell them that, and a whole lot more about the way I felt, and . . . and . . .

"She's okay—for a girl."

That's all I said.

Despite the sly smile that curled his lip, Daddy just lay back on the pillow and held the magazine in front of his face.

"Well, if she's okay . . ." He paused to turn the page. "I guess you wouldn't mind if we stayed an extra day, and went to Water World with the Sullivans tomorrow."

❧ Chapter 12 ❧

Soccer camp was fun.

Six Flags was fun.

Water World was . . . it was . . .

Well, there simply weren't words to describe it.

The Sullivans checked out of the motel the same time we did and followed us to Water World. Parked right next to us.

We swam and played and dunked each other. We talked about friends and school and Grandpa's puppies. We talked about fun stuff and even serious stuff. We ran to every single ride in the whole park—then laughed and talked some more.

It was almost dark when Mama and Daddy said it was time to start home.

Mr. Sullivan, Daddy, and I changed out of our wet clothes in the bathhouse. We waited for Angie and the moms, then headed for the cars. While the grown-ups were saying their good-byes, I went to stick my bathing suit and towel in the trunk.

I reached up to close the lid, but my fingers slipped off when I tried to pull it down. It was like the thing was stuck or something. I glanced up. Angie stood behind me, holding the trunk lid. She put her free hand on my shoulder and turned me so I was facing her. Then she let go of the trunk and put that arm around my neck and . . .

She kissed me—right on the mouth.

Vicky Fargus tried to kiss me one time, on the playground. I'd shoved her away, shook my fist in her face, and told her if she ever did that again, I'd bust her right in the nose.

Now I just stood there. Darned if Angie didn't kiss me again.

She stuffed a little piece of paper into my hand. "I know we'll probably never see each other again. You can e-mail me, if you want to. But you don't have to."

I looked at the little piece of crinkled-up paper, nodded, and smiled at her. "I will."

She arched an eyebrow.

"I will. Promise."

"Thank you," she said. "You made this the most wonderful vacation I ever had."

When she smiled, her eyes sparkled like stars flickering in a cloudless night sky.

I could still see them when I looked up at the clear . . .

"Tom?"

"Yes, dear," I breathed.

"Thomas!"

The sound of Grandpa's gruff voice made me jerk. I blinked a couple of times. I wasn't looking up at the stars twinkling in the clear night sky. I was staring up at the roof of the barn. Grandpa stood beside me, his head tilted far to the side, his eyes opened so wide, it almost made him look like he had hair on the front of his bald head again.

"What, Grandpa?"

"Got the lead rope wrapped around my legs." He pointed. "And you're choking the dog."

"Sorry." I unwrapped the rope, then knelt and rubbed the dog's throat until he stopped coughing. "I was thinking about something else."

"It's like you're a hundred miles off. Been that way all morning. Now pay attention to what we're doing, so we can work these last two dogs and . . . and . . ." He paused a moment, looking around, then sighed.

"Tell you what, Tom. I got a better idea. Why don't you go help your grandmother with the puppies?"

I puffed my chest out and stood straight. "I'll pay attention, Grandpa. Really. I'm serious."

"I'm serious, too." His smile was gentle—not mean or irritated. "This dog doesn't fight the rope, so I won't have to pull or strain. Besides that, I'm starving. If you go move Angie's pups for Grandma, she can start dinner. Then we can eat."

Frowning, I studied him for a moment. Sure he was being honest with me, I smiled back at him. "Yes, sir."

I'd only taken a step or two when I heard a

weird snort. Glancing over my shoulder, I caught Grandpa clamping his lips shut so tight that even his nose was turning white.

"You okay, Grandpa?"

He snorted again and kind of waved a hand, as if shooing me away.

"Just glad you said 'Yes, sir' instead of 'Yes, dear.' Kinda had me worried there for a minute."

I felt the heat rush to my face. My ears burned. They were probably so red, Grandpa could see them glowing. I didn't even turn around. I just took off, like a shot, to go find Grandma.

Grandma was in the old brooding house. The walls were thick, to help keep it cool in the summer. An electric heater was about halfway up the west wall, high enough so neither the mama dog nor the puppies could get too close to it and hurt themselves.

Kind of dark inside, it took a moment for my eyes to adjust to the dim light. Grandma sat on top of a big wooden box filled with old blankets and burlap bags. Holding one of the pups in her lap, she stroked its head and back. Cooing and talking sweet to it, just like it was a real baby. When she noticed me standing there, she ruffled the puppy's head and put it on the floor.

"Grandpa sent me to help move the puppies so you could go start dinner."

She made a grunting sound when she struggled to her feet. "Reckon they are old enough to wean," she said. "But it's always kind of sad when pups have to leave their mama." She knelt and held Angie's face between her hands. "You're a sweet girl," she said, softly. "You've been a good mama. But it's time for them to go." She sighed. "Guess it's just part of growing up," she added—more to herself than to me or Angie.

She picked up two of the pups and nodded toward the others. I got two, then followed her outside.

There was a portable chain-link pen, about thirty yards to the south of the brooding house. Not far from the creek, big trees threw shade across part of the area where it stood. We put our pups down, pushed them back so we could get the gate shut, then went for the last three.

Once all seven of the pups were in the pen, we

went to the barn to get a couple of food bowls and a bucket for water.

"You take the water in and put it on the far side of the pen—there in the shade," she told me. "I'll stay here and try to keep the little rascals from getting out, then hand the feed bowls over the fence to you."

Just getting in the gate was a challenge. The puppies kept jumping at my legs, trying to get me to play with them or let them out so they could run. I figured—real quick—that if I slid my feet instead of walking, it would be easier to get across the pen without stepping on one of them. The bucket was big around, but the sides weren't very tall. That way the puppies could reach over the top to get a drink. What with the wide bucket and the puppies jumping against my legs, I ended up spilling about a third of the water before I could set it in the shade.

Grandma handed the three food bowls over the fence. "Spread them out." She motioned with a wave of her arm. "That way they won't all clump up at one bowl, and they'll each have plenty to eat."

Careful not to step on anybody, I put down the food bowls and made my way back to the gate.

Tumbling over one another, the pups followed me—scampering in front of me, bumping into my feet, and making it next to impossible to walk. It took both Grandma and me to keep them shoved back and get the gate closed.

They stood with their paws on the chain-link, wagging their tails, yapping and bouncing. But for only a moment. Then they took off for the food bowls. Well, not the food *bowls*. Despite having three bowls spread out in the pen, they all managed to clump around one bowl.

Guess I hadn't taken the time to look at them before. In the bright sunlight, with me standing outside the pen where I didn't have to worry about smushing one of them, I finally had the chance.

One pup didn't race to the bowl with the others. He sat at the gate—very straight and proper—and watched us.

"Grandma. Look at this little guy. He's got blue eyes. I never saw a dog with blue eyes before."

When we asked Grandpa, he stopped what he was doing, rushed to put the dog he was working with back in her pen, and took off.

Grandma and I had to trot to keep up with him.

☙ Chapter 13 ☙

"Doe-eyed." He smiled.

"Doe-eyed?"

Grandpa nodded. "Yep. Doe-eyed."

Growing up—even before Grandpa had his surgery—we came to visit a lot. And although I wasn't into bird hunting, I knew a little bit about pointers.

There were liver-eared pointers. Those dogs were mostly white with dark brown or liver-colored markings on their ears, sides, and rumps. Angie's litter had a few of those. Then there were lemon-eared pointers. They had pretty much the same markings, only their spots were lighter—sort of a yellow color. Finally were the black-and-whites. They were a fairly new breed. Well, not a new breed—they were still pointers. But their spots were a jet black color, instead of brown or yellow. Three of Angie's pups were black-and-whites.

But all the time I'd been hanging around the kennel and around Grandpa, I'd never heard the term "doe-eyed."

"Doe-eyed?" I wondered out loud.

Grandpa nodded. "When he gets older, the eyes will turn from blue to a light brown color. Kind of like a deer. A doe? You know—doe-eyed."

The other pups were still eating, but the doe-eyed pup sat at the gate watching me. When Grandpa flipped the latch and picked him up, he wiggled, and wagged his tail, and tried to lick Grandpa. But as soon as he closed the gate, the pup spotted me and tried to climb out of Grandpa's arms.

"All the years I've been raising and training pointers, this is only the third one I've seen. The other two were spectacular dogs. Probably the best bird dogs I ever trained. A little neurotic, but still spectacular."

"Neurotic? What's that?"

"Ah—well—," Grandpa stammered. "Different. You know—weird. Nutty. Temperamental.

"Rock was the first. That dog could find birds quicker than any I ever hunted behind. But the old rascal wouldn't retrieve, no matter what.

"He'd pick a bird up and toss it in the air, so I'd know where it was. But I had to go pick the bird up myself, while he went on about his hunting."

"How about the other one?"

Grandpa glanced at me. "Other one?"

"Yeah. You said you only saw two other dogs with blue eyes. What was the other one like?"

"Well, he's not quite as fast to find the birds as Rock was. But in my entire life, I never saw that dog bust a covey."

"What's bust a covey, Grandpa?"

"Flush or scare the birds up, before the hunter gets there. It'll happen to even the best dog. But all the years I hunted with him, not one single time did he scare the birds up before I got there. And that, Tom, is just downright miraculous."

"Did he retrieve? You know, bring the birds back to you?"

"Sure does. Drops 'em right at my feet. Real soft mouth, too. Never chewed a bird."

The pup was leaning so far out of Grandpa's arm, I thought he was going to fall. He stuck out his long pink tongue and licked my arm. I petted him and reached out. He squirmed his way out of Grandpa's arms and into mine.

"You still got him? Is he still around?"

Grandpa nodded and pointed to where Angie stood watching from her pen.

"Yeah. It's Angie's sire. Old Gabe."

I jerked. Without even thinking, I drew my arm away from the pup and his pink tongue, and shoved him back at Grandpa.

"I'm hungry. Let's go eat dinner."

It wasn't that I didn't like puppies. I think every boy does—at least all the guys I knew. And it wasn't that I didn't like that one particular pup. He was kind of special. He caught my attention right off.

Thing was . . . what if he grew up to be like his grandfather—like Old Gabe?

That dog had a sixth sense when it came to

knowing when I wasn't expecting an attack. Since that first week, he'd gotten me at least three more times. His attacks didn't scare me as much as the first one—I didn't drop the hose and go flying out into mud and dog poop this time. But still . . .

What if that pup turned out to be like Gabe? There never was a meaner, sneakier, nastier dog in the whole world.

So when it came to taking care of the puppies, I left that pretty much to Grandma. And I kept my distance.

Well . . . for a couple of days, anyway.

Since there were seven pups, the puppy poop piled up pretty fast.

After church on Sunday, we all went to Grandma's for dinner. We ate, sat around and visited, watched TV for a while, and waited for Grandpa and Daddy to wake up from their naps. When they started to stir, Grandma said we probably needed to move the puppy pen.

She wouldn't let Grandpa come, because he still wasn't supposed to lift stuff. He grumped a little, but sat in his chair on the porch. Grandma,

Daddy, Mama, and I got at the four corners of the chain-link pen and lifted.

"Careful," Grandpa called. "Raise it too high, and the puppies will get out. Just scoot them along with it as you walk."

Guess Daddy wasn't listening. First thing we knew, there were puppies flying all around the yard. Grandma managed to grab one and tucked it under her arm. Yelling and shouting, she took off after another. Mama and Daddy were calling and whistling for the others, but they were totally ignoring them.

Pointer bird dogs *love* to run. It's just part of their nature. They can't help it.

I started to take off and join the chase, but something bumped my foot. I glanced down.

One of the pups was right beside me. Sitting very straight and proper, he looked up with those blue eyes. When I reached for him, he didn't take off like I expected. He didn't start squirming or trying to lick me like I expected him to, either. Instead, he just kind of nestled his head against my chest, wagged his tail, and looked up at me like I was some kind of yummy doggy treat or something.

Grandma still had only one puppy. She stood in the middle of the yard, so out of breath that her sides were heaving. I trotted to her and handed her the pup.

"I'm still in pretty good shape from soccer camp," I said. "If you hang on to this guy, I'll go help Mama and Daddy catch the others."

Grandma was huffing and puffing so hard that she couldn't answer. She just nodded.

I *was* in good shape from soccer camp, but by the time I got through running down four of the pups, I was ready to drop. What made matters worse was, once we got home, Mama reminded us that the carpet cleaner guy was coming the next day.

I had to straighten my room while Mama and Daddy dusted. Then we stayed up another hour or so moving furniture and taking turns with the vacuum.

Altogether it took about two hours. The house was spotless and I was pooped. I took a quick shower, got my pajamas on, and hopped into bed. The sheets hadn't even settled on top of me when I heard a tap at my door.

"Yes?"

Mama peeked in. "Wanted to let you know that you have the day off tomorrow."

I grinned. Mama smiled.

"Someone has to be here to let the carpet cleaners in, so I told your grandfather that you wouldn't be there to help work the dogs. I'll come and get you after I get off work."

"Okay," I nodded.

Holding on to the doorjamb with one hand, Mama kind of leaned around the corner. "This somebody's e-mail address?" she asked, tapping the corner of my dresser mirror with her finger.

Squinting, I saw the little piece of wrinkled paper she was pointing at. I remember slipping it between the wood and the glass on my mirror—so I wouldn't lose it. But I'd almost forgotten that it was there.

"It's Angie's."

She smiled. "I noticed it when I was dusting in here. Have you written to her?"

"Not yet."

Mama shrugged.

"You're not doing anything tomorrow."

When I didn't say anything, she turned off the light. "Good night, Tom."

" 'Night."

With a smile, I tucked the sheet around my shoulder and nestled my head into my pillow. I did promise Angie that I'd write. And having a day off from working with the dogs would be a restful and fun change.

I could hardly wait.

❧ Chapter 14 ❧

Grandpa reached into the coop, grabbed a pigeon, and stuffed him into the small wire box tucked under his arm. He closed the spring-loaded lid and slipped the pin into the latch. The thing kind of reminded me of a hand grenade—what with the pin and all.

"Give me a couple of minutes to plant the box. I'll whistle, and you bring Rex. Keep him on a short lead until you're past the kennel, then let him out to the end of the rope."

Rope wrapped around my hand, and Rex tugging at the other end, I leaned back against one of the barn poles and waited for Grandpa to whistle.

Helping with the dogs was a *whole lot* easier

than e-mailing a girl. I was glad to be back. But as I stood there, leaning against the pole, that stupid letter kept rattling around in my head.

Dear Angie,

That's how I'd started. Then I'd sat there and stared at the monitor for what had seemed like an hour.

When the carpet cleaner guy came, I'd let him in, then gone back to my room . . . and stared at the screen some more.

I don't know how long I sat there when I finally wrote:

I'm fine. How are you?

It should have been simple. I mean, when I was with Angie, talking and laughing with her was easy. It seemed like the most natural and comfortable thing in the world. But trying to write to her . . .

I had probably punched the DELETE button and started over again at least five times. When the carpet cleaner guy left, I came back and stared at the screen. Then Mama got home from work.

And all I'd written was:

Dear Angie,

    I'm fine. How are you?

    I have been helping my grandfather with his dogs. He needs help because he had some kind of operation on his heart and isn't supposed to work too much. So I help him.

    What have you been doing?

    Well, time to go. Bye.

Sincerely,
Tom

Instead of punching the SEND button, I left the screen on, got up and walked around the room for a minute. Then I looked in each drawer of my dresser—didn't straighten anything—just looked.

Back at the computer, I added:

P.S. I had a great time at Six Flags!

Then I paced around some more, opened my closet, and stared aimlessly in there for a while. I was just about to close the door when I noticed my backpack on the floor. Snatching it up, I reached in and pulled out my list of spelling words. It still brought a smile to my face. I was sure glad Mrs. Nash found them. It made me even happier to think about her being my teacher again, next year.

Throwing the backpack into the closet, I took the spelling words to my desk. For some reason I wanted to keep them, but not in the backpack. I flattened the two pages, folded them neatly, then went to my drawer to hide them behind my undershirts. Seemed like a good hiding place. A place where no one would know they were there but me.

Just as I placed them in the far corner of the drawer, I noticed the writing on the back.

Writing skills. Journal. Letters.

I remembered Mrs. Nash telling us that we would be working more on our writing skills next year, and I'd jotted it on my paper. A sly smile curled my lips. I shot back to the computer.

P.P.S. I got an idea. Why don't we write letters instead of e-mail?

Elbow propped on the desk and chin resting on my fist, I sat and stared at it. When Angie read it, I didn't want it to sound like an assignment, but . . .

I smiled at my computer.

P.P.S. I got an idea. Why don't we write letters instead of e-mail?

Then I added: *It's a little more private.*

Happy, confident, and almost downright proud of myself, I punched SEND.

Grandpa's shrill whistle finally came. Like a rescue, it pulled me back from thinking about the e-mail I'd spent all day yesterday on and into the present.

When Rex and I went around the dairy barn, all of the other dogs barked and bounded against the fence. They wanted out, too.

On the far side of the barn was a big pasture. The way it was mowed made it look like a giant checkerboard. Areas of tall grass and weeds were the squares. The clear-cut paths, where we walked, were the borders between them. Grandpa waited for us at the near edge.

When Rex went tearing into the tall grass squares, he yanked on the end of the rope so hard I almost lost my grip. He ran back and forth in big, sweeping arches. Grass bent as he dragged the rope across, only to spring back and wave in the gentle breeze. We let him run for a moment or two, then Grandpa nudged me with his elbow and pointed.

"He's running wild. Give him a little tug."

I nodded. "Rex! Easy!"

When he didn't slow, I yanked the rope. Not hard enough to flip him or even turn him—just hard enough so he'd feel it.

"Rex," I repeated. "Easy!"

He slowed. Instead of racing through the grass squares, he stuck his nose to the ground. Moved slow and steady. Sniffing all around each square thoroughly, before he raced across the mowed part to a different patch of tall grass and weeds.

A little over midway through the big pasture, Rex charged past a square, and was almost to another one when he turned.

He didn't really turn. It was like something grabbed his nose and turned him. His nose stopped. Then his front legs turned and stopped. Then his hind end slipped in the short grass, until I thought he was going to fall over. Throwing dust and grass clippings in the air, his rump slid to a stop—in a straight line with his nose and front end.

"Good boy!" Grandpa shouted. "*Eeeasy.* Easy, Rex."

The dog stayed, totally frozen, as we walked up slowly behind him. His head didn't move. His tail didn't move. But the closer we got, I could see the muscles in his shoulders and hips quivering.

"Easy," I ordered, sliding my hand up the rope and tightening my grip. *"Eeeasy."*

Rex lunged. I yanked.

"Rex! Hold!" Grandpa barked.

Again Rex froze. He was still trembling, though.

Grandpa stepped up beside him. He reached out a hand and ran it down Rex's back and tail. Rex didn't move.

"Good point." Grandpa smiled. "Soon as I pull the pin, let him go."

He stepped in front of Rex. Pulling the starter

pistol from the holster, he swept his foot back and forth through the tall grass. At last I could see his foot poised above the metal footpad where he had attached the cord from the pin. He stomped on it. The spring clicked and the wire box popped open. The pigeon, feathers flying as his wings knocked against the sides, burst from the box and flew off.

Rex charged after him. Grandpa fired the pistol a couple of times. It made a loud sound, but smoke from the blanks was the only thing that came out.

We let Rex chase after the bird a few seconds, then Grandpa nodded for me to call him back.

"Rex!" I yelled. "Rex! In!"

The pigeon was already high in the air. While Rex came trotting back to me, the bird circled a couple of times. Once he had his bearings, he flew back to the coop in the barn. Grandpa and I both patted and praised Rex when he came, wagging his tail and his whole rear end.

We put Rex into his pen and repeated the same thing with Sis. Only Grandpa hid the box in a different part of the checkerboard pasture. We were just taking her back when Grandma flung open the front screen door.

"Food's getting cold," she called. "You two quit messin' with those dogs and get in here."

After dinner, Grandma decided Grandpa needed to rest. He fussed a little, but finally settled down on the couch. I flipped through the TV channels, but there was nothing worth watching.

Grandma must have heard me clicking through the soap operas and talk shows. Dish towel in hand, she peeked around the corner from the kitchen.

"Why don't you go play with the pups?" She smiled.

I smiled back and took off like a shot.

Chapter 15

I stopped at the edge of the barn. Six of the pups were piled up—all curled around and flopped across one another—sleeping in the shade. But just like I expected, one pup stood with his paws on the gate, wagging his tail. I hadn't made a sound. Still, somehow he knew I was coming.

When I'd asked Grandpa about naming the puppies, he told me that their new owners would name them. He and I would just call them each Pup.

I named him Tad. I just didn't tell Grandpa.

It was really cool the way I came up with his name, too. I used the initials: *T*homas and *A*ngie *D*anfield. But if anybody ever asked, I was covered. That's because my middle name is Andrew—so

I could just tell them I used the initials for *my* name, and nobody would ever know.

"Hi, Tad," I whispered. "How you doing, boy?"

When he heard me, his ears perked high. His tail whipped so hard, I was afraid he was going to knock his hind feet clean out from under himself.

Quiet as I could, so as not to wake the other puppies, I opened the latch and let him out. He shot past me, ran a wide circle around the pen, then came back to jump up and put his paws on my leg. I petted him. He wiggled all over, then took off again.

Pointers *love* to run.

A jet took off from the airport. The sound still made my neck scrunch down between my shoulders, but just a tiny bit. I was so used to the sound, I hardly heard it anymore. The puppies didn't stir. Tad didn't seem to notice, either. While he made another circle, I moved away from the pen.

There was a little clearing, near the creek. An enormous stump stood in the middle, just about the right height for sitting.

Perching on that stump gave me a pretty good

view. I could keep an eye on Tad, no matter where he went.

Not that I really needed to.

Tad could run like a streak of lightning. He could cover more ground and cover it faster than any of the other pups. But he always managed to keep me in sight. And he always circled in, sort of like touching base. He'd run to me, get a pet, then go racing off to explore someplace else.

Sure enough, my bottom had barely touched the stump, when he came racing back. Standing on his hind legs, he put one paw on the log beside me. The other paw patted my leg, as if he were tapping me on the shoulder—saying something like:

"I'm here, Tom. Say hello, so I can go run some more."

I reached down with both hands, wobbled his head between my palms, then scratched behind his ears. He gave my wrist a quick lick, then shot off down the slope to go check out the creek.

When Tad came back, panting and tongue hanging out of his mouth, I picked him up. He lay across my lap for a while—head and front paws draped over my left leg, rump and hind legs dangling off my right. After he rested a couple of minutes, he sat up so he could lean his head against my chest.

"I got another letter from Angie, yesterday," I told him. Tad leaned away so he could look up at me. "That's the second she's sent since I e-mailed her. I should probably write her again, but I haven't. So then today—here comes a *third* letter from her."

Tad arched his ears and tilted his head to the side.

"The first letter she sent was a little bit scary. She told me she thought it was 'really romantic' to write letters instead of e-mails. I thought I was in BIG trouble. You know . . . she'd get all mushy and stuff like that. But I think she's okay now. In this letter she told me she's taking dance and playing on a girls' soccer team. She said soccer doesn't last much past the end of September in Minnesota, because of the snow. So when soccer season's over, she's supposed to take piano." One of Tad's ears drooped, but the other stayed up.

"Then she told me about her dog, Lady. She

was a cocker spaniel. She was seventeen years old. Angie said she was really sick, and last week, she got so bad she couldn't even get up. They had to take her to the vet and have her put to sleep.

"It was really sad. You know . . . the way she talked about how it made her feel. I'd write her back, only I don't know what to say."

When I glanced down, Tad wasn't listening anymore. He was draped across my lap, leaning forward to sniff a big ant who scurried across our stump.

I snuggled him again, then took him back to the pen with the others. They were awake, so—careful where I stepped—I managed to fight them away from the gate and get inside.

All of them wanted to be petted. They wiggled and squirmed and went crazy when I picked them up, and tousled their fur. As soon as I put them on the ground, they wagged and bounced against my leg so I'd pick them up again. I couldn't help laughing and smiling at their antics.

Sure that I'd given each of them some attention, I picked Tad up and petted him a minute, then reached for the gate latch.

"See you tomorrow, pups," I said, putting Tad on the ground and ruffling his head and ears. "Be a good puppy, Tad."

"Tom."

Grandpa's voice made me jump. I turned and spotted him standing near the side of the barn. He pointed at the pen.

"Before you come out, bring two of those pups over here. They're old enough to start staking 'em out."

Staking 'em out? I repeated inside my head. *Sounds like some kind of torture technique.*

"What are we doing?"

"Staking 'em out," he repeated. "Teaching them not to fight a collar and leash. Bring 'em, two at a time. I'll show you."

It was downright challenging to hold two puppies, fight the other five back, and latch the gate— all at the same time. Somehow I managed.

One pup tucked under each arm, I found Grandpa. He was inside the barn, standing in front of a long board with big nails hammered halfway into it. A bunch of dog collars hung from the nails. He found one for each pup and fastened them securely around their necks. Then he took one pup and motioned me to follow with the other.

Outside the barn, the side closest to the house, was a big log chain. Its links were bigger around than my thumb. About ten feet long, it was held down at both ends with big iron stakes. Smaller chains, with clips, lay on the ground at intervals along the big log chain. Grandpa clipped his puppy's collar to the first chain. Then he took my pup and clipped him next in line.

"Go get two more."

Glancing over my shoulder, the way the pups looked, made me cringe. The two that were already there were throwing a regular fit. They leaped against the chain. They cried. They bit at the smaller chain. They jerked and hit the end of it, flipped themselves clear over, and whimpered and whined when they couldn't follow me.

When I left Tad, he didn't fight the chain or flip himself over. He just looked at me with those big blue eyes. A sad, pleading look that seemed to say: "I like you. Why are you doing this to me? What did I do wrong?"

I felt like a total jerk!

❖ Chapter 16 ❖

About thirty minutes later, after Grandpa and I had worked with another of the older dogs, we went back for the puppies. At the edge of the barn, he held out an arm to stop me. Together, we leaned forward.

All seven of the pups were calm as could be. Three were lying down. One stood, watching toward the house. Tad and the last two sat on their haunches. All seemed alert and watchful, but none were chewing on the chain or struggling to get free.

Then Tad must have sensed that I was nearby. He sprang to his feet, looked all around, then started lunging at the chain again. When he jerked, all the others jumped up and started barking and twisting around.

Grandpa and I stepped back.

"Next time we stake 'em out, they'll still fight the chain," Grandpa explained. "But not as much. The following time, hardly any at all. After that they're ready to put on a collar and lead. Using the chain is safer, too. No leash to get tangled up in, and nobody yanking on the other end to scare them.

"Dogs are pretty bright animals. They learn real quick that once they quit pulling and fighting—you know, keep a little slack on the collar—it isn't all that bad. That way we can work them on birds without hurting them. And when the new owners come next week, to pick out their pup, they'll be ready to go home with them."

"New owners?"

"Yeah," Grandpa answered, with a jerk of his head. "Let's go put them back in the pen."

"What new owners?" I asked, suddenly stopping at the end of the log chain.

"Well, Jeb Owens is coming Monday. He gets the pick of the litter. Then there's a fella from Weatherford, Texas, and another hunter from Tulsa who told me he wanted one of Angie's pups when she had another litter. They should be here Tuesday or Wednesday."

Grandpa took one of the pups off the chain and handed her to me. For some reason, I couldn't follow. I just stood there, holding the puppy in my arms, with my mouth open. He had to walk back to hand me the second pup.

"Who's Jeb Owens?" I asked.

"His dog, Willie, is the sire. You know, the pups' father. I think Willie's real name is something like Sir Lester Fonsworth of Wilstershire— or some such highfalutin name. Bloodline goes clear back to England. Field Dog Trials champion two years running, and National Open champion about three years back. Jeb just calls him Willie. Good dog, but a little too high-strung for me. That's why we decided to cross him with Angie."

"You mean he can come and pick any puppy he wants?"

Grandpa tucked a second pup under his arm, and motioned me to follow.

"That's the way it's done. Since his dog is the sire, he either gets a breeding fee, or his pick of the litter. I'm glad Jeb went for the pup. Last time

I checked, Willie's breeding fee was somewhere in the neighborhood of five thousand dollars. Even with our insurance—after paying for my open-heart surgery, your grandmother and I couldn't afford that kind of a fee."

Grandpa opened the gate, just wide enough so I could stuff my two puppies in, but not enough so the other two could get out. After I crammed them through the opening, I sprang to my feet and sprinted back to the log chain.

By the time Grandpa latched the gate and turned, I already had Tad's collar off. I held him in my arms. He rubbed his head against my chest.

It's always hot in August. That's why I couldn't quite figure why my teeth were chattering, and why my arms and legs shook like leaves trying to escape a fall tree. Tad just cuddled closer. I clamped my lips between my teeth to keep them from rattling inside my head.

"Grandpa. I was just wondering . . . I just thought that . . . that maybe I could . . . maybe . . ."

He stopped right in front of me. When I looked at his face, I couldn't quite tell what I saw.

Grandpa's eyes were gentle and loving. His

lips curled to a caring and understanding smile. But the set of his chin and jaw took all the joy from that smile. They were stiff, hard, and unmoveable as a mountain boulder.

"I know, Tom," he said, his voice barely a whisper. "You want to keep Tad."

My head snapped back.

"How did you . . . ?"

"I've heard you calling him, when you thought I wasn't around. I've seen the way you look at him. And I've seen the way he looks at you."

Grandpa sighed. His chin jutted out once more. Then he took a deep breath.

"Tom, Jeb Owens decided on the pick of the litter. I agreed. I gave my word."

I heard the gulping sound inside my head when I swallowed.

"I could take Tad home. That way he wouldn't be here when the man came."

Grandpa just looked at me.

That look hurt. I wished I hadn't said what I did. Just the thought was dishonest. It was lying and cheating and sneaky, all rolled into one. The second those stupid words came tumbling out, I wished I could grab them and stuff them back inside my mouth.

My mind raced. My eyes darted from Grandpa to Tad and back again.

"Maybe you could talk to him, Grandpa."

He didn't even blink. "Tom, what you're suggesting isn't right. Jeb gets the pick of the litter. You can't tell a fella that, then add: 'You get the pick of the litter, except for this dog, and that dog with the black spots, and that dog over yonder.' It's not right."

I squeezed Tad closer to my chest.

"Okay, maybe *I* could talk to him. If he knew how much I liked that pup—if he could see us together . . . He's probably a nice man, Grandpa. Isn't he? Even if he's not, he couldn't be that mean. He couldn't take a puppy away from . . . maybe . . . maybe we could . . . Grandpa?"

Little puddles formed at the bottom of Grandpa's eyes. Still, his jaw and chin didn't budge. "Jeb Owens is a good and decent man. He's not the kind who would separate a boy and his dog. But Tom, there's always times when not telling the truth, or hedging just a little, looks a whole lot easier. Safer. And there's times when keeping your word or doing what's right—hurts."

He brushed a sleeve against the side of his head. I couldn't tell whether he was wiping the sweat that beaded up on his forehead, or the little drop that raced down his cheek.

"When you get right down to it, Tom, a man doesn't have much in this world that is truly his own. Friends come and go. You can't always depend on them. And there's tons of people who will lie to you. Always somebody trying to cheat you out of something. A fire can burn your house down. Death can take away the people you love." He traced a finger down the center of his chest. I could tell he didn't even realize he was doing it.

"The only thing a man has—the only thing that's really his—is his word. That and his faith in God."

He cleared his throat and took a deep, wheezing breath.

"It hurts me as much as it does you. Maybe even more. I know how much you love that pup—I knew probably even before you knew it yourself. I could see it in both of you.

"But Jeb Owens will get his pick of the litter. All we can do is hope and pray that he won't take—"

"I hate you, Grandpa!" I raged at the top of my lungs. "Jeb Owens may be a nice man. He wouldn't separate a boy and his dog. But *you* would!"

Clutching Tad close to my heart, I ran for the creek.

❦ Chapter 17 ❦

On my hands and knees, I reached into the bottom of my closet, shoving the soccer ball out of the way. Quiet, so as not to wake Mama and Daddy, I moved some shoes aside, felt around, even shuffled through a pile of my old toys.

Finally I found my backpack.

When Mama bought notebook paper, she always got the big economy size. At the beginning of school, then again around January or February, I filled my notebook. There was always paper left over. So I kept that on the side of my dresser.

Trouble was, the letter I'd been writing to Angie used up the last two sheets from my pile. I had to get my notebook, because there was still more I needed to tell her.

I set the backpack beside me on the bed and reached in. Digging around, I finally found my notebook. Shoving my backpack aside, I opened the notebook in my lap, picked up my pencil, and . . .

Went totally blank.

I had no idea what I was going to say to Angie next. So, finding the letter, I started reading to see where I'd left off.

Dear Angie,

 I was really sorry to hear about Lady. The way you talked about her in your letter I could tell she was a good dog and you loved her a lot. It made me sad to read that your mom and dad had to put her to sleep. She was very sick and it was probably the best thing you could do for her because she doesn't have to suffer now. But I know it hurts.

 Until yesterday I didn't know how much it hurts. I told you about helping my grandpa with his dogs. I told you about Angie having puppies too. I remember because it made you mad. One of her pups has blue eyes. He's real smart and as cute as he can be. He is my favorite. I think (no I know) that he likes me too. Only I didn't know until yesterday how much I love him.

I told Angie all about Tad—how he wormed his way into my heart so quick that I didn't even know it was happening. How he always knew I was near, and no matter how far or fast he ran, he always came back to me. I even told her how I got his name. I told her about screaming at my grandpa. And how I took Tad and hid out in the creek and the back pasture for over an hour. And how I thought about running away—at least until that Mr. Owens was gone. And I told her how I was almost twelve and going to be in sixth grade. And how I was getting kind of grown-up because I had already had my first kiss, and I didn't even think about punching her in the nose.

I told her how, instead of acting grown-up, I'd behaved like a little four-year-old, throwing a temper fit because I didn't get my way.

I told Angie about bringing Tad back and handing him to Grandpa. About trying my hardest to make sure he understood how much I loved him, and how scared I was about his surgery, and that

I didn't mean to hurt his feelings. Only I knew I had. And I told Angie how rotten that made me feel inside. And I left off with:

I know Grandpa is right. I know he's doing the right thing. The only thing a man can do. But it

That's where I ran out of paper. So I started writing on the fresh notebook page:

still hurts!
I don't know what I'm going to do next Monday when Mr. Owens comes. I think what I'll do is tell Mama and Daddy I'm sick and stay home. If the man picks Tad, I'll end up crying. And I don't want to do that. So

I stopped a moment and stared up at the ceiling. Then I glanced at the clock. It was five minutes till one. I stared at the paper for a long time before I took my pencil and marked a big *X* over the lines that began "I think" and ended with "So."

I will go help Grandpa with the dogs tomorrow, because I told Grandpa I would. But when the man comes I don't know what I will do. I really don't.

Sorry I made this such a l o n g letter. I hope you don't think I'm crazy for all the dumb stuff I said. I couldn't tell Grandma or Grandpa. I couldn't even tell Mama and Daddy how I'd acted and how it made me feel. But I had to tell somebody, and I thought you would understand.

Yours,

Tom

P.S. Sorry if I didn't spell stuff right. I didn't take the time to check my spelling.

P.P.S. Don't tell anybody how I got Tad's name. Okay?

I folded the paper in thirds, addressed the envelope, and made sure it was sealed. Then I went to bed.

☙ Chapter 18 ❧

Friday morning, Grandpa and I got two of the older dogs from the kennel. While he held them at the side of the barn, he sent me to let some quail out.

The quail box was at the far edge of the pasture. I don't know what I was expecting, the first time we went to get quail, but that box *wasn't* it.

It was just a tall, green, wooden box with a slanted roof on the top, like outhouses I'd seen. Only the door didn't have a new moon shape cut in it like Shrek's outhouse did.

I opened the door just wide enough to stick my head in. The whole floor was full of bobwhite quail. As they scrambled to escape the "monster" who was invading their home, they climbed and fluttered over one another. They stepped in the big water thing on the left wall, near the door. They knocked feed out of the metal trough on the right wall. One even climbed on top of some of the others and ended up falling out the ramp.

The opening for the little ramp was about six inches above the floor on the right wall. When the birds came back to the box, they could find the opening outside, because it was at ground level. They would walk up the ramp, and hop down to the floor. But once inside, they weren't smart enough to get out. That's because the opening inside was above their heads. Quail aren't the brightest animals in the world. Guess they didn't have sense enough to look up.

Reaching in, I caught one and set him behind me on the ground. Three more shot from the opening, raced between my feet, and escaped. I tossed out a couple more, then latched the door.

Quail love to stay together. The ones outside were already calling—whistling—to find their way back to the covey. If the birds were too close to the box, the smell would confuse the dogs. So I walked in a circle around the thing. Two birds flew off toward the creek. I made a wider circle the second and third time. Three more birds flew off—I'd almost stepped on the last one before he burst into the air. Those birds landed near the cedar trees on my right.

The last circle—even wider than the others—got another bird up. Not remembering how many were out, I figured that was good enough, so I jogged back to Grandpa and the dogs.

We spent the morning watching the dogs sniff and run. They pointed, stayed solid as a rock, until Grandpa or I kicked a bird from its hiding place.

I kept as close to Grandpa as I could. We talked about a lot of things. Most I don't remember. But I wanted to be with him—to let him know how much I liked him and cared for him. And even though neither one of us said a word about the little temper fit I'd had, I hoped that being with him would let him know—would help him under-stand—well, how sorry I was.

After lunch, Grandma asked if I wanted to go play with the puppies.

"Not today." I tried to smile. "I think I'll just rest instead."

I tried to sound light and happy. But Tad would have looked at me with his blue eyes and he'd know. He'd be able to tell how scared I was—how much I was hurting. He'd wonder why I didn't hug him and love on him like I always did. It was because I couldn't.

Loving on him and being with him would hurt too much if Mr. Owens took him from me. But there was no way I could make a pup understand.

So I watched TV instead, and waited until Grandpa was ready to go again.

That afternoon, Grandpa and I got two other dogs out of their pens. One was an older pointer named Sid that he was keeping for a friend who was on vacation.

Rex was the other dog. I liked him. Grandpa and I had worked with that pup a lot over the summer. Rex's color and the way his spots were arranged made me think of Tad, only Rex's eyes were dark brown.

Grandpa said we'd work them together because Rex belonged to the same man, and we needed to finish him.

When I asked what "finish him" meant, Grandpa

explained that Rex could point pigeons. He could find quail, and he was good about holding a point—not scaring the birds up before we got there. But since these two would be hunting together come quail season, we needed to make sure Rex was ready—"finished" with his training.

That's what Grandpa told me.

But while he was keeping the dogs on the far side of the barn as I jogged out to let more quail loose, I figured out the real reason.

Same as this morning, watching the dogs work with quail was a whole lot more fun and interesting than working them on pigeons, or training them to "heel" or retrieve. Grandpa thought this would keep my mind off Mr. Owens.

It helped—a little. But not much.

Sid and Rex found the first two birds within just a few seconds of each other. Sid on our left, pointing. Rex frozen solid and pointing another bird on our right.

Grandpa and I went to Rex. He stayed, paw raised and tail frozen like an icicle, until I scared the bird out of a clump of tall grass. Wings fluttering ninety-to-nothing, it burst into the air. Grandpa fired his starter pistol, and let Rex chase after the bird a few seconds before he called him back.

Grandpa was pleased with him.

While Rex was working his way back to us, we went after the bird Sid had found.

An older and smarter dog, Sid didn't race after his. Well, he took a couple of hops toward it when the thing flew. But then he stopped and watched where it landed in the bottom of the creek bed.

He didn't chase it as soon as it hit the ground, though. Instead, nose to the ground, he swept back and forth in front of us—just to make sure there wasn't another bird hiding nearby.

I could tell by the grin on Grandpa's face that he was pleased with him, too.

But when Sid found his bird the second time, Grandpa was *not* pleased.

That's because—just about the time Sid raised his paw and his tail froze straight and stiff—Rex plowed into the back of him.

Both dogs tumbled. Sid yelped and spun to see what had hit him. Rex didn't even slow down. He just climbed over the other dog, and went off chasing the bird that he had just scared up.

"That's what I was afraid of," Grandpa muttered. "Go grab his rope. We'll try something else."

This time I held Rex. Following behind, we waited until Sid found another bird.

"Bring him up slow," Grandpa said. "Right behind Sid. When he's about five feet away, give him a tug and say 'Hold.'"

Rex didn't hold. Even when I tugged the second time, he still kept straining against the collar, trying to find the bird. I could tell by the way his nose flared—how it made that popping sound—that he knew there was a bird there. Instead of stopping, he just kept trying to see it for himself.

The next time, Grandpa followed Sid and me. He didn't have any more success than I did. Rex never so much as looked at the other dog, or slowed to see what he was pointing. When Grandpa finally got him stopped, and loosened his hold on the rope, Rex shot past Sid and scared the bird.

Grandpa threw up his hands. "Guess we're gonna have to do it the hard way, pup." Then to me: "Call 'em in. We'll wait till Monday. Take him out with Old Gabe."

Just the thought of letting Old Gabe out of his pen sent a chill up my back. I didn't say anything, though.

Mama was there when Grandpa and I got back to the house. She told Grandma that we were driving to Spiro to see Daddy's folks, but we'd be out for Sunday dinner. After they were through visiting, we went to clean kennels and feed. I talked Mama into letting me feed the puppies.

Chapter 19

Daddy was already home from work when Mama and I got there.

"Tom." He cleared his throat and pointed to the coffee table. "You got another letter from Angie."

When I turned toward the coffee table, I heard Mama giggle, then she whispered, "Quit that."

I knew better than to glance back. So I picked up my letter and went to my room.

Dear Tom,

I have a new puppy. I haven't thought of a name for him yet. Oh, by the way, he's a boy dog. Maybe I'll name him Tom, because he's so cute and sweet. But I'm not sure.

Lady was an outside dog. We've never had an inside dog, but I talked Mama and Daddy into letting him stay in my room.

Right now he's snuggled next to me, watching me write this letter.

Here's a picture of him.

Yours,
Angie

For a long long time, I sat and stared at the picture. He was a beagle, with big brown eyes and floppy ears. They took the photo with him lying on a couch, and the little guy looked more like a fuzzy lump than a dog. But he *was* cute.

I could tell from the letter that Angie hadn't gotten *my* last letter. The way she wrote, I could tell she was happy. I could tell from looking at the picture that the little beagle puppy was happy, too.

And I was glad for her.

But it also hurt. I couldn't keep from thinking about Tad. How maybe he could sit on my bed when I wrote her the next time. How we could run and play. How he could nestle his head against my chest when I hugged him.

How—maybe—I'd never see him again.

I stuffed the letter back in the envelope and put it with the others, in my drawer. Then I went outside.

The patio had a big aluminum awning over it. I sat in one of the wicker chairs. Leaning forward, I rested my elbows on my knees, my chin in my hand. For a long time, I sat staring out at our backyard.

It was a small backyard. No, it was tiny. The nearby streets were busy and from the patio, I could hear the rumble of cars and trucks running up and down the freeway, which was only two blocks off.

What if Tad got out? What if . . .

I squished my eyes shut as hard as I could and shook my head, trying to chase the thought away.

Then for the next thirty minutes, I sat there, trying to convince myself how Tad wouldn't be happy here. Bird dogs love to run. Our yard was way too small. They love to hunt. I don't like guns. What would I do with a bird dog, anyway?

And I tried to tell myself that he'd be better off with Mr. Owens.

Then I went to bed.

But I didn't sleep very well.

We left early on Saturday morning, because it was about a three-hour drive to Spiro, where Dad's folks live. I guess with all the flipping and flopping and twisting and turning I'd done last night, I pretty much wore myself out.

I slept most of the way.

Grandma and Grandpa Danfield were quite a bit younger than Mama's mom and dad. After all the hugging and kissing, they sat in the living room and visited. It was pretty boring.

Then Grandpa Danfield got Dad to reset the clock on the VCR, because he still couldn't remember how to do it. We went to eat at a restaurant in Fort Smith. When we got back to the house, they visited some more. I went outside to look at the cows.

But all I could think about was Tad. How he'd love it here. The farm had lots more hills and brush than the land around the kennel. There was room to run—not like our tiny backyard. And Tad would . . .

I bit my bottom lip so hard, it almost brought blood.

Then I went back inside and sat down to listen to them talk, and be totally bored—because it was easier than thinking about Tad.

Monday morning, I still didn't know what I was going to do when Mr. Owens showed up.

Usually Grandpa would be drinking his coffee and waiting for me on the front porch when I arrived. This morning there was no sign of him. I waved bye to Daddy, watched him drive off, then headed to the house to see if Grandpa was sleeping late. Or maybe he was sick again, or . . .

A knot tightened in my stomach. I almost wanted to double over.

Maybe Mr. Owens was already here. Maybe . . .

"Tom! Stop!"

The shout came from near the barn. I spotted Grandpa standing there, waved, and took a couple of steps toward him.

"Tom, stop!" he repeated. "Don't move a muscle. Just stand there."

The urgency in his voice froze me in my tracks.

Suddenly I heard a barking, snarling roar. Hard as he could run, a liver-eared pointer raced toward me.

It was Old Gabe!

Eyes darted to the house—the door—back to the charging dog—then to the safety of the house once more.

If I was fast enough . . . If I ran as hard as I could, I might just make it.

Gabe's lip curled. Long, sharp, yellow teeth caught the morning sun and glistened like daggers.

Chapter 20

My legs wanted to run. It took every bit of courage I could muster to stand.

Snarling and snapping, Gabe slid to a stop, his yellow teeth less than an inch from my leg. I didn't move. I didn't even breathe.

From the corner of my eye, I could see Grandpa walking really fast, carrying something in each hand. I couldn't tell what he had because my eyes were locked on the snarling dog. His hair bristled down his back when he looked up at me.

Maybe Grandpa had a couple of clubs or brooms or something. Maybe he was going to have to beat the dog, to get him off me.

Gabe wagged his tail. But a deep, nasty growl came from behind those up-curled lips, from someplace down deep in his throat.

I needed to swallow, but I couldn't even do that.

"Here," Grandpa said, handing whatever he had in one hand out to me. "Take it slow and easy, then hold it down at your side, like I'm holding mine."

Without looking, I slowly raised my hand. Grandpa put something in it. And even more slowly, I began to lower it to my side.

It was a shotgun, well, not really a shotgun. It was made entirely of wood.

Gabe sniffed my leg. He raised his head and sniffed the wooden shotgun.

"Come on, Gabe." Grandpa's voice was excited and happy. "Let's go find us some birds."

Long, pointed tail whipping the air, Gabe took one hop toward him. He sniffed Grandpa. He sniffed the shotgun that dangled at his side, then . . .

Gabe took off for the far side of the barn.

I don't know what surprised me more—the fact that Gabe *didn't* bite me, or the fact that, for an old dog, he bounded off hopping and as excited as a little puppy.

The air whooshed from my lungs and I gasped

for another breath. Grandpa let out a blast of air that flew up his forehead. It didn't wiggle the hair on his head, because he didn't have any. But I could see the wild, bristly, burly hairs that stuck out on his eyebrows jiggle.

"Craziest old dog I ever saw in my life," he said. "Huntingest old dog I ever saw, too. Long as he thinks we're hunting birds, that's all he cares about. Come on."

Still breathing heavy, I followed Grandpa toward the barn.

"What is this?" I asked, looking at the wooden shotgun.

"My grandfather carved that for my dad, when he was ten years old. Dad played with it a bunch. Reckon that's why the trigger is broken off. Dad waited until I was twenty-one before he passed it down to me. Guess he figured if I played with it, I'd break the hammers off. When you come of age, I'll pass it to you. Try to take good care of it. It's hand-carved from solid black walnut. Thing's kind of a family heirloom. But today, it's mostly for Old Gabe. Like I said—long as he thinks we're hunting, he won't bother you."

I couldn't help but marvel at the thing. When he first handed it to me, I thought it was a toy gun. The more I studied it, the more it looked like a work of art. Its barrels were perfectly smooth, almost like the steel on a real gun. The hand rest and where it was connected to the stock were intricately checkered, just like Grandpa's shotgun. There were even designs carved onto the breech. A picture of a deer in the forest on one side, a flying pheasant on the other.

I was so busy looking at it, I bumped right into Grandpa.

"It's not real," he said, glancing over his shoulder. "But real or not, always treat any gun like it's loaded. Keep it pointed away from any other hunters and dogs. Put it down when you cross a fence. All that stuff. Just like it's real."

"Yes, sir."

Sid and Rex were tied to the fence. Grandpa leaned to loosen one of the lead ropes, then suddenly straightened.

He looked toward the house.

My breath caught. He stood real straight, stretching his neck as if looking at . . .

Suddenly my stomach tightened. A knot came into my throat that I couldn't swallow.

I couldn't look.

What if Mr. Owens's car was there?

What if he was ready to pick his dog?

Tad was the best dog of the whole litter. I didn't know much about bird dogs, but even I could tell that.

What if Mr. Owens chose . . .

Eyes cast down—frozen to the dirt—I walked to the fence, untied Sid's rope, wrapped it around my hand, and ever so slowly raised my eyes toward the driveway.

Grandpa must have noticed. He turned and smiled at me.

"Thought I heard a car drive up. Must have been a private plane, or something, taking off from the airport."

My sigh came clear from my knees. It raced around my stomach, up through my chest, and came wheezing out my throat.

I thought I heard Grandpa sigh, too. Only his wasn't nearly as deep or desperate. "Let's see if these dogs can find some birds."

❧ Chapter 21 ❧

While we walked behind the dogs, Grandpa told me that he had already let some quail out. He had tied Sid and Rex by the barn, and was just getting ready to put a collar on Old Gabe, when Daddy and I drove up.

From the time we left the barn until we got to the pasture where the dogs were hunting, he must have apologized about ten times for not having Gabe under control.

The dogs were fun to watch. Sniffing and racing back and forth in front of us, they hunted and searched every inch of the pasture.

"Most of the quail landed along the creek," Grandpa told me. "We'll let 'em hunt up here a couple more minutes. Get a little of the running out of Rex's system. Then we'll head down there."

When we turned, the dogs stayed in front of us. Gabe went to the far side of the creek. Sid and Rex stayed on our side.

Rex was the first to find a bird. He was in some tall grass, and all I could see was his tail whipping back and forth. Then, suddenly, the tail froze in mid-swing. Stood straight and stiff.

"Got one," Grandpa said.

I nudged his arm when I saw Sid.

"Looks like Sid's found one, too."

Stopping, Grandpa frowned and shook his head.

"Nope. That's an honor."

"Huh?"

"He's pointing Rex. Honoring the other dog's point. See how his head's up, not down like he's looking at something in the grass. And if you'll look at his eyes, they're pointed straight at Rex."

Studying them for a moment, I remember Grandpa talking about honoring before. I kind of had an idea what he meant, but I didn't really understand—not until I saw it with my own eyes.

When we kicked the bird up, Grandpa fired. The shotgun was a lot louder than the starter pistol. It made me jump, but just a little.

"You miss on purpose?" I teased.

"Yeah," Grandpa admitted. "But I'll have to bring one or two down before too long. Otherwise, the dogs start getting frustrated or discouraged."

The quail were fun to watch, the way they ran and darted around, the way they flew, beating their wings so fast I couldn't see. I didn't like the thought of Grandpa shooting one of the cute little things. But I understood.

Rex found the second bird, too.

Just like before, Sid stopped and pointed.

"Honor?"

"Honor," Grandpa answered.

Gabe must have figured the huntin' was better on our side of the creek. Before Grandpa and I reached Rex, Gabe came leaping over the ridge at the edge of the dry creek bed.

In midair, his eyes flashed. Legs stiffened. Tail didn't wag—it didn't even spin to help balance him. The instant his paws touched the ground, he was frozen—motionless—in a solid point.

"Now that's an honor," Grandpa whispered.

Sid found the next bird. Only Rex went flying right past him and scared it before we could get there.

"Call him in." Grandpa snorted.

"Rex! Come here, boy."

"No," Grandpa said. "Call Sid."

"Sid? He didn't do anything wrong."

"Call him in."

Sid came running. Grandpa put his shotgun down and knelt. He wobbled Sid's head between his hands, petted him, and kept saying, "Good boy. Good boy, Sid." Then he handed me the lead rope and told me to keep him beside us.

Sid didn't understand. He kept pulling at the rope, wanting to find more birds. I didn't understand, either.

Not until Old Gabe found the next bird.

The old dog was making a turn when he locked up. Kind of leaning *way* to one side, it's a wonder he didn't fall over. Sid stopped tugging at the rope in my hand. When I glanced down at him, he wasn't pointing, but he did stop.

When I looked again, Rex was about ten yards

behind Old Gabe. He came racing up right on his tail, sidestepped to get around him, and just as he was about to shoot past . . .

Old Gabe pounced.

Roaring and growling and snapping, he lit into that pup like a tornado. He was all over him. Knocked him to the ground. He snarled. Snapped. Bit.

Even when Rex rolled over on his back to expose his tummy—that's what dogs do to show another dog they don't want to fight—Gabe kept right on snarling and snapping at him.

"Aren't you going to stop him, Grandpa?"

Grandpa shook his head. "Gabe's not hurting him. Just talking to him."

Far as I could see, it sure looked like a vicious, mean, and nasty way to talk. But as soon as Gabe let the pup up, Rex raced to us for protection. He hid behind us, kind of peeking around to make sure Gabe wasn't still after him.

Grandpa was right. He had slobbers all over him, but there was no blood. Not so much as a scratch.

The bird Gabe was pointing had flown off, so

he went right on about his business, trying to find another. Rex stayed on our heels for only about a minute or so. Then his instincts took over. He couldn't resist trying to find another bird.

"You want me to let Sid go?"

Grandpa shook his head. "Usually takes twice." He sighed. "Hold on to him until Gabe finds another bird."

Sure enough.

After being attacked twice, Rex was a little slower about leaving his hiding place behind Grandpa and me. But when I let Sid loose, he took off, too.

Sid found the next bird. Gabe wasn't far behind. When Sid pointed the bird, Gabe pointed him. I cringed when Rex came flying toward the two dogs. About four feet away, he stopped and pointed Gabe.

Grandpa smiled. "Yep. Twice usually does it."

We hunted a while longer. All three dogs took turns finding birds. And all three dogs took turns honoring.

Once Rex came down on a point. Only it didn't look quite right, because his tail kept wiggling. Gabe stopped, too.

"What's he doing?"

Grandpa let out a little chuckle. "Field mouse or a rabbit. Old Gabe knows it, too. See how he keeps looking at us?"

All of a sudden, Rex pounced. Front paws together, he hopped on a clump of grass. He must have missed, because just a second later he pounced at another clump, then started sniffing around to see where the mouse went.

"Come on, Rex," Grandpa urged. "Find a bird. Birrrd."

"Grandpa, I don't get it. If Gabe knew it was a mouse or a rabbit, why did he honor the point?"

Grandpa shrugged. "It's what he's supposed to do."

"Even if the other dog's wrong?"

"Even if he's wrong. Guess Old Gabe figures that he can't expect the pup to honor *his* point if he doesn't honor the pup's point."

We found about three more birds before Grandpa said he was getting tired, and suggested we go see what Grandma had for dinner.

I hated the walk back to the house. For the

longest time, I was afraid to look. Even when we put Rex and Sid in their pens, I kept my eyes down. Finally I got up enough nerve to glance at the driveway. A smile tugged at the corner of my mouth when I didn't see a car.

Grandpa took the shells out of his shotgun and handed it to me. While he went to put Old Gabe in his pen, I headed for the house. The house with no car parked in the driveway.

I walked around the edge of the barn. I was still smiling when a movement caught my eye.

There was a man in the puppy pen.

He held something in his arms. I took another step before my knees felt weak and began to wobble as if I might fall.

He was holding Tad.

When he saw me, he smiled and nodded. Then he lifted Tad a little higher.

"Fine-lookin' little pup you got here. Don't you think?"

It took two seconds before I could breathe. Another second before I looked him square in the eye and answered:

"He's probably the best one of the whole litter."

Chapter 22

For the life of me, I couldn't believe I had said that. I couldn't understand why.

It's amazing, the thoughts that come, the visions that flash through the mind's eye, in an instant of sheer panic.

I remembered thinking how bad I wanted to SCREAM at that man. "NO!!! He's *my* dog! Put him down! You can't have him!"

I wanted to race to him. Tear Tad from his arms. Run to the creek and hide. Run clear home. Lock Tad inside the house, so the man could never touch him again.

My eyes blinked faster than a quail's wings

beat. Each time I blinked, pictures flashed through my mind.

I could see the car driving away. I could see Tad standing with his paws on the back window, watching me, wondering why he had to leave, wondering why I didn't do anything.

I could see Tad, all alone in a pen with no one to play with, and no one to love him.

Despite all that, all I'd said was:

"He's probably the best one of the whole litter."

Mr. Owens held Tad up, admiring him. A little shudder raced through me. I closed my eyes. And . . .

I could see Grandma, the day we put the puppies in the pen by themselves. See the look of loneliness in her eyes when she petted the little pup, put it down, and said, "I guess it's just part of growing up."

I could see Grandpa—not crying, but with little puddles beneath his eyes—and I could hear his voice when he said, "Keeping your word ain't always easy."

I could see Old Gabe tearing into Rex. And I could see Gabe honoring Rex's point—even when he knew Rex was wrong.

I could see Mrs. Nash. See her standing in front of the room. Hear her say, "You are an honorable young man, Thomas. I should have believed you."

I thought all that. Saw all that. Felt all the hurt. All the worry. All the uncertainty that went with each thought and each vision. And it was all there— like a giant spark that shot from my head to my toes and back again. And . . .

I knew why I answered like I had. I understood.

It was the only thing I could do.

I'd had to answer, truthfully, and without hesitation:

"He's probably the best one of the whole litter."

❧ Chapter 23 ❧

When I walked to the pen, the man opened the gate and slipped outside. Once he was sure none of the other puppies had escaped, he tucked Tad under his left arm and offered his right hand.

I shook it.

"You must be Andy's grandson."

"Yes, Sir. Tom."

"Pleasure to meet you, Tom. I'm Jeb Owens."

Letting go of my hand, he kind of stepped to one side, moved around me, and held his hand out again. Grandpa was there. He looked worried, but when he took Mr. Owens's hand, he managed a smile.

"Hi, Jeb. How you doin'?"

"Doin' fine, Andy. From the looks of you, a fella wouldn't even know you'd had heart surgery. Lookin' spry as ever. How you feelin'?"

Grandpa patted his chest. "Little sore every now and then, but comin' around. Where's your car? We didn't see it in the drive."

Tad was wiggling and trying to get to me, and Mr. Owens had to hold him with both hands. I moved behind Grandpa, so he couldn't see me.

"Flew down. I mean, what's the sense having your own private jet if you don't never get the thing off the ground? Caught a cab from the air-port."

Guy's got his own private jet, wears blue jeans and old boots that look like they've been in a cow lot or something. Mr. Owens wasn't what I had expected at all.

Grandpa motioned toward the house. "We been workin' a couple of dogs. Just headed to the house to see what Beth's got for dinner. Might as well join us."

Mr. Owens shrugged. "Love to, Andy. Problem is . . . well, I'm qualified on instruments—you know, flying the jet without actually seeing the ground, when it's dark or dusty. Only it's been so long since I've done that, I don't want to. Best pick out a pup and head for home, while there's still light."

Grandpa kind of nibbled at his bottom lip. "What were you and Tom talking about when I come up?"

Mr. Owens held Tad up for Grandpa to look at. "Just admiring this pup. He's a good-lookin' dog. Good conformation. I know the bloodlines are excellent. When I asked your grandson what he thought, he told me he was probably the best pup of the litter. What do you think?"

Grandpa shot me a startled look when he glanced over his shoulder. Then he cleared his throat and turned back to Mr. Owens.

"Well . . . ah . . ."

Guess Grandpa was having a little harder time answering than I did.

"Well . . . I reckon he's a good dog. 'Course you never *know* until they been trained."

"Well, what do you *think*?"

Again, Grandpa hesitated. From behind him, I could see his shoulders sag.

"I think the boy's right. I think he's probably the best one of the litter."

The smile stretched clear across Mr. Owens's face. He puffed his chest out.

"That's exactly what I thought."

In that instant, I knew Tad was leaving. It would hurt—not for just a day or two, but for a long time.

But I also knew that it would be okay. The hurt would go away. If I'd lied to him, if I'd so much as hinted how much Tad meant to me . . . well, that would have stayed with me. It might have lasted forever.

"Problem I got, though," Mr. Owens went on, "is Willie's been my prize dog for years. Don't get me wrong. He's still a good stud dog—just not quite as active as he used to be."

"Happens to the best of us," Grandpa whispered, like I couldn't hear.

"Week before last, I flew to Germany and got me a new dog. His bloodlines are good. Sire won best of breed at the International Dog Show in

Zurich last year. The . . ." He paused a moment. Kind of glanced around Grandpa at me. "The . . . ah . . . the dog's *mother* was the National Field Trials champion at Atlanta two years ago. So . . ."

He turned, opened the pen, and set Tad on the ground. All the other puppies tried to bounce against his leg so he'd pet them or play with them like I did. He looked around a moment, then swooped up one of the black-and-whites.

"What I really need is a female. Kinda hard to be a successful dog breeder if all I got is male dogs. It just don't work."

He latched the gate behind him. Held the puppy up and looked her over again, then held his hand out to Grandpa.

"Think I'll take this one. Okay?"

Grandpa shook Mr. Owens's hand so hard, I thought he might yank the man's arm out of its socket.

"Okay."

We'd only gotten about ten feet from the pen when Mr. Owens turned and looked back.

"Tell you what, Andy. How about I buy that male pup from you?"

My eyes almost popped out of my head. I think Grandpa's did, too. He shook his head.

"What do you usually get for a finished dog, Andy, two thousand?"

Grandpa nodded.

"He's just a pup, but I like the looks of him. Don't even know if he can hunt birds or not. But I'll still give you two." Mr. Owens didn't wait before he said, "Nope. Tell you what. I'll double that offer. Four thousand dollars!"

Chapter 24

Dear Angie,
   I got a new puppy. His name is Tad.
                              Your friend,
                              Tom

P.S. Forget all the dumb things I said in my last letter. Okay?

That's all I wrote.

I didn't tell Angie how Mr. Owens offered Grandpa a whole bunch of money for my pup, and how Grandpa just laughed at him and said he'd have to talk to me—because he had promised that, if Mr. Owens didn't take Tad, Tad was mine.

And I didn't tell her how Mr. Owens's jaw went slack, and his mouth fell open. And how he shook his head and told Grandpa that he had no idea I wanted that dog. Then he shook my hand, and said something about how much courage it must have taken—not to let on until after he made his decision.

And I didn't tell her how sick I felt when I saw him holding one of the pups. And how I wanted to die when I saw that it was Tad.

I didn't tell her about how, when he asked me if I thought Tad was a good dog, I told him Tad was the best dog in the whole litter.

And I never told her about all the feelings, and thoughts, and things that flashed through my mind's eye in those three seconds it took me to answer him.

I didn't tell her that he picked one of the black-and-white girl dogs so he could breed her when she got older. I didn't tell her because I didn't think a boy should be talking to a girl about stuff like that. Not even Angie.

And I didn't tell her how, after Mr. Owens took all of us to eat at a fancy restaurant and we got home and loaded in the car to leave, Grandpa came running out of the house, yelling at us to stop. He had me get out, hugged me, and gave me the hand-carved wooden shotgun that his grand-father had made.

"I told you this would be yours, when you came of age," he said. "I figure you're there."

When he hugged me, he was smiling, but wiping tears from his cheeks at the same time. And I didn't understand why.

I took one last look at the letter.

Dear Angie,

 I got a new puppy. His name is Tad.

        Your friend,
        Tom

P.S. Forget all the dumb things I said in my last letter. Okay?

That should do it, I thought. All the important stuff is right there. I folded the letter, stuck it in the envelope, and sealed it. Then, with Tad following and bouncing against the back of my leg, I took it to Mama and asked if she'd mail it for me in the morning.

The light was still on in their bedroom. I tapped at the door.

"Come in," Mama answered.

She was sitting up, reading a book. Daddy was curled up on his side. The light on his side of the bed was off. But when I asked Mama if she'd mail the letter for me, he rolled over and sat up.

"With all that's been going on today, I totally forgot. You have another letter from Angie. It's on the coffee table."

I told them good night, then Tad and I trotted to the living room and got my letter.

Dear Tom,

This letter probably won't reach you until after the man picks his dog. I hope you get to keep Tad. I've been praying for you every night since I got the letter. Mom says we shouldn't ask God for dumb stuff, like toys or candy bars or even pets. But I could tell from your letter that Tad is more than a pet. From your letter I can tell you love him and he loves you. A pet may not be something I'm supposed to pray for, but I think love is.

Just in case, I decided not to name the new puppy Tom. His name is Tad.

I'm kind of like you. I don't know what you should do when that man shows up. But I DO know that you will do the right thing. You are very brave. I decided that when you turned around in the log at Six Flags and made me talk to you. You knew I was kind of mad at you, but you still did it. Most boys wouldn't be brave enough to try.

Write soon so I'll know what happened.

Love,

Angie

I just shook my head.

"I don't get it," I told Tad. "What is it with all this courage stuff?"

When I looked at him and said something, his scrawny tail thumped the bed.

"Courage is like soldiers who have to go to war. Got people shooting at them and trying to kill them. Or courage is firemen who run into burning buildings to save people.

"Or even Danny—that time when he wouldn't let Harry Mottson copy off him during the math test. He knew Harry was gonna get him after school, but he still wouldn't do it. You know—standing up to a bully.

"That kind of stuff is what I always think about when somebody talks about being brave or having courage.

"What do you think?"

Both ears cocked. Thumping his tail on the mattress, Tad just looked at me.

I turned the light out and lay down beside him. He crawled up, wedging himself between my arm and my side. I had to lift my arm. When I did, he crawled higher and laid his head on my chest.

"Now, Angie signing that last letter 'Love, Angie.' *That* scares me. Handling that—if she keeps doing it—that's gonna take real courage."

Tad's tail just thumped louder.

Maybe it was brave. Sometimes maybe just doing what's right—when it's the last thing you want to do—maybe that *is* courage. Just a different kind. Who knows?

I closed my eyes. Said a short prayer to thank God for keeping me and Tad together. And with his head nestled on my chest, and my arm draped over him, Tad and I fell asleep.

You have to pull a boy
from the pond and kiss him
before you'll know whether
he's a frog or a prince . . .

Pulling Princes

Pulling Princes

THE CALYPSO CHRONICLES

by Tyne O'Connell

BLOOMSBURY

Published by Bloomsbury Publishing, New York and London
Distributed to the trade by Holtzbrinck Publishers

Library of Congress Cataloging-in-Publication Data
available upon request
ISBN 1-58234-957-6

First U.S. Edition 2004
Printed in the U.S.A.
1 3 5 7 9 10 8 6 4 2

Published in the UK by Piccadilly Press

Bloomsbury Publishing, Children's Books, U.S.A.
175 Fifth Avenue
New York, New York 10010

Printed in the U.S.A. by Quebecor World Fairfield

All papers used by Bloomsbury Publishing are natural, recyclable products made
from wood grown in well-managed forests. The manufacturing processes conform
to the environmental regulations of the country of origin.

*Dedicated to Cordelia O'Connell,
my muse, my consultant . . . well, let's face it —
my adviser in all things stylish!*

ST AUGUSTINE'S

ST THERESA'S CONVENT

PRIEST'S HOUSE

APPLE ORCHARD

HOCKEY FIELD

CHAPEL

THE OLD OAK

NETBALL COURTS

SPORTS FIELD

PAVILION

MAIN HALL

TUCKSHOP

PET CEMETERY

SPORTS HALL

SALLE D'ARMES

PHIPP'S FOREST

1
2
3

FENCING SALLE

MILLPOND BRIDGE

MILLPOND

MILL HOUSE

SWIMMING POOL

TEACHERS' HOUSES

MAP by ERIC HEWITSON

SCHOOL FOR LADIES

ONE

Saint Augustine's

Talk about random. This was the *worst* worst-case scenario in my long history of worst-case scenarios. But then, my entire life is a random series of worst-case scenarios.

At fourteen, you start to realise these things.

On the flight back to school after the Easter break, wedged between an enormous professional-mom type and a smelly backpacker, I had weighed up my tactics for turning my life around during the summer term at Saint Augustine's.

Life at Saint Augustine's had been hell since Day One, which was why I'd made a decision that I would do everything I could to get the cool crowd to accept – if not respect – me. I mean, OK, so I suppose I knew deep down they were shallow and mean, but . . . well, there is only so long you can spend as the form freak before you actually go mad and start wanting to be part of the cool set.

I knew I had a tough term* ahead of me if I was going to finally start fitting in. I knew I was going to have to reinvent myself. That is, become the sort of girl who can pull boys – particularly really fit ones.

So it was sorted; I was on the case.

I knew radical action was needed.

But it was cool – I had a radical plan.

I had even factored in the possibility of things getting worse before they got better.

In short, I was prepared.

But even I, the Queen of the Doomsday Prophesies (my mom's nickname for me – what can I say, she's hilarious), hadn't considered the possibility that I would be forced to share a dorm room with The Honourable Georgina Castle Orpington . . .

The girls, all dressed in our hideously evil Saint Augustine's uniform – maroon pleated skirt and green ruffled shirt – were all crowded, with their toff parents and toff valets in tow, in the dimly lit, wood-panelled entrance hall, peering at the noticeboard to find out which dorm they were in and who they'd be sharing a room with that term.

'Oh great, I'm with the American Freak,' I heard Georgina whisper sarcastically to Honey O'Hare, a member of her cool pod of friends.

That's what they called me – American Freak. They do

For this and other Britishisms, turn to Calypso's special glossary on page 215.

these horrendously bad piss-takes of my accent, which is ironic, really, because when I go back to Los Angeles during the holidays everyone starts talking like Dick Van Dyke, imitating what they perceive to be my proper English accent. You can't win, really.

Standing at the back of the crowd, waiting for my chance to see the list, I pretended not to have heard Georgina's lament and tried to think of something really cutting to say in reply. (I rarely actually say the cutting things that I think up in my head, though, because I have discovered that it is better to stay under the radar and keep my witty remarks to myself.)

Both Georgina and Honey were holding their Louis Vuitton pet carrier bags containing matching super-cute pet rabbits, Arabesque and Claudine. They'd have hated it if they'd known, but I was always stopping by the pet shed to cuddle their rabbits; particularly Georgina's, Arabesque, who was really adorable and had the sweetest pink eyes and the softest, floppiest ears. Honey's toffee-coloured rabbit, Claudine, was always biting me (no surprises there).

I would have loved a rabbit of my own, but one of the things about being an American freak at an English boarding school is that you don't get to have a pet because of the totally cruel quarantine laws. My parents probably saw this as character building, like everything that depresses me.

My parents are big on character.

Both my parents are writers in Hollywood. I long to write myself – only not the sort of dreary stuff they write.

They think of themselves as really hip and liberal because they say I can call them Sarah and Bob (like I'd ever do that!). Besides, they are so *not* cool. For a start, they drive a Volvo and say things like 'swell' (Dad) and 'super' (Mom). My mom is a senior staff writer on a crappy soap that doesn't even air in the UK, so no kudos there. My dad is writing the Big One – that's Hollywood-speak for the script that will finally make his name, but currently brings in no money.

They didn't think LA was the place to bring up a teenager. They told all their friends that they were afraid I would become 'too Hollywood.' They sent me to *Le Lycée Français de Los Angeles* when I was a kid, which is where I picked up my fencing problem. But the real reason I was in this hell was because my mom is British and she went to Saint Augustine's, and she ADORED it.

'It'll be super, darling. You'll make friends for life – just wait and see,' she promised me on the flight over three years ago.

All I'd come up with in the friend department so far was Star. She's the daughter of a rock star who was huge in the eighties and even though he was mega (and is still adored by several million tragic people with bad hair worldwide) and is one of the richest men in Britain, Star was too random and unconventional to be accepted at Saint Augustine's, or to have any kudos like Antoinette did. Antoinette's entire family are famous pop stars. Even though Antoinette was in the year below us, she was considered the trendiest girl in school – unlike Star, who was a total goth with a lot of weird habits: 1) wearing only black, 2) fencing, 3) having a freaky extended family, and 4) being friends with me.

Honey pointed one of her long, French-manicured fingers at the list and said, 'Oh yaah. But, darling, look, it's not *just* the American Freak. Guess who else you've been roomed with? Only her weird friend, Star!'

Georgina's eyes almost popped out of their long-lashed sockets. 'Darling, are you serious? I am so going to get Daddy to complain,' she declared loudly as she looked despairingly down the list and held her own perfectly manicured hand to her brow.

Honestly, I thought, it's a wonder these two don't wear tiaras . . . whoops – they do on occasion!

This was going to be a great term.

My despair at having to share a room with Georgina was somewhat diluted by the thought of Star being in my room too. I had asked to share with Star, but, as Georgina now knew, you don't always get to share with your first choice.

Star's my best friend. As I said earlier, she was my *only* friend on account of us both being the form freaks.

We had bonded the first day of Year Seven (my first year at Saint Augustine's) in fencing. We spent so many hours alone together in the *salle d'armes* practising (i.e., escaping the other girls and, in Star's case, fancying Professor Sullivan, our fencing master) that we grew pretty close — especially when we both chose sabre as our weapon. The other girls were beginners, so had to start on the foil, but because Star and I had been fencing since we were quite young and were showing so much enthusiasm, Professor Sullivan allowed us to advance to *épée* and then on to sabre.

Sabre is the most aggressive of the three fencing weapons; it has a really cool full-fist guard and a flat cutting blade, with a folded-off end rather than the tragiclooking bobble that you have on foil. Sabreurs have a bit of a reputation for being a swashbuckling, ruthless lot.

In our ignorance, Star and I thought ruthlessness and swashbuckling would be agonisingly chic qualities to foster. But that was before we realised that being sabreurs would make us stand out — something that wasn't done at Saint Augustine's.

Things that make girls stand out (and therefore make them the object of ridicule and derision) at Saint Augustine's School for Ladies:

1) **Not being willowy and not having really long hair (preferably blonde).**

2) **Not having a title or at least a double-barrelled surname (although *using* your title was considered tragic).**

3) **Not owning a massive house in the country and a quite big one in a really smart area of London.**

4) Having a spot problem (i.e., any spots whatsoever).

5) Being overweight (i.e., being of average or above-average weight for your height). Note: even bulimia and anorexia were more status enhancing than being a chubba.

6) Having unusual amounts of body hair (i.e., any).

7) Having a funny accent (i.e., any accent that wasn't madly posh and English).

8) Not being asked to be a debutante (i.e., being presented to the Royal Court). Perversely, actually agreeing to be a debutante marked you out as even more uncool than if you hadn't been asked in the first place.

9) Not being attractive enough to pull fit boys (preferably older ones) who then went on to leave messages on your mobile for other girls to listen to.

10) Not being completely obsessive about sweets and fags.

11) Having clothes that no one else would buy (i.e., non-designer, like mine).

Number 9 was the clincher.

Pulling fit, older boys is vital for all girls, but especially for girls who live in an all-girls school, where the ability to pull fit boys confers status like nothing else can.

I knew this because of what happened to Octavia, a girl

in the year above me. Octavia had very little social cachet and stood out like a sore thumb with her short, dykey hair. She also had this body hair problem (i.e., she was *covered* in the stuff) that had earned her the nickname Pubes.

Like me, Octavia had been one of the girls who hid in the cupboard at lunchtime to avoid being confronted by her total lack of friends. (Who sits next to whom at lunch says everything about your status at Saint Augustine's.) Then suddenly after the Christmas break, Octavia was transformed into one of the most popular girls in the school and one of Georgina's best mates – all because she pulled a Lower Sixth boy from Eades. Eades College is the madly posh school where the world's grandest boys are educated in privilege and the art of effortless charm (well, that was how Star put it). One exeat (that's a weekend when you are allowed home) he even came and picked her up on his Ducati motorbike. We never saw her again.

You could fail every other test, but developing a reputation for never pulling boys was the end. Like providing the alcohol at social events, pulling boys was always the girl's responsibility and consequently we talked of little else. When I say 'we,' I mean the cool girls – not me, but the girls I wanted to be like.

Failing to share stories about the boys you had pulled was as bad as not sharing your tuck. It was vulgar.

Over Easter, I tried to explain the imperative of pulling a boy by the time I was fifteen, but my parents went totally ballistic about it – as if I'd said I wanted to start having sex.

Naïvely imagining that it would calm them down, I explained what pulling actually meant, i.e., kissing and that sort of thing. I mean, *hello*! They work in Hollywood for goodness' sake! Kissing is PG-13 there! But instead of saying something sensible like, 'Oh, yes, darling, of course we understand. Get on to that pulling business right away! If there's anything we can do to help, just let us know, dear,' they delivered this really long dissertation about how you can get mono (glandular fever) from kissing. Until eventually I nodded off into my carb-free meal.

As an American with parents who have virtually impoverished themselves (in Hollywood terms, not real terms, obviously – I mean, they could still afford to pay for the fees, the flights and the tragic uniform; it just meant they had to do without a pool) in order to send me to boarding school in England, I pretty much flunked all eleven tests. I suppose I am tall and thin and my hair is blondish (if I spray myself stupid with Sun-In). But it's not sleek and straight like the cool girls' hair; it's wavy and has little fluffy bits at the front that stick up like horns no matter how much I try to stick them down.

In Year Seven when we were all eleven, the dorm bedrooms had six or more girls in them, but as the years went on, the number of girls per bedroom was getting smaller and smaller, and it became harder and harder to hide what a freak I was compared with all the other girls who were pulling boys left, right and centre.

Years Nine and Ten were housed in shared bedrooms of

three per room in a building called Cleathorpes. It was an ancient house with a gabled roof and mullioned windows. In some ways I guess it looked kind of spooky and Addams Family-ish, but I had always longed to be roomed there. It was away from the main building where all the other dorms were.

Cleathorpes had good points and bad points:

Good points: It was away from the main building and meant we could sneak out at night through the bursar's window, which was conveniently never locked. This meant that IF we could dodge the guard dogs and armed security guards, slip through the electric, barbed-wire fence and sprint through the woods (where it was rumoured flashers and rapists lurked) and take the 23:23 train to London, we could go clubbing at one of the really cool London clubs like Fabric (that is, if you knew someone who knew someone who knew the doormen). Not that anyone in my year had done anything as cool as that yet, but all the Lower Sixth girls claimed they had done it all the time when they were in Cleathorpes.

Bad points: The House Mother (or as we referred to her, House Spinster) was the horrible Miss Cribbe. Not only was she bearded and mad and always trying to get all chummy with us like we were her real children or something, but she had a disgusting incontinent springer spaniel called Misty, who was constantly sneaking into the dorms and weeing on our duvets.

All Miss Cribbe ever said was, 'Oh, Misty, you are a naughty little doggins, aren't you.' (Miss Cribbe always spoke to Misty in a baby voice.)

The whole of Cleathorpes smelled of wee, even though we all made a concerted effort to get Misty to run away by spraying her with Febreze.

I lugged my trunk up the narrow, dimly lit, oak-panelled stairwell that wound around the central hall. Each of the cold stone stairs had been hollowed in the centre from about two hundred years of wear. As I struggled alone, behind all the parents, guardians and valets carrying up the other girls' trunks, I took in the smell of beeswax and floor cleaner.

The stained-glass window depicting Saint Theresa doing something miraculous cast a wintry half-light on the stairwell, even when it was fabulously hot and sunny outside. Bent double under the weight of my trunk, the strap of my fencing kit cutting into my shoulder, I looked up at her peaceful features – and wished she'd do something miraculous for *me*, like carry my wretched trunk up these stairs.

My parents lived in LA, so I suppose they couldn't accompany me every time, but also they claimed lugging a five-thousand-tonne trunk on my back was character building. Clearly the fact that I was going to end up looking like a hunched-up old woman by the time I was eighteen didn't concern them in the least.

T W O

Friends for Life

Georgina's full title is The Honourable Georgina Castle Orpington, but she was far too grand to use it (as I explained, using your title was considered vulgar). So she went by Georgina Castle Orpington. Obviously, though, Georgina was not so grand that she didn't want everyone to *know* that she was titled and grand and should be treated as such.

By far the best bed in the room was the one by the window. It had drawers underneath and a view over the ancient oak woods (known as Puller's Woods) where all the illicit high jinks went on.

We were only a couple of miles away from Eades. Although Eades was too grand to have a formal relationship with any girls school (especially a Catholic one like Saint Augustine's), because we were the nearest one, we shared loads of activities. We had an *amicabiles concordia*, as our Latin teacher loved to call it.

I totally hate Latin. What am I supposed to do with *amo, amas, amat?* We were always telling Ms Mills, our Latin teacher, that Latin is a dead language, to which she replied, 'You'll be dead if you don't finish your declensions' – even though, as a Catholic, she shouldn't be threatening the physical manifestation of our souls.

The teachers at Saint Augustine's are such hypocrites – apart from the nuns, who are mostly really cool and devout (or at least old, deaf and indifferent). The dead ones are all buried in the nuns' graveyard near the apple orchard. When I'm feeling really sorry for myself about being the form freak, I sometimes go and sit there and ponder the strangeness of their existence compared to my own.

You couldn't see the nuns' graveyard from our window, but you could see the most beautiful spread of bluebells, like a carpeted pathway through Puller's Woods.

'Do you want the bed by the window, then, Georgina?' I offered, when all the toff parents and toff valets had departed.

I knew Georgina would take whichever bed she wanted anyway, on account of her being head of the Year Ten cool girls, but I was just trying to make conversation.

I've *so* got to stop doing that.

'Whatever,' she replied, mimicking my American accent. Nevertheless, she threw Tobias (her ancient teddy bear) on the window bed.

Tobias had his own mini-trunk of designer outfits and his own passport. Whenever Georgina hated something or someone, she'd say, 'Tobias can't bear that/them!' All her friends found Tobias and his temperamental personality hilariously funny.

You can see what I was up against.

I was counting down the seconds until Star's arrival.

It's not like I thought that Georgina, Honey and their kind were fantastic role models or anything tragic like that. It was just that I was sick of being the class freak. I was sick of being mocked about my accent, sick of having nasty Post-it notes stuck on my back, saying mean stuff about what a tragedy I was.

Also, another part of me wanted to know what it was *like* to be part of the cool pod of girls, whose ingrained sense of entitlement both excluded and intrigued me.

My plan to start fitting in first came about when I was talking to my mom's PA. Once he got over the hurdle of his amazement that I get teased for sounding American ('But you sound sooo British!'), he started to come up with some really cool ideas. Personal assistants can be very wise.

Jay had been assigned the task of looking after me on the studio lot during the Easter break. My mom's PAs were usually Valley Girls who just wandered around the lot talking on their mobiles while I followed them around like an old dog they've been asked to walk. But Jay chatted away to me like I was an actual person and he even let me drive the golf cart around the lot, something my mom would never allow.

I could tell Jay felt really sorry for me when I told him about how I locked myself in cupboards to avoid things like lunch or makeover parties where I knew I'd be excluded. I might have made it all sound worse than it was. I mean, everyone locks themselves in the cupboard sometimes – even Georgina (although she only does it to avoid Mass and lame stuff like that).

I suppose I didn't bother to explain to Jay that my parents sent me to boarding school because they wanted the best education for me. Also I didn't tell him about the sacrifices that my parents make in order to send me here. Or that we would have lived somewhere nicer than East Hollywood and had a pool and a Mercedes like everyone else in Hollywood if they hadn't had to spend what amounted to most of their salaries on flying me to and from my exorbitantly expensive school in England.

But boarding school isn't the 'done thing' in America – especially in the socially liberal world of Los Angeles – and when I told him about how unpopular I was on account of being American and having no money and no pulling history, he came up with the idea of turning my social fortunes around by posing as a worldly wise *Sex and the City* type, who pulls lots of fit boys.

So this was the term when things were going to change. I was never going to be asked to be a debutante and curtsy to the Queen, I might not own a mansion in the country or a posh house in Chelsea, but I didn't see why I couldn't pull a boy – preferably an older, fit one.

First step, Jay said, was all about creating the illusion that I held a fatal attraction for the opposite sex.

'Hey, isn't this great?' Star squealed dementedly when she finally arrived. Ray, her father's valet (enveloped in his trademark stench of patchouli), was trailing behind her with her trunk. 'After all this time we finally get to share!'

She was referring to *me*, not to Georgina, who hates Star almost as much as she hates me – and don't worry, the feeling is mutual.

Georgina glared as Star stumbled in and threw her arms around me in a big hug.

I do love Star.

Georgina pretended that she was chucking up at the sight of our cuddle and started filling up the tiny wardrobe we were all meant to share with her numerous expensive designer outfits.

Star pulled away and said, 'Gosh, you've grown again! I wish I was tall and skinny like you, Calypso.'

Oh yes, that's another thing – my name: Calypso Kelly. I have the crappiest name ever. My mom let my dad choose it so he could feel more 'involved' in the parenting process. He clearly thought giving me a freakish name and packing me off to boarding school was all the parenting he needed to do.

Star's the only girl at Saint Augustine's who doesn't make fun of my American accent, which is strongest after breaks.

It totally sucks being an American in the twenty-first century.

It's not as though I was the only American in the school or anything. There were twelve Americans in the Upper Sixth, known at Saint Augustine's as The Manhattan Apostles (because there were twelve of them). As far as I know they never got stick for their accents, but then they didn't really talk to anyone outside their group – not even the other Americans. They all came from the same junior school back in New York. All their school fees were paid for by one girl's father, who didn't want his pampered daughter to feel lonely at school in England.

Which brings me to the ultimate DBI (Daddy-Bought-It) accessory – friends.

My daddy couldn't afford any friends for me.

He couldn't even afford to give me a decent allowance, which means I had to buy all my clothes secondhand off the girls in the year above who were always dropping by with their hardly worn designer clothes. The saying *'Mi casa es su casa'* (my house is your house) is translated as 'Daddy's plastic is my plastic' at Saint Augustine's. *My* daddy didn't buy into this philosophy – he claims not to believe in plastic!

'You can't not believe in plastic,' I told him. 'It's there, it exists! Like trees and grass – it's out there, everywhere. Face it, Dad, we live in a world of plastic!'

He told me he didn't want me to grow up spoiled. He's always changing the subject like that.

My mom actually applauds the idea of me having to buy secondhand clothes off the other girls because she's so environmentally aware (and not as rich as all the other parents who send their kids here).

Ray, Star's dad's valet, dumped the trunk by Star's bed and grunted something incomprehensible before handing Star a bundle of twenty-pound notes.

'Tiger said to give you some readies.' (Tiger is Star's dad, but at least he doesn't ask her to call him that.)

Ray was wearing tight black leather trousers and a black T-shirt with *Roadie* written on the front and back. His long black hair hung in a limp ponytail down his back. He used to tour with Star's dad's band until it had its first bust-up (now a bi-annual event, as apparently it pushes up album sales). After that, Ray and all the rest of the roadies became staff at Star's parents' enormous Derbyshire estate. And even though they still tour every few years, once the tour is over the roadies always return to their valeting and other duties in Derbyshire.

I sometimes spend exeats with Star, which is cool because no one supervises us – basically because they are all usually stoned.

My dad is a massive fan of Dirge, Tiger's band, and thinks it's 'swell' that I spend time there. I've heard him boasting to his LA friends about it. He would totally freak if he knew what actually goes on in that house. And I'm not just talking about the perilous quad-bike racing Star and I get up to.

Once I saw her father fall backwards off his chair at

breakfast and all Star's mother said was, 'Tiger, I wish you wouldn't do that.'

I was like, HELLO, your husband is on the floor in a dressing gown with cereal all over his face. Don't you want to *do* something? It was gross – his penis was peeping out of his robe – but everyone just kept munching on their toast like nothing had happened. He was still there on the floor, snoring away, when we came in at lunch and we all had to step over him.

I am so never doing drugs.

'Cheers, Ray,' Star said as she handed him one of the twenties back. He held the note up to the light as if he thought it might be a fake or something, then gave her head an affectionate pat and told her not to drink or drug too much before loping off.

THREE

My First Fake Boyfriend

'Cute guy, Star,' Georgina said, sarcastically referring to Ray as she flicked through a copy of *Tatler*. (Georgina had appeared in the social pages once and ever since she always had a copy on her.) 'Is that your new boyfriend, then?'

Star sneered. She wasn't intimidated by Georgina the way I was. She was quite happy to get into total screaming bitch fights with Georgina and her mates if they pissed her off – which of course they did all the time.

And now we were all going to be sharing the same room! Even more reason to start fitting in, if just for the sake of peace.

So, while Georgina read *Tatler* and Star began to unpack, I nonchalantly started pinning up a large photograph of Jay and me driving around in a golf cart on the Paramount lot.

I could tell Georgina was peering over her *Tatler* as I

pinned up a second photograph – a glam head shot of Jay that he had given me for just this purpose.

'So who's that, then?' she asked fake-casually, still flicking through her magazine.

I acted as if I hadn't heard the question and set about pinning up my *pièce de résistance* – a close-up shot of Jay and me, Jay staring into my eyes adoringly. (We both fell apart laughing after the shot was taken. Have I mentioned that Jay is gay?)

'Oh my God,' Georgina cried out, no longer capable of faking indifference. 'Did you actually pull *him*?' She scrambled onto my bed and scrutinised his gorgeous face more closely. She was wearing an expression I had never seen on her before. . . . I think it was amazement.

I just shrugged. Not being effusive was another part of my makeover. I was determined to stop being an idiot chatterbox and be more mysterious and enigmatic like the cool girls. That was Jay's idea too. He said that sometimes 'less is more.' I told him that less of Georgina and Honey would definitely be more, but he just laughed and told me to trust him.

Georgina obviously hadn't worked out that I had developed a mysterious side over Easter because she asked me again if that was my boyfriend. By this stage Star had plugged in her electric guitar and was messing about with her own blend of minor chord compositions.

Star utterly worships Morrissey, who was this totally morose musician in the mid-eighties – I mean, she wasn't even born then! As an homage to him, Star writes and performs her own songs about hating her life as a rich rock star's kid and wet, suicidal afternoons at boarding school. Her father thinks she's a total genius and lets her use his recording studio, even though her songs would make the most positive person want to self-destruct.

Georgina gazed at my photo gallery. 'I can't believe you pulled someone so hot, darling!' she announced.

I had to hide my amazement. Georgina and Honey and their friends always called one another 'darling.' But she had certainly never called *me* 'darling.'

I wasn't sure if this meant I should 'darling' her back. What is the etiquette on that? I wondered. So I merely shrugged enigmatically.

Star stopped playing her guitar and peered at the photographs. 'Nor can I!' she agreed – somewhat disloyally, I thought.

I disappeared into the en-suite and started unpacking my woeful little selection of toiletries and make-up. I'd managed to decant some vodka into some empty Body Shop bottles when my parents were out. I knew from experience that these were vital components to being part of any dorm party. The cool girls always take Body Shop Specials down to the woods and I wanted to be prepared for my first invite to this exclusive club of dissipation. Georgina had already claimed the entire cupboard with about ten thousand little Body Shop Specials, so I just stuck mine on the wobbly shelf above the sink.

'Calypso!' Star called out to me. 'Is this for real? Like, did you really pull this guy when you were back with your folks in LA?'

Star knows only too well how deeply dull my trips to LA normally are, because I'm always moaning about them.

'Yaah, of course,' I told her breezily, as if fit, older boys falling madly in love with me was an everyday occurrence.

And then Georgina said the words that I had wanted to hear ever since I first arrived at Saint Augustine's. 'He's seriously fit, Calypso. I'm impressed.'

So that was that. I knew then that whatever else happened in my life I would always have this memory to cling to. *I* had impressed *Georgina Castle Orpington* – the most deeply unimpressed girl in our year. First she darling-ed me and now *this*! A little imaginary slide show started playing in my head:

Georgina, her cool gang and me sitting together at lunch.

Georgina, her cool gang and me climbing out of the bursar's window for late night dashes through the woods to take the 23:23 train to London to some ultracool club like Fabric.

Georgina and me, waxing each other's legs and giving each other facials on Saturday nights.

Georgina and me, spraying Sun-In on each other's hair.

I don't even really like Georgina, but I couldn't help wanting to be liked by her . . . maybe even be a little bit like her. Because girls like Georgina lived the good life. Girls like Georgina were always at the centre of things and I was so *over* being on the periphery. In just over a year I would be sixteen and I had never been kissed.

I wanted to be respected enough to be accepted by the core of girls at Saint Augustine's who made things happen.

I just hadn't expected it to be this simple. If I'd known, I would have done it ages ago. I mean, how easy could this be? Three photographs and I had already impressed Georgina Castle Orpington, a girl who had never just randomly spoken to me – apart from when she was trying to flog her clothes for exorbitant sums of money or telling me what a freak I was.

She shook her head. 'I mean it, Calypso. I am seriously impressed.'

I tried to look all nonchalant and casual.

'Are you coming out for a fag, then?' she asked – and she didn't even do a piss-take of my American accent or anything. She spoke in her normal Sloaney voice, just as if she was talking to one of her It-Girl friends.

'Erm, well . . . the thing is, erm, I don't actually smoke,' I replied before I could stop myself. '. . . much – that is, I'm trying to give up,' I added, thinking on my feet. 'I mean, cancer and all that – you know how it is.' I gave a little cough.

I can make a total arse of myself when I try. Sometimes even when I don't try.

Georgina looked at me strangely for a moment, but then she just said, 'Yaah, you are so right, darling,' in her drawly way. Then she added that she was thinking of giving up too. I was so amazed I almost fell backwards like Star's dad!

'I've really got to give up trainers,' Star declared from her position on the floor, breaking the spell of my little bonding moment with Georgina. 'They are totally taking over my life.'

Georgina and I watched as Star jammed the last of her six hundred black trainers in her cupboard and slammed the door with her foot.

Georgina looked Star up and down – from her shoes to her hair and then down from her hair to her shoes again. She has a lot of dismissive looks like this down pat. All the cool girls have this ability to shrivel your confidence with withering looks.

Star didn't shrivel easily, though. I guess the fact that her father was way richer than Georgina and her cool pod of friends put together gave her confidence a boost – or maybe she really just doesn't care.

Star had a saying which had always helped us survive the slings and arrows of Georgina and her friends' jibes: 'Wear Your Pain Like Lip-Gloss.' The first thing any girl does when she's in a jam or stuck for words is reach for her lip-gloss. So whenever we're nervous or someone says something bitchy to us, we pull out our lip-gloss and apply.

I pulled out my lip-gloss and applied, but Star didn't notice because she was busy giving Georgina her own withering look, which, as looks go, is like a cross between the gym mistress's pre-menstrual scowl and a tiger growling – i.e., pretty damn frightening.

Then Georgina gave Star another look of *her* own.

I'm telling you, it was a war of looks.

I have always admired Star for standing up to Georgina and the other girls, because I was completely terrified of them. It's not like Star was bursting with confidence either. I mean, she was fully self-conscious about her weight – not that she was a chubba or anything, but like I said, Saint Augustine's had a reputation for producing tall, willowy girls, whereas Star was more your classic ordinary-sized girl with red hair (she calls it Titian, but it doesn't alter the fact that she's always being teased for being a ginga).

Star always says that she envies my figure. I keep telling her she has nothing to worry about because she has a lovely figure and beautiful hair, but she still says she'd rather trade with me. I suppose I *am* tall – although I'm more gangly than willowy. My mom says I've got stunning cheekbones, but the older girls were always coming up to me and pinching my cheeks and saying stuff like, 'You've got the cutest little chubby cheeks.' I hated that.

'God, you're a loser, Star,' Georgina sighed as she put her Gucci sunglasses on (presumably to save her eyes from the glare of our ugly rays).

I wanted to defend Star – not that Star would have wanted me to, and anyway, anything I said would only have made things worse – but then something almost magical happened. Georgina turned to look at me through her sunglasses and smiled. 'Bet he was a great kisser, darling,' referring to Jay. 'You can always tell by the lips.'

'Definitely,' I lied, trying not to puke at the thought of kissing Jay. I mean, yes, he's fit and all, but HELLO, he is SO gay. He practically walks on tippie-toes.

Georgina lowered her glasses down her nose slightly so she could give me the searchlight look, only without the dismissive sneer that she used on Star. I could tell she was genuinely awestruck by my pulling prowess. Well, maybe not *awestruck* exactly – I mean, Georgina is no beginner in the art of pulling. At the last social she pulled five boys!

But she was rattled, I could tell.

I was shaking my duvet into its cover when Honey and Arabella came in and slumped on Georgina's bed. 'Hey, check this out, darlings,' Georgina urged, pointing to my photographs. 'Calypso has pulled an actual hottie.'

The girls clambered over onto my bed and scrutinised the photo. 'Wow! Calypso, he's *really* fit,' Arabella agreed.

'So what's his name?' Honey asked nastily.

'Erm, Jay.'

'*Jay?*' she squealed. A look of undiluted disgust flashed across her flawless It-Girl face. 'How tragically American is that?' Then she started saying 'Jay' with an exaggerated American accent, which set the other girls off.

I went bright red.

Star looked over at me pityingly, then made psycho

stabbing motions behind the other girls' backs, which almost made me giggle.

'Did you seduce him on your teen duvet, then, Calypso?' Arabella asked bitchily, referring to the Club'N cover I was trying to shove my duvet into.

It was the cover my mom had bought me when I first came to Saint Augustine's – back when Club'N were cool. I know, tragic. OK, so maybe I had begged her for it at the time, but I was only eleven! The picture of Club'N was fading, but it was still a Club'N cover and way embarrassing. It was also made of synthetic fibres, and a single bed duvet, not a goose-down double like all the other girls had.

I should have made my mom get me a new cover, but I'd hardly seen her the entire break. I should have made up a cooler name for Jay too, but I was so thrilled about the photo gallery success that I hadn't given the matter any thought. Stupid, stupid, stupid, Calypso.

'Actually, Jay is just short for James,' I lied, suddenly inspired (James being a much posher name than Jay).

The cool girls nodded, clearly satisfied with this explanation.

Star flopped onto my bed with the others. 'I snogged that Rupert guy,' she groaned. 'My tongue got caught in his braces. It was so embarrassing.'

'*You're* embarrassing, Star,' Georgina said with another sneer. 'I can't believe I'm going to be sharing a dorm with someone called Star. What's up with that anyway? Were your parents stoned out of their heads?'

I was shocked. Not about how nasty she was – I was used to that – it was just that usually it was me she said stuff like that to.

Star didn't seem bothered. That's what I love about her. Even with her name and her weird parents she's really chilled about herself. Also, like I said, she thinks Georgina and Honey are the freaks.

Honey did her screechy little fake laugh. She looks like a hyena when she laughs, although it was obvious that she'd had Botox (to give her eyebrows 'a lift') in the break. She'd already had collagen injected into her lips at Christmas.

Honey is a total psycho toff; in fact, she makes Georgina and the other posh girls seem positively friendly. I always got the impression that even they sometimes find Honey too much. But Georgina's father and Honey's bio-logical father go to the same hunting meets and the two of them had to stay overnight together at a hotel for posh tots in Chelsea called Pippa Pop-Ins. Then when they were four they were packed off to the madly grand Hill House in Knightsbridge, which was where Prince Freddie, his father, Prince George, and, well, all the grandest chil-dren went. Georgina and Honey even learned to ski together at the school's Swiss annex. So when anyone dared to question Honey's behaviour, Georgina always stuck up for her.

Honey's mother is a way-famous It Girl who presents a programme on celebrity homes for a cable station called

'E.' She had Honey when she was about seventeen, so she still looked incredibly stunning.

Georgina might have had a somewhat grander-than-thou way about her, but Honey was a genuine Class-A bitch. She was always giving Georgina a really hard time about her weight and her looks, even though Georgina was really stunning and slim. Also, everyone knew that Georgina's had huge food issues, mostly on account of her parents' divorce.

Just about everyone at Saint Augustine's has issues with food – and not just because they feed us slops that taste like sewage. In fact, the nuns tick your name off at lunch and dinner and check your tray when you stick it in the cart to make sure you've eaten everything because anorexia is so rife. If you miss two meals, you have to speak to Sister Dempster in the infirmary about how anorexia can make your bones brittle and even kill you.

Last year when Georgina's parents separated she became bulimic. Star says that sometimes bulimia and anorexia are ways to control something when you feel everything else is out of control. Star actually tried to be really helpful, pointing out that anorexia and bulimia can cause your hair to go thin and fall out and make your skin go all old and wrinkly looking, but Georgina just told her to piss off. We heard she stopped throwing up her lunch and supper, though, so I think Star might have hit a nerve. Georgina's hair is beautifully long and straight and luxuriously thick and I know she'd hate it to fall out.

'I'm going for a fag. Anyone coming?' Star announced, stuffing her cigarettes in her bra and her Febreze in her bag.

The smokers always sprayed themselves with Febreze to take the smell away after a visit to the tennis courts for a fag. Then they'd come up to non-smokers like me and ask, 'Do I smell?' and I'd have the responsibility of sniffing them. Of course if a teacher later smelled smoke on them, I'd get the blame.

At least Star smokes, I thought enviously. At Saint Augustine's everyone smoked, even the nuns. I tried to smoke once, but I threw up because I'd just come from an interschool fencing tournament and was totally starving. Anyway I actually don't want to smoke because it would affect my health and even though I haven't even told Star this, I really, really love fencing, and I actually dream of fencing in the Olympics one day.

The smokers trailed out of the room, leaving me to finish my unpacking. I was just about to take my fencing gear down to the armoury when Clementine Fraser-Marks came running into the room. 'Oh, it's you,' she said, clearly disappointed. 'Erm, hi, how was your break?'

'Oh, yaah, fine,' I replied, pretending that I believed she actually gave a shit.

'Great. Where's Georgina?'

'Up on Puller's Hill.'

'Fair enough.'

I could tell she was uncomfortable having to be alone in the room with me but was too well brought up to show it.

'You sharing?'

'Uh-huh.'

'Cool. Well, Antoinette is selling listens if you want.'

'Cool.'

'Is that your boyfriend?' She pointed to the photographs.
I shrugged. 'Guess.'

'Fit. He looks like an adult sort of thing.'

I said, 'Yaah, well, that's on account of how he is . . . an
adult sort of thing.'

'Wow. Well, it's Blake from Cell anyway, if you're interested. She's only charging fifty p on account of how it's the
first day back.'

Cell was the hottest new band of the year. They'd had
two number ones already and had also admitted taking
coke. Blake, the lead singer, was Antoinette's brother.

It was a Saint Augustine's custom to sell 'listens' of
mobile phone messages left by famous family members or
really fit brothers or boyfriends. They didn't always have to
be famous, but you got more money for a famous listen.
After the social last term when Georgina pulled five guys
and they all left messages she made a small fortune and the
queues snaked down the corridors.

Jay had promised to leave a message on my phone.

I was actually starting to believe that he was my
boyfriend.

FOUR

The Royal Sport

There were only about twenty girls who fenced at Saint Augustine's and only three were on the sabre team – Star, Portia and myself. None of the willowy cool girls took fencing that seriously, which made the fact that I was the captain a badge of shame. Tennis, lacrosse or riding were the sports that were taken seriously by Saint Augustine girls. The other girls only did it because, aside from drama, it was the only opportunity to have contact with boys during school.

I couldn't help myself, though. I loved fencing. I was fifth in Britain in the under sixteens – and I wasn't even fifteen yet.

It was my mum's idea that I take up fencing when I was a little kid at the Lycée. In those days I didn't realise I could have a say. Now that I was almost fifteen, I could have stand-up screaming matches with her if I wanted, but it was too late for me to chuck it in now and make a fool of myself on the tennis courts.

Actually, forget that. What am I saying? It's never too late for me to make a fool of myself.

In Year Seven, Star had a tragic crush on our fencing master, Professor Arthur Sullivan. Neither of us mentions it anymore, although I suspect that Star still carries a torch for him. I mean, he's a nice guy and everything (although there is a rumour that he once wore a cravat), but he's at least thirty-five or something ancient like that. He's extremely grand and only teaches fencing because of his love of the sport. He's absolutely loaded and drives four Jaguars (not all at once, obviously) – a racing green one, a powder-blue one, a black one and a silver one. I like the powder-blue one best.

Professor Sullivan always spoke to us in French during fencing training because he thought it made us think harder. 'Fencing is a physical form of chess, an intellectual debate between two bodies.'

He was always telling us stuff like that . . . only in French.

Once he drove Star and me to Star's house on an exeat (in the powder-blue Jag) and for a brief nano-moment we were the envy of all (being driven to London by a teacher conferred a special status, especially if the teacher was even mildly fit).

As it turned out we had the whole house in Chelsea to ourselves because Star's parents forgot to show up. Star said it was probably because they were too stoned. I guess she was used to it, and anyway it meant we could do anything we wanted!

I'd like to boast that we threw a wild party with fit boys and alcohol, but we were only twelve and largely friendless so we just ate loads of sweets while Star enjoyed the luxury of smoking cigarettes without spraying herself with Febreze.

On the Saturday night we went out to the cinema covered in make-up and managed to talk our way into a 15. Later we wandered down the Kings Road, which is where boarding school kids went to pull on exeats. They do a sort of promenade up and down the street, trying to look cool, checking one another out and trying to get into pubs. All Star and I managed to do was strike up a conversation with a homeless guy and his bedraggled dog, Ralph, whom we patted and fed Jelly Babies to.

I would have loved to have a dog, or any pet, for that matter. We are allowed to keep rabbits and hamsters and things in the pet shed, but then we have to take them home in the breaks and I can't exactly take a rabbit back with me to LA all the time. Also customs would confiscate the poor little thing and shove it in quarantine.

Star had a pet rat called Hilda and a python called Brian. Even though we weren't officially allowed to keep snakes they made an exception for Star after her dad donated loads of money to build a new music wing. Georgina and Honey were always threatening to sue if Brian so much as hissed at their rabbits, Arabesque and Claudine.

I wasn't too keen on Hilda and Brian myself, but out of loyalty to Star I always made a huge fuss of them when we went up to see them and asked if I could hold Hilda.

'I'm worried Hilda's got a cold,' Star told me as we were doing our warm-ups in the fencing salle. The salle or rather *salle d'armes* was the latest addition to our sporting complex. It was like a squash court only far, far bigger. The floor was sprung, there were three pistes and the surrounding walls were flanked with fencing masks, weapons and ancient photographs of Saint Augustine's teams triumphing at tournaments.

'Poor Hilda,' I said, in my best fake-sympathy voice.

Star was always paranoid that the rat had picked up an infection even though Hilda was the healthiest pet in the pet shed. She fussed over it all the time, treating her as if she were a gentle, nice animal like a hamster or a bunny instead of a vicious rodent with beady eyes.

We always had to give Hilda vitamin drops in her nasty little mouth and she would sometimes bite me while I tried to part her yellow teeth so Star could squeeze the dropper in.

'Yaah, she had a little sniffle when I went in to visit her at lunch,' she said sadly as she lay on the floor doing her leg raises.

'Oh no. Poor Hilda,' I sympathised as I stood up and moved on to my stretches and my lunging exercises.

The Eades College boys were here for an interschool tournament, but most of the Saint Augustine team girls were too busy flirting to bother with warm-ups, so it was left to Star and me to make fools of ourselves with our sidelong leaps down the fourteen-metre piste while the others looked on sneeringly. Like I said, the other girls mostly only did fencing as another way of meeting boys – also I was pretty sure they weren't immune to the fact that the all-white fencing outfits made tall, thin, gorgeous girls look even more stunning.

The Eades boys were mostly there for the girls too (rugby is the serious sport of Eades), but there were a few who were serious about the sport. Eades is *the* most exclusive boys boarding school in the country – maybe even the world. Royalty and rich people from all over the world send their sons there for a pukka British education. So do lots of ordinary rich people, some of whom made their money in their own lifetime (slightly tragic by Eades standards), doing not-so-pukka things.

The school has been around for hundreds of years, so they can get away with their mad traditions, and with making the boys wear tailcoats and funny shirts with stiff collars and things called 'ribbons' around their necks.

Loads of the girls at Saint Augustine's have brothers at Eades, which gives them extra status (but only if their brothers are older, obviously).

Honey said that Eades has gone awfully downhill since her father went there. She said it is full of plebs and the sons of East End gangsters, known collectively as kevs. My father asked me why we called these boys kevs and then got all champagne socialistic and hot under the collar when I told him that Kevin was a lower-class name in England and so kev was an alternate word for pleb.

Honestly, I don't know why he thrust me into this elitist world if he didn't want me to pick up elitist slang!

Less than three miles apart from each other, Eades and Saint Augustine's tend to share fencing and drama activities, so while not many of the pupils take the activities themselves seriously, they take the inter-gender aspect very seriously indeed.

The Eades fencing team is known to be totally rubbish, even though they have a huge pool of boys to pick talent from. Most of the team were chatting to girls, but a few of them (mostly the Europeans, and Billy, their sabre captain) were valiantly warming up on the piste beside Star and me.

I was surprised to notice that one of them was Prince Freddie. I mean, everyone knew he fenced, but he'd never struck me as being particularly keen on the sport. I'd figured he, like his mates, was only on the team to meet girls.

Freddie was second in line to the British throne, after his dad, Prince George, so naturally there were girls clustered about watching him. He was clearly loving the attention, even though he pretended not to notice them.

His security men were loitering with intent. They were dressed in polo shirts and chinos, as if they were just out for a stroll, but they so looked like bodyguards with their squaddie haircuts, massive muscles and little earpieces.

The security guys in the fencing salle weren't all for Prince Freddie, though. There are more international royals at Eades than there are tiaras at a debutante ball. And then there are the regular famous people – a lot of them have scores of bodyguards. Prince Freddie seemed to be able to manage with just two. I quite respected him for that, especially given that he was always being hounded by the media.

Some of the security guys were hired by the kevs just so they could show off how wealthy they were – a bit like sporting a gold bracelet or a sovereign ring, according to Honey. Boys can be just as status-tragic as girls, I suppose.

You get used to seeing bodyguards hanging around Eades boys. A few girls had them at Saint Augustine's, but they were made to keep a much lower profile. I don't think the nuns are that keen on having them around.

So anyway, once the warm-ups were finished, the president started calling the bouts. I'd seen Prince Freddie fencing *épée* before and he hadn't been very good, so I was surprised when our names were called together.

FIVE

Flirting with Princes

The president called Freddie's name first, and as I watched him lope down the piste to the *en garde* line in this really sexy way, I couldn't help but think he was fit. Not just fit, actually, but sooo fit. He'd grown a lot since last term and was now a good few inches taller than me. He was also much cooler-looking, as this time he wasn't sporting a gross pimple on his forehead.

Even though I knew I was going to slaughter him on the piste, I started to feel a bit nervous. I was even blushing because he was so utterly . . . well, there's no other word for it . . . fit. Thank God for the fencing mask covering my burning cheeks.

To fence sabre, you needed a metallic jacket worn over your plastic plastron, to register hits and to avoid serious injury to vital organs, sabre being the only cutting weapon used in fencing. Officially, you are not supposed to hurt your opponent too badly, but in practice sabre is a dirty weapon. Sabre is the most aggressive and impressive type of bout to watch. Most sabreurs like to make the most of their weapon, and as a result we were usually all pretty bruised and sore by the end of a few bouts.

Our teammates had helped us hook up the backs of our jackets to the electrical apparatus that was linked to a box on the ceiling and registered our hits with coloured lights and a buzzer.

Freddie and I saluted the president first and then each other, casually lifting our blades to our lips and back down to the fencing position. Whenever I salute my opponent before a bout, I think how strange it is that there is this much etiquette involved before two people try to kill each other. But there we are, or as Sister Regina would say, 'Diddley-dee.'

Then we put our masks on and waited for play to be called. *'Prêts, allez!'*

I advanced down the fourteen-metre piste first, figuring the Prince, being a bit of a wimp, would either retire or parry. But instead he riposted, attacking into my offensive, which took me a bit by surprise. I made my attack swiftly, though, scoring a hit. The buzzer rang and the president called my hit.

There's this thing called a captor inside the sabre guard, which allows hits to be recorded on the electrical apparatus, but only if the blade arrives on the *lamé* by way of a cut or a point – any other hit is invalid in sabre. Sometimes, with everything happening so fast, you don't really know if your hit is valid or not until the buzzer sounds and the president calls '*Halte*' or 'Stop,' at which point the clock is stopped until play is called again. A bout lasts for around five minutes of actual combat time, but it seems a lot longer.

Freddie scored the next hit with an obvious attack, provoking me into a parry of quinte (neck) by threatening me with a cut to the head and then disengaging the parry and rotating his blade to cut at my flank. 'An old one but a gold one' as Professor Sullivan likes to say (in French, of course, even though it doesn't rhyme).

Freddie's balance was excellent and his coordination reasonable, but he was no match for my compound attacks or disengagements, moves that require skilful wrist action (which you'd think he'd be brilliant at . . . being a boy). Actually, Professor Sullivan wasn't wrong – fencing *is* like chess. But it is so fast that your brain must be completely focused. That can be difficult when your opponent is a totally fit member of the opposite sex. There was a moment when an image of me wilfully committing a *corps-à-corps* (literally body-to-body, a totally illegal move) flashed through my mind, and Freddie scored another hit.

The rest of the hits were all mine – although to be fair, Freddie was pretty cunning and his parries and ripostes were totally respectable. But as Star always said, in sabre you can parry and riposte all you like, but you're only putting off the ultimate moment of your slaughter.

Fencing might be chess of the body, but the sword is a

weapon and in sabre it is often a case of the most aggressive, fearless player winning – especially at our level. I was totally wired. Hit after hit went to me.

'Cheers,' Freddie said as we shook hands after the bout. He'd taken off his mask to reveal dazzling cornflower-blue eyes and ink-black hair.

I took off my mask, revealing the fluffy bits at the front of my hairline, which I didn't need a mirror to know were sticking up like horns. 'Yeah, erm . . . thanks, well played.'

'My name's Freddie, by the way.'

Like I wouldn't have known that? *Hello*, second in line to the throne and the constant topic of media speculation. Where does he think I'm from – the Moon?

'Erm, m-mine's Calypso,' I stuttered.

Please don't mention my name. Please God, don't let him mention my name, I thought. Why do I have to have such a stupid name?

We grinned stupidly at each other as they detached us from the electrical recorder.

God must have been listening because Freddie just said, 'You were terrifying out there! You really rinsed me.'

'Gee, erm . . . thanks.'

'Quite cutting, aren't you,' he drawled.

Was that a flirty look in his eyes?

'Thanks,' I said stupidly. 'I didn't know you fenced sabre.'

'I've only taken it up recently. Which probably explains why I'm such bollocks, right?'

'Well, you were pretty fit, actually – I mean . . . erm, competent. Like, your flunges weren't horrendous or anything. And your renewal was sort of, erm, impressive.'

My father reckons when I'm in a hole I like to keep digging.

I was saved from further bad dialogue by Honey and Arabella and a few of the fencing girls who'd already fought their bouts and been seeded out from the pools (which meant more time to chat with boys).

'Wow, Calypso, that was so amazing, darling. Well done,' Arabella squealed as they all clustered around the Prince like atoms.

Yeah right, like they were actually even watching me.

'Thanks,' I muttered as I was squeezed out of the circle.

They were fluttering their eyelashes at the Prince so hard I thought they were going to knock themselves out. I watched him closely as he chatted amicably in that charmingly deferential Eades-ish way and I couldn't help but feel a tiny frisson of something. Probably dehydration, I thought. I decided to leave the It Girls to it and went over to the refreshment stand for a drink.

Star was there, getting into her plastron. 'Cool bout, Calypso. Freddie wasn't bad either. I mean, seriously, at the tournament last year I thought he was totally tragic. I didn't even know he did sabre.'

'Yaah, it was OK. I thought he was pretty good, actually.'

'Even though you rinsed him, right?' she laughed. 'Listen, after we've finished our bouts do you want to come to the pet shed with me to check on Hilda? I'm really worried, her eyes looked all sad and bleary this morning.'

'Sure,' I agreed, even though I would have preferred to chat a bit more with Freddie.

When almost all the bouts were over and tea was served, Freddie came over and stood near me – only he was still enveloped in a bubble of Honey's friends so I couldn't get to talk to him. We were watching Star trounce a member of his team. I thought for one second Freddie was looking at me, but then it turned out he had something in his eye.

Honey helped him to get it out.

Star dragged me away before I even had a chance to say goodbye, which was completely irritating because when we got to the pet shed Hilda was running around on her rat wheel like there was no tomorrow.

We still had to give her a cuddle, though.

SIX

Dorm Party Heaven, Duvet Hell

That evening during study period all I could think of was Freddie. I had to stop myself writing his name on my folder. Everyone was weirdly nice to me that night and Clementine, Arabella and Honey invited our room to their room for a makeover party.

It was normal for one room to be invited to another room, but in other years Star and I hadn't been included in these invitations and would only go to each other's rooms and hang out, ignoring whoever else was in the room. When Arabella and Honey burst in with their invitation, which clearly included all three of us, Star and I caught each other's eyes. I bit my lower lip, terrified that Star would tell them to piss off, but instead she shrugged her shoulders in a 'why not?' sort of way and off we went.

Georgina called up for a pizza from the Pizza Express

in Windsor, which you're really not allowed to do, but everyone does, because you can't survive on the inedible grey slops they feed us. Smuggling the Pizza Express guy in isn't that hard, and as long as you tear the box into a thousand pieces and distribute them in lots of different bins around the school, you never get caught.

Later we pooled our tuck in the middle of the floor. Everyone was really impressed by all the American sweets that I'd brought back this time. Jay had taken me to this really cool candy shop in the Beverly Hills mall and I'd just bought everything that looked different.

Georgina said, 'Wow, Calypso, darling, these Hershey's Kisses are so delicious.'

'I like the Pixie Stix,' Star added as she tipped one up and sucked the sugar out of the tube.

I was thinking about saying that Jay had bought them for me, which was kind of true, but for some reason I didn't want to talk about Jay anymore. Maybe I was afraid of jinxing the mileage I'd already got out of him or maybe it was because I couldn't stop thinking about Freddie and how fit he looked in his fencing gear. I especially liked the way he had his hair – all sort of longish on top but not floppy like some of the Eades nerds. It was all bunched up like it was gelled – only it wasn't, because gel is so tragic. His hair was just thick and cut in a really cool way.

We gave one another homemade facials, using porridge and bananas and honey and other goopy stuff we nicked from the kitchen. Georgina even offered to wax my legs!

Star rolled her eyes, but I couldn't have been more thrilled. Even though the pain was almost too horrendous to describe I kept my grin fixed on my face.

Star let Clemmie rag her hair so she could have ringlets and then Star braided Clemmie's hair, which looked really cool.

'You look stunning,' Arabella told Clemmie – and she did. Her long, dark hair braided down her back seemed to bring out her gypsy looks. I felt proud of Star because it was her idea.

Star and Clemmie's family estates were near to each other, so despite their differences, Clemmie often blagged a lift home with Star on exeats.

Looking around the room now, I realised why Star had never really felt like an outsider in the same way I did. She'd grown up in this world, she'd gone to prep school with these girls, they spoke the same language. For her there was no inside or outside – for her it was a case of 'choose to refuse.' But for me, that night was like being in an entirely new country – the cool country.

Later we snuck down to the science lab to steal some of the condoms they used for sex education lessons so we could practise putting them on over bananas, the way they always taught us.

Ms Argos had come in from a local comprehensive school, as a concession to the curriculum, especially to give the Sex Ed talks, because . . . well, it wouldn't really do to have a nun rolling a condom over a banana, would it?

Although it would be quite funny! I suppose a non-nun teacher could have done it, but then the really, really Catholic parents would have thrown hissy fits.

I'd hardly ever been invited to someone else's dorm party and definitely never had someone as cool as Georgina offer to wax my legs. This was the longest any-one apart from Star had gone without mocking me and the way I spoke.

Star kept rolling her eyes at me as if to say, What are we doing with these freaks anyway? But I just pretended not to notice.

'I can't wait to do this to Freddie,' Honey announced as she was rolling a condom over a banana.

'Are you serious?' I asked before I could stop myself. Firstly I was horrified at the thought of her with Freddie. And secondly I hadn't realised that anyone had actually gone that far yet in our year – apart from Lucy, who was one of the druggie girls that Georgia *et al.* didn't talk to. There was a rumour going around that Lucy had even slept with one of the plebs from the village, which was considered as tragic as it could get at Saint Augustine's.

But obviously not as tragic as being unable to pull anyone!

'Oh yaah,' Honey went on. 'Freddie was totally into me, darlings, as I'm sure you all noticed. He asked me all this really personal stuff about our holiday in Kenya last year. Like, we only know about *everyone* in common. I could tell he wanted to invite me out, but no one would leave him alone. It was like that time we went to that club in the

limo and everyone kept asking me if I was a model –
remember, Georgina?'

'Darling, your hair was out-of-this-world amazing that
night that we ragged it,' Georgina said, applying eyelash
dye to Clemmie's eyes.

'It would be so cool to pull Prince Frederick, darling,'
Clemmie sighed wistfully as a drop of dye rolled down her
cheek.

'But would you . . . you know, actually *do* it with him?'
Star asked, speaking directly to Honey for the first time
that night – or maybe even ever!

All the girls looked at Star as if she were from Year
Seven or something. '*Hello*, we *are* talking Prince Frederick –
second in line to the throne!' Honey reminded her, rolling
her eyes in disbelief.

'So if he asked, you'd actually, well . . . ? Darling, that's
quite a big step,' Arabella added, and then she giggled as
the banana burst through the condom.

'Darling, I heard Lucy's already given a boy a blow job,'
Clemmie added.

'She's such a slut, though – she'd give one to Mr
Morton if he asked,' Georgina remarked. Mr Morton was
the octogenarian groundsman.

'Are you going to pull him at the social then, Honey?'
Georgina nudged Honey's leg with her toe.

'I don't see that I have much choice,' she sighed, as if
kissing Prince Freddie would be such an effort.

'I thought he fancied Calypso, actually,' Star interjected,

giving me a supportive smile.

I went bright red. If I was caught fancying a boy that Honey planned to pull, it could destroy me.

'Pah-lease. As if,' Honey sneered, flicking her perfect blonde tresses over her shoulder. 'Can you honestly envision a member of the royal family with an *American*?' Then she started laughing in a really nasty way and everyone apart from Star joined her. Star looked over at me and pulled out her lip-gloss. I pulled mine out too and applied liberally.

'Well, what about Mrs Simpson, that woman King Edward married?' Star reminded them.

'My point exactly!' Honey said.

Wait, were they comparing me to that prune-faced old woman?

'I'm not being horrible,' Honey said. 'Calypso, you know that. It's just, well, you know how it is.'

Did I? I shrugged. Maybe she was right, though. Princes are probably really restricted in who they are allowed to fancy. I seem to remember that they totally loathe Catholics. I thought of reminding Honey of this, but decided against it.

'Besides, you've got Jay, haven't you, darling?' Georgina reminded me, offering Tobias a Hershey's Kiss.

I'd temporarily forgotten about my tragic fake relationship with gay Jay. 'Yaah, totally,' I agreed.

'Has he called you or anything yet, darling?' she asked kindly, popping the chocolate into her own mouth.

'I haven't actually checked my phone messages, erm, and . . .'

She smiled at me and passed me some of her coconut and passionfruit cream to put on my legs. 'This smells just *so* divine, darling. Try it.'

I looked at my legs. They were still all red and blotchy.

'I know a girl who spent a night in a sleeping bag with Freddie's cousin Alfred,' Arabella remembered.

I rubbed the cream into my legs and wondered what it would be like to share a sleeping bag with Freddie. I wouldn't even mind if he were sweaty.

When we got back to our room, it was clear that Misty had been there. The stench was horrific. And when I went over to my bed I found out why: she'd weed all over my nerdy Club'N duvet.

'Bugger, Misty,' I cursed, just as Miss Cribbe walked in to say it was time for lights out.

'Language, Calypso!' she trilled.

'Miss Cribbe, it's not fair. My duvet is all wet. Misty's weed on it.'

She put her hand on my soggy duvet to feel if it was wet. 'Don't be silly, you don't know for certain that it was Misty.'

Hello, it smelled of dog wee and Misty was the only dog living in Cleathorpes!

'Now, stop fussing. Give it to me and I'll wash it. It's a warm night and you can sleep with a sheet just for tonight.'

Star waded in to my rescue. 'Miss Cribbe, that is so

unfair! Poor Calypso will freeze. And anyway, it *was* Misty. You know it was.'

'That's enough cheek from you, young lady. Apologize immediately.'

'I will not,' Star shouted. (She can be very stubborn.) 'Misty's always weeing all over the dorm – it's disgusting.'

'Star, I'm warning you, that's enough,' Miss Cribbe replied with a wobble in her voice. 'Misty is a lovely dog. She adores you girls – why, you're like family to her. She'd be devastated if she heard what you were saying.'

'It's OK, Miss Cribbe. I don't mind sleeping under a sheet,' I assured her. I hated it when Miss Cribbe cried. It meant someone had to cuddle her and she'd completely soak you in tears. I gave her the duvet and she grabbed me for a beardy kiss on the cheek.

'You don't really think Misty did this dreadful thing, do you, dear? It was probably a dog from the village.'

Yes, that would be right. A dog had walked the two miles from the village, managed to get through the electrified, barbed-wire fence, negotiated its way past the hordes of roaming attack dogs and armed security guards, found its way inside our locked building, just in order to pee on the faded faces of Club'N.

'Yes, you're probably right,' I comforted her as I patted her back, hoping to escape from her bosomy embrace sooner rather than later. She smelled a bit like dog wee herself.

'Now, Miss Cribbe will bring you a nice clean sheet and

tuck you in, dear.' She often referred to herself in the third person, as if she were royalty or something. I wondered if Freddie referred to himself in the third person. I didn't think I'd want to pull a boy that did anything to remind me of Miss Cribbe.

'You can use my spare duvet, Calypso,' Georgina offered.

'See what a lovely friend you have in Georgina, dear.' Miss Cribbe wiped away a tear with her sleeve. 'You might take some notes from Georgina, on how to be a good friend yourself, Star.'

'As if,' Star muttered. But Miss Cribbe didn't hear, or pretended not to, anyway.

'Now, I know you don't mean to be unkind, but it's very hurtful when you talk about dear Misty like that. I love you girls as if you were my own – you know that, don't you?'

'Yes, Miss Cribbe,' we all said – anything to shut her up.

'Good girls. Now, say your prayers and go to sleep.'

Georgina and I nodded solemnly. Star turned over to face the wall and muttered something under her breath that no one could hear.

'As for you, young lady,' she said, referring to Star. 'You can see Sister Constance tomorrow after supper for a suitable punishment for cheeking me.'

'What did I do?' Star yelled.

'I won't have you cheeking me, young lady.'

'Fine,' Star replied, but when Miss Cribbe left the room she blew a big raspberry.

'What a freak,' Georgina said, climbing out of bed to get me her duvet.

'Sorry about getting you in trouble, Star,' I told her.

'You didn't get me in trouble. I hate her stupid old dog. Everyone knows Misty is always weeing everywhere. This whole building stinks. It's foul. Besides, all Sister will do is make me sweep the corridor.'

'And give you a big fat Mars Bar afterwards, darling,' Georgina added, and all three of us laughed. It was nice laughing together. Star even gave me a look as if to say, Maybe Georgina's not that bad *really*.

The nuns were never particularly interested in punishing us. Not unless we got caught taking drugs or fighting in the corridor or smashing school property or something heinous like that. We all quite liked the nuns, actually, mostly because they were very old and seemed to live in their own little nun world, complete with its own sweet little cemetery.

Georgina threw the duvet over me and then pretended to tuck me in like Miss Cribbe. 'Now give my moustache a big sloppy kiss, Calypso dear.' She put loads of saliva on her lips so they glistened, and then puckered them up the way Miss Cribbe did.

After the lights were out I snuggled into the lovely, plain, white Egyptian cotton-covered duvet, said a few silent Hail Marys, and asked Mary if she would petition God on my behalf so that a horrific accident might befall my teen duvet (something more permanently destructive than Misty weeing on it) so that I could have a nice grown-up duvet like this one. Then I fell asleep.

That night, Star walked and talked in her sleep. It wasn't a new thing. As long as I've known Star she's talked in her sleep, although usually she only did it when she was at home. We woke up to find her sitting on Georgina's bed, babbling on about not wanting to die. Georgina helped me get her back into bed.

She was quite sweet about Star's sleepwalking, really, considering she'd been woken up. I would have expected her to go ballistic and scream about what a freak Star was, but all she did was giggle.

Maybe Star and I had got Georgina all wrong before, I mused as I drifted off to sleep.

But then Georgina whispered to me, 'Hey, Calypso. Tomorrow let's tell Star she was going on about pulling Professor Sullivan.'

SEVEN

Food Fight Fiasco

As it turned out, there was no time to tease Star for sleeptalking about Professor Sullivan, because the three of us slept through all six bells and finally Miss Cribbe came into our room, bashing away on her wretched copper gong.

'Wakey, wakey, girls! Wakey, wakey!' she cried out in her special morning sing-song voice.

There was a mad scramble to dress, then we all clustered around the sink in our en-suite bathroom to clean our teeth before tearing down the stairs in time to grab a dry croissant each from the canteen. We shoved these in our pockets, planning to eat them surreptitiously during first period, which was English literature with Ms Topler. Yawn.

I swear, Ms Topler is the Antichrist of literature. Theoretically it should have been my favourite subject, given how I love reading and writing. I've had two letters published in *Teen Vogue*, but my dream is to write articles in the witty, satirical vein of Nancy Mitford or Dorothy Parker.

Ms Topler doesn't appreciate my wit or satire, though. If anything, she is ethically opposed to wit and satire. Where there is literary joy she can be relied upon to throw cold water on it through critical analysis, and if she happens to prescribe a classic like Simone de Beauvoir, you can rest assured she will slaughter it with one of her diabolical deconstructions.

Mostly, though, she loved giving us tragic books to read, like *Little Women*, and as if this weren't bad enough, she made us discuss them *ad nauseum* in class.

Every time I was about to put a piece of croissant in my mouth, she'd ask me something lame about the tragic Jo. I told her that 'despite an indefatigable independent streak, Jo was the classic L to the power of three – a Literary Lady Loser.'

I wasn't even trying to be funny, but Star and Georgina and a few other girls laughed – and no, not in a piss-take sort of way. Georgina's crowd were acting like I was actually one of the girls now, and then to top it off, Georgina announced that Tobias couldn't bear *Little Women* and had refused point-blank to let her read it.

The class fell into paroxysms of mirth.

Ms Topler gave me a 'blue.'

A 'blue' handed out by a teacher means having to write lines, like 'I must pay closer attention in class,' one hundred times or something annoying like that. It's called a blue because you write the lines on blue paper. Older girls can hand out blues too, but we could usually slack them down – although not when we were in the younger years. In Year Seven once Star tried to slack down one of the older girls who gave her a blue for something really minor, and the older girl reported her, then Star ended up having to write lines from six a.m. to seven a.m. (Pre-breakfast lines have now been deemed too barbarically cruel, even for boarding school.)

When we got lines we could petition Sister Constance and usually get a transmuted sentence, something really easy like sweeping the corridor. As Georgina pointed out, the best part of getting Sister Constance involved was that she always gave you a sweet reward afterwards – which sort of defeated the point of giving a punishment, but like I said, you don't need to be rational to be a teacher, let alone a nun.

Having missed breakfast, my mouth was watering at the thought of a Mars Bar.

By the time class was over I was starving and the already-stale croissant was a pile of flakes in my pocket. Our sadistic dorm matron was going to go mental when I put it in for wash if I didn't remember to get every minis-cule crumb out. I would try to remember to flush my pocket out tonight, but deep down I knew I would forget and get one of Matron's lectures about my manifest lack of wash-bag respect and how I would end up being ridiculed by my children – if I ever had the good fortune to have any, which she seriously doubted because what sort of man would want to marry a slattern like me, who eats food from her pocket?

A sense of proportion isn't part of the job description for working at Saint Augustine's.

Because of the wretched Ms Topler keeping me back late in order to give me my stupid blue (Star and Georgina had both waited for me), we were late for everything and on the charge to the canteen at lunch, we were all clutching our stomachs with exaggerated hunger pains. Even though it was unprecedented, it just seemed natural to sit with Georgina and her group to eat. Georgina, Arabella and Clementine all seemed fine with that. Clemmie even squeezed over, practically sitting on Arabella's lap, so that we could all fit on the bench. Even Star seemed fine with it, but Honey glared at me when I sat down with my tray.

'Are you sure you have enough there, Calypso?' she asked nastily.

I had encouraged the dinner lady to pile the fish nuggets pretty high, because they were one of the few edible things they served us at Saint Augustine's and I was famished after missing breakfast.

Star grabbed one of the fish nuggets off my plate and threw it at Honey. She riposted with a chip. And that was it. The food fight was on . . .

Clementine tossed a broad bean from her salad at Arabella, who chucked it across at Star. Georgina wiped a glob of mayonnaise on my nose and I flicked a pile of peas at her with my spoon. Within seconds it was a free-for-all. Food was being pelted around the canteen by everyone.

We were told to report to Sister Constance in her office after supper.

Sister sat in silent prayer under the massive gruesome crucifix that loomed above her desk. Its ivory Christ with an enormous spear jutting out of his bleeding side always made me feel really guilty and a little scared. In this setting, Sister Constance looked quite scary too. Generally, she has a very stiff, formal manner (although sometimes you catch her suppressing a smile).

Her office was lined from floor to ceiling with holy texts. The ancient literary feel was rather spoilt by a nasty, grey metal filing cabinet, supporting an enormous wooden statue of Our Lady of Lourdes. I don't know why, but Sister Constance's office always smelled of an old church Bible, that mixture of mustiness, wax, frankincense and furniture polish.

Seconds turned into minutes and I swear I heard Christ groan with the agony of it all as he hung from his cross. Although maybe it was just my tummy – I hadn't actually got to eat any of my fish nuggets, because of our food fight. And at supper they'd served us the grey slops, which I had vowed never to eat after a rumour went around the school that it was made from dead pets from the pet shed.

Eventually Sister broke her meditation. She looked up at the six of us standing in front of her table and told us how disappointed she was. We bowed our heads solemnly, striking what we hoped was a remorseful pose.

'How wantonly wasteful to treat food in such a cavalier manner.'

'Yes, Sister,' we all said together.

'Did you even spare the slightest thought for the poor little hungry children of the world who haven't got enough food to fill their distended bellies?'

'Yes, Sister,' we repeated. I was looking out of the window and was slightly distracted by the sight of a group of girls heading off through the bluebells towards Puller's Hill.

But I was brought back to attention by Sister Constance, gasping in shock.

'Well, if you thought of those poor little hungry children and their desperate need for food, what possessed you to throw it about?'

We looked at one another, startled. Star spoke for all of us. 'We meant no, Sister.'

'No what?'

'No, we didn't spare the slightest thought for the poor little hungry children of the world who haven't got enough food to fill their distended bellies.'

'I thought as much,' she said with a sigh, disappointment etched in every line of her face. 'Your mother would be especially sorry to hear of you abusing food, when she does so much good work in her capacity as a senior fundraiser for War Child, Miss Castle Orpington.'

'Yes, Sister.'

'However, I can see you are all deeply ashamed about this affair now.'

'Yes, Sister,' we all agreed.

'Yes, Sister what?'

'Yes, Sister, we are deeply ashamed of ourselves,' we recited.

'Well then, let's press on. What do you think your punishment should be on this occasion?'

'We could . . . erm . . . sweep the corridor, or something nasty like that, Sister,' Star suggested.

'Actually, Star, that was going to be your punishment for cheeking Miss Cribbe last night. She was very upset about your suggestion that Misty may have been responsible for wetting Calypso's bed.'

Star didn't even struggle with herself. 'Sister, she wees all over the place.'

'Star!'

'It's true, Sister,' Georgina piped up. 'Mother says it's really unhygienic.'

'I've no doubt it would be if it were true, but then so is throwing food all over the canteen. No, I'm afraid sweeping the floor won't be a suitable penance for this severe wickedness. I've decided to assign you a special task.'

We looked at one another and swallowed. This sounded ominous.

Sister Constance went on. 'I want you to come up with some fund-raising ideas for the Children of the World charity. Last year, the Lower Sixth raised six thousand pounds. We're aiming to improve on that figure this year.'

We all weren't quite sure what to say – or what it meant. Even though six thousand pounds wouldn't even pay for a term's fees at Saint Augustine's, I knew it was a lot of money.

My parents are always going on about money. I am always reminding them that I wasn't the one who came up with the idea of flying across the world to an exorbitantly expensive boarding school – to which they always reply that nothing in life is really free. They say they are more than happy to make sacrifices in order to give me a rounded education, and if that means driving around in a crappy car and forgoing pools and holidays, it's a small price to pay. Parents have a very odd sense of logic.

Just the same, I realised that six thousand pounds was a drop in the ocean compared to what it would take to help all the suffering children of the world.

'Here are some brochures to inspire you.' She pushed across some pamphlets that depicted sad-eyed children clustered around an empty bowl. I suddenly felt miserable and pointless as I scanned their hungry faces.

'Now, I know it's too soon for you to be thinking about gap years, but later on this week one of Saint Augustine's Old Girls will be visiting us and giving a talk at assembly about the wonderful inspirational opportunities that Raleigh International offers to girls like yourselves; opportunities to meet girls and boys from different backgrounds;

opportunities to give something back.'

My stomach rumbled really loudly, which was desperately embarrassing given how I'd only missed lunch and these kids were like missing their whole lives, basically.

'That will be all, ladies,' said Sister Constance.

'Thank you, Sister,' we replied.

'Star, you will also have the duty of sweeping the Cleathorpes corridor.'

Damn, I thought, I'd forgotten to present my blue and now I'd missed my chance to transmute my lines to floor sweeping.

'Yes, Sister,' Star agreed, her eyes downcast – even though I knew she must be whooping it up inside because she didn't have to do six double sides of lines.

'I'll come and see you shortly, to see how you've got on.' (In other words, to bring you your Mars Bar.)

We backed out of her room, heads still bowed, the way we'd been taught to when we first arrived at Saint Augustine's. Sometimes we did it to other teachers who weren't nuns, just to wind them up.

'This is so random,' Honey complained, once we were out of earshot.

'I think it could be quite fun,' Star argued. 'Doing something worthwhile.'

'Worthwhile?' said Honey. 'Are you insane? Rattling a tin around like a beggar. You are such a plebeian, Star.'

But Star wasn't backing down – she never does. 'No, think about it. We could do some really cool things, like have parties and stuff. I mean, it would be the perfect cover for all sorts of cool outings. And anyway, it would be for a good cause.'

Clementine had to agree, reluctantly. 'She's right. We could use it as an excuse to hire a minibus to take us to the Feather's Ball. We could raffle places on the bus.' So typical of Clemmie, who was the most boy-mad girl in our year. She rarely spoke unless there were boys around and even then she mostly only ogled and giggled.

'Whatever,' Star said dismissively. 'Personally I think the Feather's Ball is the lamest thing out. The bands they have . . . pah-lease!'

'Didn't stop you pulling that gross boy from Worth Abby at the Valentine's Ball, as I remember,' Honey riposted.

Star curled her upper lip and looked Honey up and down. 'I'm surprised you can remember, after all the vodka you drank. As I remember, you were staggering around cutting in on everyone. In fact, hang on, I remember you cut in on me, *darling,* and pulled him yourself. But perhaps you were having one of your blackouts and don't recall.'

Honey was about to open her mouth when I heard someone say, 'Oh, shut up, both of you!' Actually in the brief silence that followed I realised that the words had come out of my mouth, but no one said anything. Instead Clemmie merely continued with her line of thought, adding, 'We could charge some random amount like double or triple?'

The discussion went on and no one seemed to notice I was there. I felt completely invisible. Being the school freak and not having parents with a madly grand house in Chelsea, I'd never been to any of the Capital VIP balls. But I knew about them. In the weeks leading up to a ball, it was all anyone spoke of. The balls are usually held at the Hammersmith Palais or some other huge venue and they are a highlight of the boarding school calendar. Although no alcohol is allowed, only the boys are frisked, giving girls like Honey a free hand to smuggle in whatever they wanted. Absolutely everyone who matters goes to at least a few, because it's a great place to pull. There are bands and DJs, and goodie bags at the end. Even Star had been to one, although she said the tongue of the boy she kissed felt like a small fish. But I know she only said that to make me feel better.

'Charging more is a fab idea, darling; actually we could charge different prices depending on how rich and important you are,' Arabella threw in. 'Although I do think the VIP balls are getting a little tired,' she added – for once agreeing with Star. By important, Arabella meant how many hyphens you had in your name. Her full name is Arabella Basingdom-Morgan-Heigbrewer-Tomlinson-Protvost-Smith. But she just refers to herself as Arabella Smith, knowing full well that everyone knows the portentous enormity of her name.

Arabella flicked her mane of carefully highlighted blonde hair, and a strand of it stuck to my lip-gloss. I brushed it away and started applying more lip-gloss.

Georgina said, 'Or we could have pulling competitions!'

'Five-quid fine if you don't pull at least two boys at the Eades social.'

'Make that ten for everyone who doesn't pull a prince,' Honey added cattily, arching one of her professionally styled eyebrows. She was always going on about her Russian eyebrow stylist, as if she were some sort of guru or something.

'See you back at the dorms, I'm going down to check the post,' Arabella told us before dashing down the stairs.

'Grab mine, darling,' everyone called back, apart from Star and me.

Obviously Star didn't expect mail from parents who are perpetually stoned. My parents' excuse is that they are too modern and technologically aware to send 'snail mail,' as they call it. They prefer to communicate with me by e-mail, which is so lame.

Honey's mother sent her postcards of herself chatting to various celebrities, and Honey had them pinned all over her board. But you can't pin an e-mail to your board when you are homesick, which means that everyone thinks you're a sad loser whose parents don't love you.

EIGHT

The Royal Summons

As soon as we got back to Cleathorpes, Star went off to do her sweeping punishment and the rest of us slumped on Clementine's bed to consider the task Sister had given us.

'I suppose it could be a blessing,' Honey conceded eventually. 'An excuse to slack off on work.'

'Got any of those cool sweets from LA left, Calypso darling?' Georgina asked.

'Sure.'

'I think Sister totally overreacted,' she sighed, pulling herself up from the bed. 'I mean, even my parents have food fights!'

I tried to imagine Sarah and Bob having a food fight, but couldn't – they are just way too Californian, and besides, they hate waste. 'Yeah, totally,' I agreed.

'You know, Tobias is growing quite fond of you, darling,' she confided as we walked off arm in arm down the corridor towards our dorm room to fetch the vodka and sweets.

'Yes, well, the affection is a . . . erm . . . a mutual-ish thing. I mean, I adore bears – well, most soft toys, actually.'

I honestly don't know how I let lame things like that escape from my mouth, but Georgina seemed to find this enormously funny and fell about laughing.

'You've got mail,' Arabella announced, in a bad impression of my accent, as she walked into our dorm room and tossed a FedEx package and a letter onto my lap.

Georgina looked up from her magazine. 'Oh, fabbie! Is that from Jay, darling?' she asked, jumping onto the bed beside me.

I turned the package over and read the sender's address. It was my mom's office on the Paramount lot. 'Looks like it,' I replied casually.

They both clambered onto the bed as I tore into the package. Inside was a DVD of a movie that wasn't even out in the UK yet and a postcard of the Hollywood sign.

Wish you were here, babe!
L.O.L. Jay xxxxx

I wasn't too impressed by the 'babe' bit, but still it had the required effect. Everyone went totally crazy about it and Clementine rushed off to show Antoinette, who had said she didn't believe I had a real boyfriend.

I didn't open the letter. Actually, I was so swamped with questions about Jay, I forgot all about it and then the study bell went and I had to run, leaving the letter abandoned on my bed.

Later that night, Georgina had a bubble bath that smelled all lovely and coconutty and we all sat on the side of the bath or on stools around the bathroom for a confab about our charity fund-raising ideas. (The bubbles were very high.) We made a list of possible fund-raising ideas. All of them included pulling boys, sweets and fags.

Honey continued to be quite prickly with me, but I decided to rise above it. Now that I was at the centre of things, with a fit boyfriend, I could afford to be magnanimous.

When we came out of the bathroom, Star had the pile of sweets she'd received from Sister Constance laid out in front of her on her bed. Unfortunately, our room still stank of wee so we sprayed everything with Febreze before piling our duvets on the floor for a vodka and sweet feast.

That was when Arabella came back from picking up her fags from her room. She picked up my letter.

'You haven't opened this yet, darling,' she said, tossing it onto my lap.

So with my mouth bulging with chocolate I tore open the envelope. I had no idea who the letter was from; I couldn't place the distinctive, flowing writing. Inside was a single sheet of heavy parchment paper with the royal seal on the bottom.

Hi Calypso,
Great to meet you yesterday. Hope to see you at the social –
without your sabre!
Freddie x

'Who's it from?' Star enquired, passing me her mug for a sip of vodka. She always mixed hers with warm milk so it didn't taste so yucky. We were allowed to keep milk and biscuits and other snacks in the small kitchen of Cleathorpes. We were even allowed to make ourselves toast, which Georgina did regularly – only not for herself, obviously ('Think of the carbs, darling'). No, she fed the toast and marmalade to Tobias ('He simply adores it, darling, and you know how he can't *bear* the food they feed him in the canteen!')

The milk was an inspired idea, though, because if Miss Cribbe burst in, Star would just show her the milk and say something really innocent like, 'I find it really helps me sleep, Miss Cribbe.'

Miss Cribbe just loved us when we acted babyish.

I stared at the letter for some time. My mind had gone totally blank. I reread it a few times before it all sank in and then I dropped the letter onto my lap in a daze. Prince Freddie had written to me? A mere mortal?

Star grabbed the letter and read it out loud before I could stop her.

To be fair, she knew what a horrible thing she'd done before she'd read out his name, but it was too late – the damage was done.

'You complete and utter slut,' Honey shouted, pulling her head back in from the window where she'd been blowing out her cigarette smoke. Then she came over and slapped me hard across the face.

Even Georgina looked horrified.

Star screamed at her, 'What the hell do you think you're doing? Get out, you absolute bitch!'

I started to cry. I couldn't help it. It was all just too much. One minute I was the envy of all, with my fake boyfriend, the next minute I was being vilified because an HRH fancied me. Also, my face stung. I'd never been slapped before.

Honey was just standing there, and I was worried she wanted to have an all-out fight, so I was glad when Georgina said, 'Look, Honey, I think you should leave.'

Honey flounced out of the room, followed by Georgina, Arabella and Clementine. Clemmie cast me a sympathetic look, but I threw myself onto my bed and sobbed.

Star was really sweet and said I should have been singing from the rooftops, having received a summons from royalty.

She was the best friend ever and suddenly I felt really guilty about ever wanting to be in with the cool girls and making her put up with Honey and the others, just to satisfy my egotistical wishes.

Actually I'd started to think that Georgina might not be so bad. And not just because she called me darling, but because she seemed to understand my humour, and she'd helped me out with my bedding when Misty had weed all over it. God, I was so stupid.

'I'm really sorry about reading out the letter,' Star told me.

'It's OK. You weren't to know.'

She passed me some lip-gloss. 'Wear your pain like lip-gloss. . . . Besides, you've still got me.' We had a big cuddle. 'And Jay!'

But that just made me start crying again.

'Calypso, it isn't that bad, really. Who cares about bloody Honey?'

'It's not that,' I told her, trying not to cry anymore. 'It's Jay.'

'What? You're not being paranoid, are you? Seriously, he just wrote to you! He must really like you.'

'I'm not being paranoid,' I told her. And then it all came tumbling out. 'He's my mom's gay PA.'

And then she cuddled me even harder, only it was a wobbly sort of cuddle because she was laughing so hard. 'You are so mad! Gay?'

She was laughing so hard now that she fell on the floor. 'Gay Jay, your mum's PA!'

And then even I had to laugh, because I hadn't realised how it all rhymed before. After that, I told her the whole tragic tale of my pathetic attempt to fit in with Georgina and her cool pod of friends. Star didn't get it – well, I didn't expect she would – but I felt better having told her, although I was now petrified that someone would walk in and hear her singing, 'Gay Jay, my *mum's* PA,' which I couldn't get her to stop doing for ages.

Eventually I turned the conversation around to parents generally, and Star did her impressions of her parents and their friends when they were stoned. 'You know . . . like, stop crying, man, you're freaking me out.'

It all felt so comfortable, Star and I alone and just being how we'd always been, that I almost forgot about Honey and the trouble I was going to be in. But then Star reminded me by asking what I planned to do. We both knew bad things were about to happen.

It is a law at Saint Augustine's that you don't pull boys that other girls have already declared their territory – especially when that girl is Honey O'Hare. In a school where bitchiness was a currency, Honey was filthy rich. I had seen her destroy girls in the past.

When we were in Year Nine, a girl from Year Seven called Josephine annoyed Honey by being disrespectful towards her. I don't even know what she said, but Honey mounted a relentless campaign against her and pretty soon Josephine was crying herself to sleep every night. By the end of term she was self-mutilating – cutting herself with blades from the art room. The school tried to get her parents to visit her more to reassure her, but they refused, saying Josephine would just have to deal with the problem, which even the meanest teacher in the school would agree was really mean. Eventually the school suggested to her parents that Josephine might not be suited to boarding school life.

Honey went around the school with a big grin on her face for weeks after that. I was pretty sure I didn't have the guts to self-mutilate, being as grossed out by blood as I am, but I was definitely going to be crying myself to sleep.

It wasn't long before Honey came screaming back into the room, shrieking at the top of her voice, 'You are so dead, bitch!'

Then she grabbed the letter from Freddie and tore it into about a million pieces. OK, maybe not a million – but only because she didn't get the chance. Georgina managed to grab it from her, so she only managed to tear it in half.

Arabella, Star and Clementine pulled her off me, because by then she had grabbed my head and started pulling my hair out, while spitting obscenities into my face and telling me about the various painful ways I was going to be murdered.

A crowd of girls was gathering outside in the corridor, trying to catch a glimpse of what was going on. I was rubbing my head and trying to gather my thoughts together, when Misty came in and started barking. Shortly after that, Miss Cribbe came in with her knitting and threw everyone out of the room, apart from Star, Georgina and me.

Misty squatted as if about to wee, and Miss Cribbe shooed her out too and went bright red. If Misty hadn't done that, I am pretty sure we would have been in big trouble.

My mobile started ringing, but Miss Cribbe took it from me before I could answer it, saying that it was time for lights out – even though it was only nine-thirty and lights out was officially meant to be ten! None of us argued, though.

I couldn't get to sleep that night.

'Are you awake?' Georgina asked me after the lights had been out for a while.

My head was still hurting from Honey pulling my hair and I could still feel the sting of the slap on my cheek. Georgina was Honey's best friend and I couldn't help being a bit scared of what she might say or do. So I didn't say anything.

Georgina went on. 'Personally, I think Honey is overreacting, darling.'

Her words seemed to echo in my head. I thought of all the benchmark moments of the term – how she'd called me darling, stood up for me, given me her duvet when Misty weed on mine. Then I recalled all the other benchmark moments of my time at Saint Augustine's and the way Georgina and Honey had isolated me so terribly and made me feel like the school freak.

Star was muttering in her sleep.

'Darling?' Georgina repeated.

I suppose I took it as a good sign that at least she was still deigning to call me darling.

'I didn't ask him to write to me,' I explained. 'It's not my fault. Can't you make Honey see that?'

'Arabella told me about the whole duelling thing you had with him.'

'But I didn't ask him to write!' I repeated.

For a long time she didn't say anything and I was left hanging by a thread, afraid of being back in the freak seat again.

'Honey has a lot of issues,' she said, after what seemed like half an hour – I'd almost fallen asleep. 'Seriously . . . a lot of issues.'

Hello, like I hadn't noticed! The insane bitch had just tried to murder me. 'Oh, I didn't know,' I replied softly.

'Yaah, there's all sorts of stuff going on between her mum and her latest step-dad-to-be, Lord Aginet.'

Good. A part of me was glad she was having a horrible time of it at home. 'Oh, that's sad,' I said.

'But Arabella and Clementine stood up for you, darling.'

I tried not to make too much of the fact that she hadn't added herself to that list and just said, 'That's sweet of them.' Then I thought, Well, maybe I'm overreacting. Maybe it would be all right. Maybe I wouldn't be totally vilified by everyone in my year and be forced to hide in cupboards for the rest of term. Maybe I would go to the social, pull Freddie and be the envy of everyone. Maybe I would be accepted for who I was and judged by more important things than my accent.

'Obviously, you still can't go to the social, though, darling.'

'Oh.'

'Yaah. Also, darling, if you did go, Honey would so totally kill you.'

The fact that she'd called me darling didn't dilute the poison in her words. 'Oh?'

'My advice is be sick and spend the night in the infirmary.'

Be sick or be dead is what she meant.

NINE

The Fine Line between Pleasure and Pain

The next morning I woke up with a pounding head and it wasn't just because Miss Cribbe had banged her wretched gong for ten minutes while I tried to hide under my duvet.

I always get the most horrendous headaches before my period's due. Eventually Miss Cribbe decided I wasn't faking it – or maybe her own head had started to ache from her gonging – so she sent me down to the infirmary where the much-hated Sister Dumpster (real name Sister Dempster) was no doubt waiting to torture me or poison me (depending on how sadistic she was feeling).

There are two sisters in charge of the infirmary: Sister Dumpster (not a nun, but an actual professional nurse who specialised in the demeaning and torturing of children) and dear little Sister Regina (an actual nun), who handed out the Co-codamol like there was no tomorrow.

My mom says you shouldn't take more than six pills in a twenty-four-hour period and that actually it's not even an over-the-counter medication in the States. But Sister Regina says 'pish' to that and plies you with them until you feel better again.

Sister Dumpster says 'pish' to the six-a-day rule as well. In fact, she says 'pish' to Co-codamol altogether. She did her nursing training in an era when child cruelty and sadism were in their heyday: 'A temperature of one hundred and fifty degrees? Why, that's nothing. In my day we said "tish-tosh" to a temperature like that. These days, you girls want it all your own way,' etc, etc, *ad nauseum*.

For some reason Sister Dumpster is *always* on duty when I am sent to the infirmary.

But miracles do happen (as Sister Constance is always reminding us) and it wasn't Sister Dumpster that morning, it was sweet little Sister Regina.

'Poor Miss Kelly, now you just lie down here, and I'll get you a sanitary napkin and some Co-codamol.'

She tucked me up in one of the horrendously uncomfortable infirmary beds, which I'm convinced are all from World War II and still smell of sick soldiers. The springs in them are so ancient, and make so much noise that you can't relax, let alone sleep.

Whenever you go to the infirmary for period pain, the sisters insist on handing out these pads that look like skis. The story is that the nuns were given shed-loads of them in the last century, and they are still trying to get through them all. Seriously though, you could go white-water rafting on them they are so enormous.

In the Easter break I'd finally got the hang of tampons, but I wasn't going to discuss such modern advances in personal hygiene with Sister Regina, who probably wasn't even aware that they'd had been invented.

I said thank you and gave her a hug, because she was just trying to be sweet, and nun hugs are so lovely, smelling as nuns do of incense and flowers that they pick to decorate the chapel and the gazillion statues of Mary and Jesus that are dotted about the school.

After I'd knocked back my pills and my headache had subsided, Sister Regina gave me another one of her little hugs and said I may as well miss the morning classes and rest until lunch break. I think she was feeling a bit bored so together we read the copy of *Teen Vogue* that I'd brought back from LA, and she said how none of the models could touch me for looks and poise.

The nuns all love the word 'poise.' Maybe because it is one of the few things they were able to hang on to when they gave up everything – like make-up and cool shoes – when they took their vows. Still, it was very sweet of her to say (even if it wasn't true).

She said she found it perplexing that any girl would want a job like that – standing about all day having her picture taken.

Actually, she's probably right. I don't suppose it would be nice being a model, apart from the money side of it, of course, although apparently lots of models make virtually nothing – just like actresses in LA. Also, I bet you'd always be worried about people saying mean things about your weight, or saying your nose was too big. Though according to Star they airbrush out all your nasty bits – and Kate Moss might be the size of a house, for all we knew.

I eventually left Sister Regina just before the bell rang for lunch, and took a detour via the pet shed so I could have a quick cuddle with Arabesque. I always felt a bit disloyal going to visit Arabesque, because I knew Star would rather my affections lay with Hilda and Brian. But the truth is, I much prefer cuddly rabbits to rats and snakes.

I did check on Hilda, though, who was running along on her little rat wheel in her usual demented fashion. But, honestly, how excited can you get about a rat? Star goes on and on about how intelligent rats are, and I'm sure she's right, but I wasn't really looking for witty repartee from a pet, so I moved swiftly on to the rabbit area where Arabesque was softly sleeping. See, that's what so sweet about rabbits – they do everything so softly.

At least I thought he was asleep, until I took him out and held him to me. Instead of his lovely, warm, little body wriggling against me, he was all cold and stiff.

I gasped and put him straight back in the cage, and ran to the canteen, bumping into everyone and knocking over trays in my search for Georgina.

'Georgina,' I panted when I finally found her. 'You have to come. It's Arabesque!'

Honey glared at me. 'You are so dead, Calypso. I've told Poppy what you did. She's going kill you.'

Poppy is Honey's older sister and, if anything, even meaner than Honey. She's stunning-looking and always appears in the social pages under the name of The Honourable Poppy O'Hare – although she always makes a massive fuss over how she told the journalists she didn't want them to use her title. Yeah right, whatever. The boys at Eades went potty for her, but as Star reminded me, it's probably not her personality that they were going potty over.

But I didn't care. I had to tell Georgina about Arabesque; that was all that mattered.

Georgina said, 'Just chill out, will you, Honey?' but she didn't look up at me; she just moved some peas around her plate dismally. I could tell that a decision had been made regarding my standing in the group. I was definitely out. Honey had won. Last night when she'd told me that she thought Honey was overreacting, I'd more or less taken a kind of cold comfort from her words. I'd told myself that although she'd have to stand by Honey because, after all, they'd been friends forever, at least she'd criticised Honey and acknowledged that her behaviour was out of order.

But now as I looked around the group I'd naïvely imagined I'd become part of, I saw how stupid I'd been. Maybe

Georgina did sort of like me. Maybe she'd decided I wasn't really that bad, but at the end of the day Honey was of her world and scored ten out of ten when it came to cool. But however nice my American sweets tasted, I was still considered a freak. And besides, I was almost out of Hershey's Kisses.

Then Poppy came over to the table. 'Hey, American Freak,' she said, slapping a Post-it note on my back. I knew it was a Post-it note, because I was always getting them slapped on me. Usually they said random stuff like *AMERICAN FREAK* or just plain *FREAK*. But when I reached my arm around and pulled this particular one off, it said, *DEAD*.

The word 'dead,' combined with the experience of finding poor little Arabesque, made my eyes fill up with tears. I wiped them away with my sleeve. Georgina and Arabella turned away, as if embarrassed.

'Georgina,' I said again, a wobble in my voice now.

'There's nothing I can do, really, Calypso,' she snapped, not even looking up as she twirled her peas.

'Oh, is poor little American Freak girl crying?' Honey asked in a baby voice.

Georgina looked up at Honey and shook her head as if to say, That's enough. I could tell she was in conflict over Honey's behaviour, so I took my chance and asked if maybe I could have a word with her alone, but she said that she was too busy.

Peas can be very demanding.

I couldn't just leave it, though. I couldn't go through the day knowing Arabesque was lying there dead in his cage and not tell Georgina. Whether we were friends or not I had to tell her, and I had to tell her now.

It was awful. I shuffled about for a bit and said 'erm' a few times but in the end, as another Post-it note was slapped on my back, I just blurted it out: 'Arabesque is dead.' Then I started crying, and then, after looking at me for what seemed like forever, Georgina started crying too and Arabella put her arms around her and gave her a cuddle.

Clemmie arrived with her tray laden down with the usual slops and asked what the matter was.

Honey rolled her eyes and said, 'Georgina's rabbit's dead,' like it was no big deal.

By now our little group had become the lunchtime spectacle. Star arrived and she must have been to the pet shed already because all she said was, 'Oh, I guess you all know, then.'

'Oh, Georgie,' Clemmie said and gave her a cuddle.

Georgina was really sobbing now and I think I might have been too, but I was too shocked by what Honey said next to really remember.

'Honestly, I don't know what all the fuss is about. I mean, he was quite old, darling. Actually, I always thought he was a bit manky. Besides, Daddy can buy you a new one. A better one.'

I couldn't believe it – Honey was supposed to be Georgina's best friend!

Georgina looked up and for a second I thought she was going to throw herself on Honey and rip her hair out. But Honey had started to file her talons with an emery board. When she eventually looked up and saw the look of thunder on Georgina's face, she seemed genuinely perplexed.

'What?'

'You are such a bitch.' Georgina spat the words out at her best friend.

Everyone looked at Honey, who blinked innocently and said, 'What?,' as if she had no idea that she was the spawn of Satan. Eventually everyone just shook their heads, like people do over lost causes, and silently filed out of the canteen, leaving their trays on the table.

Even Star went with them.

I was left alone with the bitch from hell.

'God, you're a freak,' she said with a sneer, and picked a chip off her plate and nibbled at it in her special way so that her lips didn't touch it.

I didn't really feel hungry now and I didn't want to spend another second around Honey, so I left the canteen without eating and chased after the others.

When I got to the pet shed, Star was stroking Arabesque's still little body.

'Oh, no, Arabie!' Georgina was screaming while the others held her back. Georgina's cry was so sad that I wanted to give her a hug, like Arabella and Clemmie were doing, but I wasn't sure if she'd want to be touched by an American Freak, so I just said, 'Oh, Georgina, I'm so sorry.' It sounded a bit lame, I know, but Georgina pulled herself away from the others and threw her arms around my neck. She sobbed and sobbed and sobbed until I thought she would die of dehydration.

'I really loved Arabesque,' I said. 'He was by far the sweetest rabbit in the whole shed and I used to come and see him and cuddle him. I knew you would hate me if I told you, but . . .'

'I don't hate you,' Georgina said. 'Oh, Arabie.'

It was only when Sisters Hillary and Veronica passed by and asked us what had happened that I realised I was sobbing just as hard as Georgina.

Star told them how she had come to the pet shed to see Hilda and noticed that Arabesque wasn't moving. Sisters Hillary and Veronica gave us all comforting little nun hugs.

'You poor dear girls,' they clucked, as if we were only five years old. 'Oh poor, poor, poor little things.' Then they said we should all say a special prayer for Arabesque, '. . . even though we know that bunnies don't actually have souls.'

So we all said a Hail Mary and a Glory Be to the Father and somehow that seemed to calm us down a bit.

The rest of the day was pure hell.

The death of Arabesque did nothing to dilute Poppy and Honey's Post-it note campaign. Between every class my back was plastered with variations of the *YOU ARE SO*

DEAD, CALYPSO theme. But all I could really think about was poor Georgina, and how horrible it had been holding Arabesque's still, cold body in my arms.

Georgina didn't eat anything for dinner that night and, because she hadn't been ticked off for leaving her tray at lunchtime, she was sent to the infirmary for a lecture from Sister Dumpster about the dangers of anorexia.

That evening, during study period, Star wrote me a note and slipped it in my English book.

I hope Georgina's eating disorder doesn't come back!

I hadn't thought of that, but it made me a bit worried. I gave her a nod and tore the note into a million pieces and threw it in the bin, so no one would see it.

TEN

The Fall-Out

'I think we should bury him as soon as possible,' I suggested, while we sat in our room waiting for Georgina to return from the infirmary. 'I just can't bear to think of him lying dead in his cage.'

'Yaah. It must be really upsetting for the other pets too,' Star added. 'I mean, I got a feeling from Hilda that she was devastated, you know?'

As far as I had noticed Hilda had been frantically racing along on her little wheel, looking as if she didn't have a care in the world, but I said, 'Exactly.'

'Should we go and speak to Sister Constance about having a funeral for him, do you think?' Star suggested. 'I could make a little cross for his grave.'

There was a pet cemetery in Phipp's Forest but none of us ever went there because it was just too sad.

'That's really kind. I mean, I know Georgina is a bit of a . . .'

'I don't know, she's not that bad, I suppose,' Star said. 'She's growing on me. I get the feeling that Honey wields a lot of influence over her. . . . Should we ask Sister if we can hold a funeral?'

'Animals don't have souls, remember, girls,' I replied, mimicking the nuns.

Star riposted, 'Oh, bollocks to that,' just as Sister Constance walked in the room with Georgina.

'Thank you, Star. You're right, Calypso, animals don't have souls, so there will be no funeral. But nonetheless, we will be holding the usual burial-blessing ceremony tomorrow at break for Arabesque. We think it would be a nice way for Georgina and her friends to say a final goodbye to her pet. Father Conran will preside over the blessing.'

'Thank you, Sister,' Star and I said.

Georgina didn't say anything. She didn't look very well. Her eyes were puffy and her face was all red. Sister Constance put her arm around her in the stiff, awkward sort of way that she has.

'We'll have to arrange for a coffin,' Georgina said, speaking for the first time.

Honey came in then, and I noticed that Georgina didn't even look at her, even though Honey reached out and held her hand. 'Why don't you bury her in her LVT pet carrier? They're kind of last term anyway, darling. Then we can buy those cute carriers that Prada is doing. We could even get those really cool pink rabbits that they've bred now. Wouldn't that be fab, darling? I'm quite bored with

Claudine anyway, so I'll give her away to one of the younger girls and get one of the pink ones too – or maybe mauve. Mauve is so *now*!' She said all this in the same overexcited, high-pitched voice she had when she discussed handbags and shoes.

Georgina shook Honey's hand away like it was diseased. 'You just don't get it, do you? Arabesque was my best friend, not a fashion accessory, and now he's dead and you're acting like he was just a pair of bloody shoes! You are such a bitch, Honey. I totally hate you.' Then she started to cry again.

Sister Constance spoke in her Mother Superior voice, which always makes my knees go a bit trembly. 'Now, that is quite enough, girls. I appreciate that this is an emotional time for you, Miss Castle Orpington, dealing with the loss of Arabesque, but screaming at your friends is not going to help.

'As for you, Miss O'Hare, I would like you to go straight to the chapel and pray to the Sacred Heart of Jesus for the mercy you clearly require in order to enable you to empathise more appropriately with your friend's sad loss.'

Honey rolled her eyes and said, 'Whatever,' and then stormed off.

I didn't know what to say to Georgina after that, but then I knew saying nothing would be really lame, so I was pleased when Clemmie and Arabella and a whole pile of other girls poured into our room to comfort her.

Honey slunk in later, and I think she realised that we were all really upset and that she wasn't going to be very welcome, but I was still surprised when she said, 'Oh, by the way, Calypso, darling, you can borrow my Juicy Couture dress for the Eades social, if you like. I'm guessing you've got nothing cool enough to wear of your own.'

I did my goldfish impression for a bit before saying, 'Erm, yaah, that would be great, thanks.'

But then Star said, 'Oh, piss off, Honey. As if Calypso would want to borrow one of your slutty toff dresses.'

I could have killed Star just then. I mean, I had *no* cool dresses – well, nothing cool enough to wear to the Eades social anyway. Also, the fact that Honey was no longer talking about killing me, but actually offering me a cool outfit to wear to an event she had previously banned me from attending, was nothing short of a miracle.

'Fine,' Honey replied casually. 'I just thought you'd look really cool in it, darling.'

Huh? Did Honey just call me darling? Was I in a parallel universe here? I knew she had to be up to something, but I figured it was her way of getting back into Georgina's good books by not acting like a complete bitch.

'Erm, is it the baby-blue one, with the strappy bits?' I enquired as nonchalantly as I could.

'That's it. You've got the figure to carry it off, darling.'

I had the figure to carry off one of Honey O'Hare's outfits? I was stunned. I simply couldn't respond.

'Anyway, it's too last term for me,' she added. 'I'm

wearing my new Earl jeans with the real diamond-studded Dior top.'

Of course she was.

'Oh, thanks,' I replied, almost relieved by her bitchy comment. It was just too bizarre having Honey being nice to me. It made my skin crawl.

I could feel Star's stare piercing through me, but I ignored it as Honey flicked her hair back over her shoulder and said, 'Fine, darling, no biggie,' and flounced out of the room without another word.

That evening we were all so emotionally drained that we couldn't even summon the energy to collect our mobiles from Miss Cribbe. I guess she must have felt a bit sorry for us, though, because she bustled in with them in her arms, which was unheard of. Most of the girls had two mobiles; a declared mobile, which they handed in before lights out and picked up after study period, and another one (their really, really cool, madly expensive ones that took photographs and everything) that they kept with them at all times. Sadly, I had only one mobile, more of a brick than a phone but Miss Cribbe returned it to me kindly as if it were a holy relic.

Everyone immediately started dialling friends and checking messages on their microscopic, fourth-generation, trendy phones.

I noticed that Georgina didn't even pick hers up.

I checked my voice-mail messages on the brick and the

clear tones of Prince Freddie announced, in a jokey, uncannily good New York gangster accent: 'So, Foxy, you don't call, you don't write, you don't come see me no more? Am I not good enough for you? You don't want your old Freddie no more?'

I tried not to laugh, but I couldn't help myself.

'Was that *him*?' Georgina asked, suddenly bright-eyed.

'Yaah,' I admitted casually.

'Are you really missing him, then?' she asked kindly. I realised then that she meant Jay.

'Actually, it was Freddie.'

Star said, 'You are kidding!' only I could tell she wasn't surprised because she winked at me as she grabbed hold of my mobile and replayed the message before I could stop her. Then she cracked up laughing and suddenly Georgina grabbed the phone and even she laughed. Then it did the rounds of the dorm rooms on our floor, with everyone chipping in the thirty pence it cost to call my mobile phone voice-mail messaging service.

It was the first time at Saint Augustine's that anyone had wanted to pay for a listen to one of my messages. Even Star had passed around listens once when her father had Ozzy Osbourne call her up to wish her happy birthday.

Later, when Star and I were cleaning our teeth, I wondered aloud how Prince Freddie had got my number.

Star gave my mirrored reflection a guilty look.

'What?' I asked.

'Are you annoyed with me?' she asked, as if she actually

thought I might be. 'He asked me at fencing,' she explained, 'and, well . . .'

But I didn't let her finish. I wrapped her in a big cuddle and lifted her off the ground with excitement.

Prince Freddie had called me. Oh my God. Oh my God.

When we were tucked up in bed and the lights were out, Georgina said, 'I guess this means you're going to the social after all, darling.'

'I guess,' I agreed, trying to keep the excitement out of my voice.

'Tobias is *so* relieved, darling. He said he simply couldn't bear it if you didn't go.'

Then, just as I was dropping off to sleep, I felt someone sit on my bed. 'Calypso,' Georgina whispered. 'Promise me one thing.'

'What?'

'I know I shouldn't say this, because, well, Honey's been my friend forever, but darling, promise me you won't trust her.'

'OK,' I agreed carefully, not that I was ever likely to trust someone like Honey anyway, but I couldn't get to sleep for ages after that. What had compelled Georgina to say that? Was she actually worried about me, or worried that I'd become Honey's friend and that she'd lose her? I decided I'd ask Star what she thought in the morning. But one thing was definite, Georgina clearly wasn't the massive fan of Honey that I'd always taken her for.

ELEVEN

The Burial of Arabesque

The burial ceremony was really lovely, even though it was raining quite hard and we all had to huddle under big black umbrellas that the nuns just seem able to produce like magic from nowhere.

It took place in Phipp's Forest, near the hockey fields, in a little glade where all the dead pets of Saint Augustine's had been buried over the years. The forest smelled of damp oak trees, which gave the occasion a sort of sacred atmosphere. I think we all felt it.

All the dead pets in the cemetery have little wooden crosses above their graves, and some of the crosses are painted in bright colours. All of them bear the pet's name and have *RIP* written above.

Star had made a cross for Arabesque, painted it black and written Arabesque's name in white, swirly Arabic sort of writing – only in English obviously because none of us can read Arabic. Most of us have enough trouble with our French and Latin.

Several of the nuns (or, as we say, a flock of nuns) were there and we all held hands, umbrellas touching, while Father Conran stood saint-like in the rain in all his vestments and said a few prayers and sprinkled holy water over us.

Mr Morton, the groundsman, wore a black overall for the occasion rather than his standard grey, although his solemn attire was slightly spoiled by his umbrella, which was a bright green contraption with *Heineken* written on it in white lettering. However, he had taken the trouble to find black satin ribbons to lower the cardboard box containing Arabesque into a hole he had dug earlier that morning. That's one of the things I love about being a Catholic – we do have a great sense of occasion and ceremony.

As the little coffin disappeared into the freshly dug earth we sang Arabesque's favourite song, which was actually a pop song by Robbie Williams, so not really sad-sounding in the least. None of the nuns knew the words, so they just sang 'la, la, la, diddley-dee' in their funny little nun-like way, but we all cried, because . . . well, you just do.

Even Honey, who was holding Claudine, looked really upset – although knowing Honey, that could have been eye-drops. Afterwards we all went back to the convent where the nuns live and had a little wake. We're often invited over for tea and it's always fun, mostly because they treat us like we're the most exciting people in the world.

They served us the sort of food you usually see at tiny

children's parties – sandwiches, butterfly cakes, fairy bread and lemonade. And they didn't even make a fuss when Claudine threw up a gherkin all over their sofa.

That afternoon, one of Saint Augustine's Old Girls came to the school chapel to give us a talk on Raleigh International and the gap year possibilities available to Upper Sixth students. She had really long, dark hair and a gorgeous tan and showed us slides of the school she was helping to build in Africa.

It wasn't a bit like the boring talks we usually get, because she had all these really funny stories about the different children and the mad things that had happened while they'd been building the school and how, even though the children were really poor, they were all still into a lot of the same things we were.

She said that she had shown them pictures of Saint Augustine's and they were really envious, or maybe just incredulous, of our art room facilities. She had even brought a painting they'd done of their class in Gambia.

Sister Hillary and Sister Veronica carried the painting into the hall. It was so bright and funny, done in a cartoon style, with all their names scrawled across the bottom of each of their faces in graffiti-style writing. I couldn't believe how cool it looked. I mean, they didn't even have walls on their school, let alone the luxuries we take for granted – like television, mobile phones and computers.

It made me feel pathetic in comparison, trying to

change my life by inventing a fake boyfriend for myself –
a gay one at that. When we were filing out of assembly,
Star and I discussed what we would do in our gap year.
Honey interrupted, bragging that her mother had already
arranged for her to do a three-month stint at Condé
Naste.

'That's what I love about you, Honey,' said Star, 'your
incredible desire to look beyond your own tiny little pointless world! Maybe they'll have you research a piece on dis-
tributing make-up tips to the starving!'

As ever, I was awed by Star's ability to carve Honey up
fearlessly, but most of all I was surprised that Clemmie
and Arabella and a few other girls who'd overheard actually
giggled.

Honey's face turned puce and I could tell that she
wanted to give Star a slap, but Georgina intercepted by
reminding us that our gap years were at least three years
away whereas we were already late for Latin.

I wrote a chatty letter to Freddie in Latin class when I
should have been translating Cicero. I thanked him for his
call and told him about how Sister had handed down this
mad punishment to raise money after we'd had a food
fight. I didn't mention how it started or anything like that.
I made it sound as madly amusing, enthralling and exotic
as I could. I deliberated forever over whether to sign it *love*
Calypso or *from* Calypso and opted for just *Calypso* so I
didn't sound too desperate.

After study, when Star was off buying sweets at the

tuck shop and Georgina was having a shower, I lay on my bed and wondered how I would cope if my parents were killed in a war and I had to rebuild my life with mud bricks and humanitarian aid.

I looked at the photographs I had put up of Jay. I know they had worked in a way, but it was all a lie and it wasn't me. I felt so angry with myself that I tore them down and shoved them in the rubbish bin. I reached under my pillow for my copy of Nancy Mitford's *Love in a Cold Climate* and began to read it for about the hundredth time.

Nancy Mitford survived the war and grew up in an even madder family than Star's. Her father had hunted her and her sisters and brother with hounds. But even while the bombs fell all over London, she had managed to write books. That's what I wanted to do – to *write*.

My other favourite writer, Dorothy Parker, also endured a horrendous childhood – her mother died when she was young, and later her brother died on the *Titanic*, but by the age of twenty-one she was working for *Vanity Fair*.

Then it hit me. Where would I be at twenty-one if all I focused on was fitting in with a cool pod of girls? I should be focusing on what I really wanted. I wanted to write and read and fence, and be accepted for who I actually *was*, rather than making myself fit into the world of posh toffs. But, OK . . . I *would* quite like to pull a boy or two or three.

I snuggled down under my duvet, but that was when I noticed that as well as the sound of water running in the shower, there was the unmistakable noise of Georgina throwing up her dinner.

I got up and tried to open the door to the en-suite. It was locked so there was nothing I could actually do. I just sat there and waited dismally with my book on my lap, looking out over the oak trees of Puller's Woods while Georgina heaved and heaved and heaved some more.

It sounded horribly painful. Finally she stopped and I heard her flush the loo. She came out with a cheerful look on her face and asked me what I was reading.

I desperately wanted to say something, but I still hadn't thought of the right words. I didn't want to sound like a teacher or a community nurse or something lame like that.

I wished that Star were here because she would definitely know what to say. In the end I asked her if she was OK in a breezy, casual sort of way and she said, 'Of course I'm OK – why wouldn't I be?' in a pissed off, back-off-and-how-dare-you-even-speak-to-me sort of way.

'No reason,' I replied and pretended to be engrossed in my book.

Then suddenly she said, 'Oh, I love Nancy Mitford!' as if the last ten minutes or so hadn't happened. 'Don't you just love *A Talent to Annoy*, darling?'

'Adore it,' I agreed, going along with her denial, and then rambling on in that way I have when I am nervous. Then out of my mouth came the words that would change everything and I heard myself saying, 'I'd love to write . . .' before I could stop.

'Well, why don't we, darling? Start a writing salon, I mean?'

I looked at her, stunned. 'You mean like the Algonquin Round Table? Erm, I don't think we could actually scratch enough girls together to go around a table.'

'No, I mean like the Hons,' she said, referring to a code word in Nancy Mitford's book used to describe a secret society the Mitford children had when they were young. A gathering of the favoured few who would sit in the closet, heated by the boiler, and talk irreverently about everything from life to death and beyond. 'Don't you think it a fabulous idea, darling?'

'Do you really think it would work?' I asked, still amazed at the sudden change in Georgina's mood, not to mention the fact that we seemed to share an interest. I mean, minutes before, I'd been considering speaking to Sister Dumpster about her throwing up and now, here she was, babbling away about a writing salon.

Georgina laughed and sat on the bed beside me. 'Oh darling, we simply must. I need something to cheer me up.'

I definitely agreed with that, anyway.

Miss Cribbe wandered past and said, 'Well, aren't we all the best of friends today then, girls?' and we fell apart laughing – more about the way she said it rather than what she had said. But I suppose that was when it first struck me that Georgina and I really were sort of becoming friends. And that even though up until recently, it had been Georgina and her type that had made my life at Saint

Augustine's sheer hell, I was seeing another side of her now. Maybe she was seeing another side of me too? Or maybe it was only when she wasn't around Honey that she was the Georgina I liked.

Whatever the reason I wasted no time in agreeing to the salon and insisting we try to find members immediately.

'Well, there's already the six of us,' she pointed out. 'Our dorm room and Honey's dorm room.'

All of a sudden a feeling of doom swept over me. The thought of having anything more to do with Honey filled me with horror. And I could just imagine Star's reaction.

TWELVE

The Lit Chick Salon

We held our first salon later that evening after lights out, by torchlight. As I'd predicted, Star confided in me while we cleaned our teeth that she had her doubts about being stuck in a writing salon with Honey. Actually what she said was, 'Are you dead or just mad? Hell can freeze over and Miss Cribbe can be made Queen but there's no way I am going to be part of a group with that evil bitch.'

I pleaded and did my jokey sad face – the one where I let the toothbrush hang limply from my mouth and make weepy-eye gestures. 'OK, but this is going to take a lot of lip-gloss,' she said. 'A lot!'

Writing has never really been Star's thing; in fact, *books* have never really been Star's thing. I've tried to get her into Nancy Mitford, but it takes her forever to read a book. She just prefers music. Sister Hillary – who simply adores Thomas Hardy (erk) – says you can't really push these literary things, you either like something or you don't. Ms Topler should listen a bit more closely to Sister Hillary on that point. When the girls snuck into our room (Honey wearing her high-heeled Jimmy Choo slippers), Star rolled her eyes and reached for the lip-gloss.

'I don't see the point of all this writing rubbish, darling,' Honey said. 'Can't we just break out the vodka and talk about boys?' Even though it was too dark to see each other properly, I could imagine the pouty face she'd be pulling.

'No, just listen, Calypso and I think it would be a fab way to raise money for Children of the World. You know, for our punishment.'

Had I heard correctly? Had Georgina just united our names in the same sentence?

Honey groaned.

'When did this happen?' Star asked.

'Erm, while . . .' For a moment I was about to say, 'Right after Georgina finished making herself vomit,' but stopped myself in time. 'You were, erm . . .'

'Look, think about it,' Georgina interjected. 'We've got to make this money somehow and Calypso came up with this fantastic idea that we could ask everyone in our House Block to write something satirical, which they would then have to read out loud at a literary party.'

My head was spinning, but Georgina didn't so much as draw breath. 'We could fine non-contributors five pounds.'

'Oh, I like that,' Honey added. She would make a great traffic warden; she's always trying to introduce fines for things. During our first term she had tried (almost successfully) to introduce a fine for girls who didn't have long, straight hair.

Star said, 'Erm, maybe I'm just being stupid, but will everyone know what we mean by satirical?' She was looking pointedly at Honey as she did this.

'Correct, you're just being stupid,' Honey replied with a sneer.

'OK, so what does it mean, brain drain?' Star challenged.

Honey, holding her torch to her face, rolled her eyes. Obviously she had no idea what it meant herself.

'Erm, well, actually, I don't know what it means,' offered Clemmie.

'It's sort of a piss-take, isn't it?' Arabella asked, looking to me for comfirmation.

'Exactly,' I agreed. 'A tease, really.'

'There, so it doesn't really matter whether people know what it means – we can simply ask them to do a tease,' Georgina suggested. 'Only cleverly done and fun, not nasty,' she added, looking at Honey as she spoke.

'Yes, funny rather than vicious,' I added, thinking of Honey although I didn't dare look at her.

Honey groaned again and flopped back on my bed, her feet on my pillow.

I rose above her – not literally, because I was lying on the floor – and suggested that we start with a reading from Nancy Mitford, the greatest literary tease of all time.

I read out the part of the book where her father hunts

the children with hounds and how all the locals thought him a total sadist. (Of course, all the hounds did was lick the children, but perhaps they imagined they tore them to pieces and ate them.)

We muffled our laughter with our dressing gowns and then Georgina read a Dorothy Parker poem about being misunderstood.

'It is awful to be misunderstood,' Georgina said with a loud sigh at the end of the piece, as if she knew firsthand what being misunderstood was all about.

Star was looking fidgety, so I asked her what was up.

'Well, I just don't think it's fair to fine people who can't write,' she announced firmly.

Everyone raised their professionally sculptured eyebrows (apart from me, of course, because I pluck my own). Fines, after all, were a part of life at Saint Augustine's – like betting, smoking and selling listens.

'Why, can't you afford it?' Honey asked cattily.

Star curled her lip. 'No – because we're meant to be raising money for charity. I don't think fining people is really the best way to go about that, do you?'

'Why not? We could raise the money in an evening if we went down and terrorised the Year Sevens.' She laughed her hyena laugh so loudly that I don't think she noticed that no one else was laughing with her.

Star shook her head in disgust. 'God, you're loathsome, Honey. Maybe we could raise money hunting *you* with hounds.' She was looking at Honey with such undisguised hatred that even I felt afraid.

'Better still, we could have your wretched rat put down!' Honey giggled. 'I'm sure the whole school would chip in for that, wouldn't they, darlings?' She looked around at everyone (apart from Star and me because . . . well, we didn't actually exist as far as she was concerned).

But Georgina started to cry. Clemmie and Arabella tried to calm things down by offering her a cigarette.

Star, Arabella and Clemmie joined her on her bed so they could blow the smoke out of the window. I sprayed the room with Febreze, just in case. Then just as I finished spraying, Honey lit one up in the middle of the room.

I wondered if I sprayed her with Febreze whether she'd explode or self-immolate.

'We could always call the fine a donation so as not to upset anyone,' Clemmie offered, poking her head in from the window.

Honey tipped the ash from her cigarette into the slipper by my bed – my pink Hello Kitty ones that I love to pieces. I was really annoyed, but I didn't know what to say.

Georgina, coming in from the window, said, 'Hey, that was Calypso's slipper you just used!'

Honey shrugged. 'Oh, sorry, darling, I didn't notice.' Only she didn't say it to me.

Star emptied my slipper out of the window and sprayed it with Febreze. Then she squirted Honey's back with Febreze. 'I can see it's a good idea for fund-raising, but all my writing is morbid and gloom-laden. Witty writing isn't exactly my strong point.'

'Funny, I wasn't aware you *had* a strong point, Star,' Honey began.

But Georgina turned to Star and said, 'Gosh darling, don't worry about not being a literary genius.' Then she whispered, 'Tobias can't read a word; he's completely illiterate, actually.' As she spoke she held her hands over his ears to save him from the shame of it all.

Honey groaned. 'Well, I think the whole thing is a waste of time anyway. It's just a stupid punishment, for heaven's sake. Let's just have our fathers donate big fat cheques – charities love those. Let's leave it at that.'

I could see my writing salon dream dissipating before my eyes. 'That's *not* what all this is about, though,' I explained.

'Oh? I forgot, your father can't afford it, can he, Calypso?' she remarked in a syrupy voice as she stood up and smiled down on me like a cat that's just licked the cream. 'I suppose the rest of us can always chip in for your share.'

I was shocked out of my embarrassment by Georgina. 'Better still,' she said. 'Honey, why don't you just fuck off!'

I couldn't believe it. I was totally stunned.

Actually, everyone was. Honey included. Honey *especially*. She stood there for a few moments, staring blankly at Georgina, wondering if it was all a joke, or if she'd heard correctly.

Everyone stared at her and said nothing, which in a

way, said everything. Honey had made a fool of herself. She had gone too far and you could actually watch the realisation hit her as it sank in. But in true Honey fashion, she pulled herself together and declared, 'I don't want anything to do with your stupid salon anyway.' She flounced off, slamming the door really loudly as she went.

We stayed silent as her Jimmy Choo slippers clipped down the corridor.

'She's losing it,' Clemmie said, looking at Star as if they'd discussed Honey together, maybe on one of their long drives back to their country piles in Star's dad's limo. 'Mummy thinks it's because her mother's still waiting on Lord Aginet to propose and blames Honey and Poppy for his hesitation.'

'Vodka, anyone?' I asked, trying to change the mood. Even though I loathed Honey with every fibre of my body I wanted to get the writing salon going and not waste the evening bitching about Honey.

'Yes, let's toast our salon,' Georgina agreed. 'You know, I think this is going to be the start of something really good.'

I nipped into the en-suite and grabbed my humble vodka stash. Once I had passed around the five Body Shop Specials, we held them up in a torch-lit toast. Georgina put her arm around Star and told her that she'd better not bottle out, and I think Star was about to collapse at the shock of it all, but then we heard the heavy footfalls of Miss Cribbe's Hush Puppies squelching towards our dorm room.

There was a mad scramble as we screwed the tops back on our vodka bottles, switched off our torches and dived under the duvets.

Clemmie and I were clutching each other and trying not to giggle as we waited for Miss Cribbe to wave her torch around the room and listened to her wheezy breathing as she moved our bin and used it to prop our door open.

None of us dared breathe.

When we finally heard her Hush Puppies shuffling back down the corridor we turned on our torches and pulled the bin away and used pillows to muffle our laughter.

Later on, Star said, 'Actually, I might have a bit of an idea. Instead of fining girls, why don't we start a school magazine, you know, like a satirical sort of thing with teases about the teachers and prefects? We could even do illustrations – and charge money for it. If it were funny, I'm sure everyone would want to buy it.'

Star's father was right. She was a genius.

'That is a great idea!' Arabella agreed, almost squealing with excitement.

'We'd need a really cool title,' Clemmie added.

'What if the teachers won't let us do it, though? Ms Topler, for example?' I reminded them. 'She'd probably think it was going against the laws of her literary snore curriculum to have fun with writing.'

'Well, then she can bugger off,' Georgina giggled.

'*Nun of Your Business*?' Star suggested.

'What?'

'*Nun* – as in N-U-N – *of Your Business*! For the name?'

Georgina held her teddy to her ear. 'Tobias just said he totally adores that!' she squealed and threw her bear in the air.

THIRTEEN

Countdown to the Eades Social

Τhe Eades social was only a day away, but we were almost too preoccupied with our salon to care. Just joking. I had received seventeen – *seventeen* – messages from Freddie. But I had only told the others about a few of them – apart from Star, obviously. It wasn't just because I was trying to be cool. It was just that I was bursting with excitement and worried that if I started talking too much about Freddie I wouldn't stop, which would be too tragic for words.

My phone's memory was now full, so I had to start deleting the messages, which was very dispiriting, as I wanted to keep every one forever, like Georgian and Victorian ladies who kept their letters tied up in pink ribbons (only I'd use blue because blue is my favourite colour).

Every time he left a message he used a different accent, which was really funny and made me feel special. His last one was a Russian accent: 'Darlink, I can't vait to share my matzo ball soup with you.'

I replied to his messages with my own accented replies – although not all of them, because I didn't want him to think I didn't have a life. Georgina said his messages were suggestive and that I was definitely going to pull him.

'Yaah – it's as bad as text sex!' Star teased.

After the incident at the writing salon, Poppy and a few of her friends from the year above came down to Cleathorpes, looking for Georgina. Poppy actually slapped Georgina across the face and called her a bitch for telling her sister to F-off. After that Honey started to hang out with her sister's crowd.

Clemmie said, 'I wouldn't be surprised if it wasn't Honey who woke Miss Cribbe and complained about us keeping her awake that night.'

We all agreed.

And so did Tobias.

There hadn't been a repeat of Georgina's bulimic episode as far as I knew, but she was smoking herself stupid every night and I was worried that I was going to die of Febreze poisoning. We were all immersed in the writing salon, even Star. Only Honey had returned to her poisonous ways, which meant my days were spent peeling Post-it notes off my back. But even that didn't bug me the way it once had. I didn't feel like a freak anymore.

Honey had issues way bigger than me.

Star was making me keep all the Post-it notes. She said

we might be able to do something artistic with them in the magazine. Arabella agreed, and said she'd write satirical pieces on us all. Clemmie said, 'I can't wait to read what you write about Honey!'

Georgina giggled and started taking the piss out of Honey. 'Yaah, darlings, why don't we simply have our daddies chip in a few thou?'

Star was busy doing little drawings of us all. She did one of me in my fencing kit with arrows pointing to my fluffy sticky-out bits of hair, which she'd drawn to look like horns. Then she did a drawing of Honey with arrows pointing to Honey's Botox, collagen and other surgical enhancements.

I was having to pinch myself at how well my life was going. Instead of being the school freak, I was part of an actual writing salon and getting a school magazine off the ground. I know it had only really come about as a result of a punishment for our canteen food fight, but still it was the first time at Saint Augustine's that I had ever really been part of something. And as well as all that, I was being pursued by phone by a real, live prince.

So why did I still feel like an impostor in an exclusive members' club . . . especially around Honey? I tried to bring it up with Star during our warm-up exercises in the fencing salle, but it came out sounding like a whine and Star lost patience.

'What is it with you and this outside/inside rubbish anyway?' she responded almost in anger as we finished our supermans. 'Being accepted for who you are doesn't come down to where you're from, like you seem to think, Calypso. Maybe you need to accept yourself for who you are before blaming your isolation on everyone else.'

My head was in a mess. Star seemed really annoyed with me, as if I had accused her of a heinous crime – the crime of being one of Them, presumably. The crime of being of Their world at least. I put my mask on and saluted, knowing I was in too much of an emotional mess to distinguish myself on the piste. The sensible thing to do would have been to retire, to say I felt sick or had a cramp. But the only thing I had a cramp in was my brain.

It was only a friendly bout, with Professor Sullivan presiding, but in my attack *au fer*, Star gained priority by parrying and I put my whole body into the counterattack, lost my balance and landed sprawling at her feet. It was so embarrassing.

'*Halte!*' declared Professor Sullivan. I gathered myself together and we went back to the *en garde* line. I was dying under my mask – *dying*. Star's words were echoing in my head: 'Maybe you need to accept yourself for who you are.' For once not even 'a physical game of chess' could grab my focus. I thought of Freddie and tried to imagine it was him I was fencing but that only made matters worse.

After she'd totally slaughtered me, when we were changing back into our uniforms, I think Star could tell I was still in a mess because she put her arm around me and went, 'Listen, I've been going to school with them all my life. Do you think that makes *me* one of them?'

'No,' I told her, laughing at the absurdity of it all and giving her a hug.

Yes, I was thinking as I grabbed my gear and left the salle.

The day before the social, the five of us – Star, Georgina, Arabella, Clementine and I – were in Ms Topler's class (yawn), reading her latest offering of Literary Realism, as she called it.

I knew it was very worthy to know all about how hard life was for women in a previous age, but honestly, didn't these people have any sense of humour?

Then Ms Topler called me up to the front and I was afraid that she was going to give me a blue for my eyebrow-raising every time we were told to bring our latest yawn-till-you-drop book out.

'So, Miss Kelly, I hear that you and your friends have organised an *exclusive* writing salon.'

I glared at Honey, who looked up at the ceiling.

'I wouldn't call it exclusive exactly, Ms Topler.'

'No?'

'No . . . well, you see, the thing is, it's more or less part of our punishment.'

'Explain.'

'Yes, well . . . erm, six of us were given the task of coming up with ways to raise money for this charity called Children of the World. They raise money for kids, like the class who –'

'Yes, yes, yes. I am perfectly aware of the nature of this charity and the good works they do for children in areas of distress.'

'Well, we have to find ways to raise money, so the writing salon was one of the ideas we had.'

'An idea – one that you didn't wish to share with others?'

Georgina, clutching Tobias to her chest, stood up. 'Ms Topler, this is so random. Why are you hectoring poor Calypso about it? It's not like we're having carnal relations with Satan or anything. Besides, the whole idea is to share the group. We're putting together a literary magazine, which is open to the whole school to contribute to.'

'I am perfectly aware of this clandestine magazine, thank you, Miss Castle Orpington. Now kindly sit down and please put that ridiculous bear in your bag. I merely wished to put to you that perhaps it might have been more Christian of you to discuss your magazine in the forum of the English literature class . . . i.e., *my* class! The one you are presently sitting in.'

OK, so this was it. Once again, I could see my dream tumbling down around me. Honestly, who was I kidding, thinking this idea would work? I said a Hail Mary without much hope, but I said it with a fervour never before applied to my prayers so that I missed what Ms Topler said next. All I heard was, 'Thank you, class dismissed. In the name of the Father, the Son and the Holy Ghost, amen.'

I trudged along behind the others towards the canteen,

listening to no one, saying nothing. Even the discovery that we had fish nuggets and chips wasn't enough to raise my spirits. I was only dragged from my well of misery by the occasional thump on the back as a Post-it note landed.

Everyone else seemed on top of the world, proving what I always knew – that I was a freak who placed far too much emphasis on amusing writing. I couldn't even get excited about the Eades social while everyone else was chattering on about it. I sat with the others and picked disconsolately at my fish nuggets while Star peeled the Post-it notes off my shirt.

'OK, this is weird,' she said, showing me one of the pile. It read:

Enjoy your dinner, Shit Face

'Whatever,' I replied. I couldn't be bothered anymore.

'Maybe it's time to show these to Sister Constance,' Arabella suggested, flicking back her blonde-streaked locks. 'Seriously, Calypso, this is harassment. Daddy's done all sorts of famous litigation cases and I'm sure he'd do you a good rate if you wanted to sue.'

I munched on a chip, too miserable to even smile at the irony of someone like Arabella (who could trace her family back to the fourth century) suggesting that I, Calypso Kelly, mount a legal suit in the High Courts against Honey O'Hare, daughter of England's most famous It Girl.

After supper, when Star and I were alone, I complained,

more to myself than to anyone else, 'I just can't believe what's happened. . .'

'What?'

'The magazine.'

'Why? It's great,' Star said. 'Didn't you hear what Ms Topler was saying?'

'Banned us from doing the magazine and probably showered us in blues.'

'Are you mad in the head or just deaf? The school is going to let us off study time to work on the magazine *and* they are going to organise the printing.'

FOURTEEN

The Night of the Eades Social

While everyone else was getting dressed up in their finery, I was in the infirmary with diarrhoea. My money was on Honey slipping a laxette in my dinner. So was everyone else's – even Tobias had his suspicions.

What was worse, the horrible Sister Dumpster was being really nasty, telling me how in her day, diarrhoea took 50 percent of the population and they didn't complain.

She was only about sixty years old so I seriously doubted it, but I said nothing.

I tried to cry myself to sleep but it wasn't working. It must have been the dehydration.

Honestly, as if being kept away from the boy of my dreams wasn't bad enough, I had to put up with Sister Dumpster knitting away at the end of my bed like old

Madame Guillotine of the French Revolution, who had knitted away in the front row while the bourgeoisie were beheaded.

I was too sick to even ask for my mobile phone to call Freddie – not that I had any credit left on it. I'd probably have to sell my mobile to survive the term (not that anyone would want to buy a brick like mine).

Having friends was lovely, but it was costing me a fortune trying to keep up with them in sweets and pizzas alone.

So I told God that I'd give up all the sweets in the world to be sitting next to Freddie at the social.

Then I ran to the loo.

Sister Dumpster looked at the little watch pinned to her chest and wrote down the time of my motion on her pad. She would make a fantastic prison warden.

'Sister, maybe I need another Lomotil?' I suggested when I came back. 'I mean, I'm going every three minutes and I feel awful.'

'You've gone from five to seven minutes, actually, Miss Kelly. That's perfectly good progress, medically speaking. Keep up your fluids and I'll reassess you in an hour.'

The social started in an hour.

There was a knock at the door. 'Oh, darling, are we poorly?' It was Honey, dressed in the baby-blue dress with the strappy bits that she had promised to me.

'You will look after her, won't you, Sister Dempster?'

'Thank you, Miss O'Hare, all is in hand. The best thing

for your friend is to keep up her fluids and wait for the squitters to pass.'

'Hmm, lovely. Well, enjoy your evening, Calypso. Chance for you to catch up on your reading. I know how you love that! Toodle-pip.'

I didn't even have time for a spiteful riposte. I was off to the loo again. This was definitely not easing up.

I came out of the toilet weak as a kitten and tearful. Self-pity was now engulfing me. Earlier I had half hoped I would be over the worst and still make the social, but seeing Honey looking sublimely divine in her/my baby-blue strappy number had destroyed all hope.

Now all I felt was despair.

'Oh, will you just look at yourself, you poor baby.'

It was Sister Regina. As large as life (in a four-foot-nine sort of way) sitting in the nurses station.

'Oh, Sister,' I moaned. 'I feel so poorly.'

'I'm not at all surprised. You take these tablets *tout de suite* and drink that jug of water with mineral salts that I've placed by your bed. I've read your chart and if this nasty business hasn't passed in an hour's time I'll be calling the doctor before you flush yourself clean away.'

An hour later we were both sitting in the horribly uncomfortable infirmary bed, flicking through *Teen Vogue*. I suppose I would survive not going to the Eades social.

More or less.

Star had popped in to say goodbye and brought a mock-up of the *Nun of Your Business* magazine to cheer me up. Sister Regina thought it was hilarious and asked if we couldn't include some of the nuns. 'We do love a giggle,' she confided. 'Especially now that the telly is on the blink. They've only gone and taken us off Sky.'

Sky television had hundreds of channels and the Sixth Formers were allowed televisions with Sky. 'Why?' I asked.

'The governors didn't think we needed it. Costs too much.' She folded her little arms across her chest and shook her head grimly. 'It's all about money these days.'

'That is so mean. How are you meant to stay up-to-date with life?' I asked.

'You tell me. They'd have us drawing water from the well like monks if it wasn't for the fearsome grief they'd get from Mother Superior.'

I can't really explain why, but I started to cry. I knew that I didn't have to draw my water from a well, but everything had been going so well and now, here I was, spending the night of the Eades social in the infirmary with a nun, discussing school governors, when I should have been pulling my handsome prince. And no doubt Honey was dancing her heart away in my dress. OK, so it was her dress, but whatever.

Sister Regina made me pour my heart out, and ten minutes later, I was sitting in the passenger seat of her old Citroën 2CV, with a stash of special tablets to 'keep the cork in,' wearing a little black dress made by some Sixth Former for her textiles exam.

She must have been a funny shape, and that's all I have

to say on the matter . . . it was miles too short and too baggy. Sister Regina insisted on using safety pins (the really big ones like they use on babies' nappies) to pin it up at back.

'Just keep your back to the wall,' she warned, 'and no one will even notice.'

It was all very Shakespearean, with a bit of Wagner thrown in for good measure. Wagner's 'Ring Cycle' was blasting out on the cassette player as we skidded around hairpin bends, through the woods and down the unlit fern-clad lanes that led to Eades. Sister Regina was singing along in her thin little high-pitched voice.

At four-foot-nine she could barely see over the steering wheel and I had to tell her when to turn. Occasionally, I even had to resort to grabbing the wheel.

'It's been very difficult driving since the governors took away our cushions,' she commented at one point.

I told Sister Regina I would write to them and complain.

We screeched into Eades and I dashed across the floodlit quad where men with sniffer dogs were patrolling for drugs and bombs.

Sister Regina tooted her horn and called out to me in her thin little voice, 'You just mind you keep your back to the wall so no one sees your safety pins, luvvie. I'll say a decade of the Rosary and you shall be the belle of the ball.'

Thank God only the security guards and the sniffer dogs heard.

FIFTEEN

The Brat of the Ball

I felt like a Lilliputian in a land of giants as I entered the enormity of the Eades dining hall, with its grand chandeliers and mahogany wall panelling. The first face I saw – the only face I searched for – was Prince Freddie. He was sitting next to psycho toff Honey. My heart thudded to the floor – I even thought I could hear it echo throughout the hall. I felt like such a fool for even coming.

The brat of the ball was nibbling away on her main course and Freddie didn't even look up. A costumed usher led me to the table where I was to be seated. As I made my way through the lines of long dining tables I saw Freddie craning his head to hear something hilarious that Honey was saying between nibbles.

I scanned the packed room for Star, but there was no sign of her anywhere.

I felt like backing out of the room and running back to

Saint Augustine's. This night was doomed, and it wasn't just because I was the Queen of the Doomsday Prophesies that I knew it. For a start there was no way I was going to be able to conceal my safety-pinned dress. I would have to sit down all night, which meant that I couldn't dance.

Nor could I eat, due to the state of my stomach.

All I could do was sit and watch in silence while Honey pulled Freddie.

Fabbo.

Oh, bloody hell, where was Star?

The costumed usher led me to a seat at the table parallel to Freddie's. In fact, I was seated directly behind him, so, in effect, the only thing my back was going to be against was him. The boy sitting next to me was spotty and clearly keener on his trout than he was on chatting. I watched, while my empty stomach rumbled, as he dissected his fish and removed its bones, placing them clinically one by one on his bread plate.

On my other side, the chair was empty. I smiled bravely at the huge portraits of whiskered men on the wall – because they were the only faces in the room prepared to make eye contact with me.

'Good evening,' the male teacher at the end of the table eventually announced. He looked a bit like Lurch in the Addams Family. I shrank farther into my high-backed, elaborately carved Victorian chair as he raised one single eyebrow at me.

I've always been intrigued by people who have the

ability to do that. I had practised raising one eyebrow a lot when I was younger, but eventually I'd realised I just wasn't the type. Still, I gave it my best shot – only I think it made me look a bit drunk.

Lurch looked down his nose at me and frowned, so I flapped my napkin onto my lap and tried to stop my face turning bright red – a nasty habit my face picked up when I was quite young.

I still couldn't see Star anywhere. What had I been thinking – letting myself be talked into coming to the Eades social, wearing a dress fastened with large safety pins at the back by a nun who couldn't even see over a steering wheel?

The voice behind me seemed to come from a long way away.

'My darlink, at last. You finally decided to grace me with your beauty.'

It was Freddie, leaning back in his chair. I could smell an intoxicating mix of limes, oranges and lemons, but that turned out to be the sorbet and I finally began to relax and even managed to ignore Honey's nasty looks.

I leaned back. 'Vy, of course, darlink,' I replied, mimicking his Russian accent as best I could – at least I think it was Russian. It could just as easily have been Polish or Romanian, or even Glaswegian for that matter. I can only really do an LA Valley Girl accent with any conviction.

For the duration of the meal we tried out every accent we could think of, finally settling on Cockney – although

I had to give up when it came to the rhyming slang. It turned out that the empty chair on the other side of me belonged to a boy called Kevin, and he actually was from the East End of London and one of Freddie's best mates.

'Oh, so you're the sabre champion everyone's been going on about!' Kev announced as he returned to his seat, which made me go so red that my head almost exploded.

Then the band started up and I finally had to stand and face Freddie – I put my hands behind my back to hide my safety pins, but the main thing on my mind was the anticipation that he would invite me to dance.

But that privilege went to Honey, who asked him first.

Kevin was really sweet and asked me if I would do him the honours, in a piss-take of an OTT posh accent – even though, like all of the Eades boys, his accent is madly posh anyway. I think the school probably offers that assurance to all prospective parents: 'Eades will guarantee that your son will leave this hallowed institution sounding like an upper-class prat' – or words to that effect.

On the dance floor, I tried to keep my back to the speakers to hide my safety pins and decided to be philosophical about things – although, to be honest, philosophy is my worst subject. What sort of madness was I thinking of anyway, imagining I could pull the heir to the throne of England?

Still, he was fit. The fittest boy in the hall, in fact.

Georgina sidled up to me just as the philosophical thing was starting to work and Kevin and I were getting on really well.

'We're just going on a mercy run with Honey – coming?'

Mercy? Honey? I don't think so.

I thought I was just thinking it to myself, but apparently I actually said it. Even Kevin, who must have overheard, looked startled at how mean I sounded.

'She drank too much vodka before we came. She's busted if one of the teachers sees her swaying on the dance floor like that,' said Georgina.

I looked around and sure enough there was Honey, totally bladdered and moments away from a suspension.

Just then, Freddie came up to us and said to Kevin, 'So, can I cut in on your trouble, mate?'

'You keep your pork pies off my trouble's bacon, if you know what's good for you,' Kevin replied.

I didn't have a clue what they were on about and my blank look must have given me away.

Freddie explained as Kevin went off. '"Pork pies" is eyes. "Trouble" is trouble and strife – wife. And "bacon" is bacon and eggs – legs.'

'Obvious, really,' I said as Freddie clasped me to his chest for a slow dance.

He asked me what LA was like. 'I've never actually been there,' he said, 'but I understand it's quite spread out.'

'Yaah, that's why it's called the city that never walks!' I told him, which made him laugh.

I rested my head on his shoulder. This was so cool.

'Hang on, what's going on back here?' he asked, feeling my safety pins.

'Erm, well, yes. Bit embarrassing, but I didn't have a dress for tonight so Sister Regina sort of gave me someone else's from the textiles class, only it was too loose and –'

'Enough,' he said, holding up his hand. 'Don't spoil the Elizabeth Hurley-ness of the moment,' then he moaned in a really turned-on sort of way. I couldn't believe that a girl like me could create an Elizabeth Hurley moment! *Hello!* The dress *she* wore (the one with all the safety pins that exposed most of her body – and made her famous) was made by Versace ... not the oddly shaped Charlotte Chapman of the Lower Sixth at Saint Augustine's. I was also quite pleased about him stopping me mid-ramble or I might have mentioned my diarrhoea – in fact, I definitely *would* have, predisposed as I am to verbally digging my own grave when nervous or embarrassed, or madly keen on a prince.

I said a silent prayer of thanks to Mary for sending an angel like Sister Regina, whose large dose of Lomotil had done the trick. My tummy wasn't even rumbling.

'Would you like to go outside for some air?' he asked, when the music stopped. Well, I almost swooned – if swoon's the right word. Anyway, I felt all light and giddy. I think the horsey girls call it skittish.

Freddie led me down a series of dark passages so we could lose his security guards. None of the musky, dark-panelled windowless corridors looked very promising. Finally, we stopped and he tapped on a heavy old mahogany door. When no one answered we entered the most magical room I had ever seen.

The entire room was lined from floor to ceiling with books. There was even a wooden ladder that slid along the shelves so you could reach the high books, and above that there was a balcony with still more books which you could examine, strolling along a little walkway. We had a fabulous library at Saint Augustine's, but it was manned (or rather, woman-ed) by the horrendous anti-bookist, Ms Parkes, who wore old men's suits that smelled like the men had died in them.

Ms Parkes always followed you around the library and if you reached for a book she would grab it before you could, and then pass it to you suspiciously as if you might be a book burner. She also stood over you while you read it (muttering things about how defacing books is a criminal offence) and if you asked to borrow it, she'd remark, 'I shall bring it to your dormitory room after lights out,' which meant we could only read it by torchlight.

It didn't make for a very comfortable reading atmosphere.

This library, on the other hand, seemed like heaven, and I would have liked to check out the books more thoroughly, but I thought it might spoil the moment, and besides, Freddie was holding my hand and pulling me along.

I wanted to ask him lots of things about what it was like being a prince, but I didn't want to seem tragic, so I relaxed into the silence that seemed to spread over us like the darkness.

He pulled off his tailcoat and asked me to hold it while he drew back the purple velvet drapes and lifted one of the large sash windows so we could climb out into a darkened . . .

Erm . . . bush, actually. A big prickly bush. But I didn't mind in the slightest because Freddie put his jacket around my shoulders and guided me gently through the bush and into a tiny clearing where he kissed me.

Sister Regina had given me a couple of Curiously Strong Mints before she dropped me off, so I wasn't worried about my breath being gross, but I wasn't absolutely positive about my kissing technique either. Of course I knew that when the other girls asked what it was like I was going to say 'amazing.' But as it was my first time, I was not quite sure what to do with my tongue and lips and the other bits and pieces of my mouth. My brain was not helping. All I could think about was kissing, and how I'd never done it. Freddie's tongue, meanwhile, was gently fencing mine. It was quite nice, actually, so I tried to concentrate on Freddie, and on his lovely boyish smell, and his soft, warm lips. Suddenly he moved his hand up my back along the safety pins and slipped his hand under my hair and rested it supportively at the back of my neck. My stomach went *whoosh*, my heart started thumping and my brain stopped and it was the loveliest feeling ever.

'Excuse me, sir, but perhaps you should step back inside.'

It was one of his security guards, reeking of CK1. 'I'm bringing His Majesty back in now, sir,' he spoke into his little ear-to-mouth piece.

It was all so unbelievably and maddeningly annoying.

'Sorry about that,' Freddie apologised as we stumbled through the bushes and out into the brightly lit quad.

We passed Honey on the way. She smelt of spew but I didn't say anything – although Freddie gave me a look that spoke volumes about what he really thought of her.

'Freddie, Freddie!' she called after us. 'Sorry to leave you like that earlier. Only I had to do a bit of a favour for a friend. I hope you'll forgive me, darling?'

'Absolutely fine,' he said, giving my hand a squeeze.

It took more than a squeeze to get rid of the sick feeling I always had when faced with Honey. She slithered up close to us and ran her arms up both our backs.

'Oh, what are these, Calypso?' Then she did her hyena laugh.

Freddie and I smiled stiffly – well, I smiled stiffly. Freddie looked right through her.

'I forgot you two knew each other, darling. All those funny messages. "You don't call, you don't text . . .,"' she mimicked the first message he had sent me – the one that had done the rounds of Cleathorpes. 'God, Calypso, you must have made an absolute fortune from those messages. Although I guess you're used to that, Freddie – having the plebs trading on your royal status. Still, a girl has to make a dime,' she joked, nudging me in the ribs. Then she wandered off, laughing insanely to herself.

Only it wasn't funny.

I really needed Freddie to give my hand one of his big

manly squeezes just then, but instead he pulled it away. 'What's this all about?' he asked tersely.

'What's what?' I replied, playing for time.

'You sold *listens* of my messages?'

It was like being slapped across the face. 'I so did not!'

'Calypso, I'm not a fool and I didn't think you were. I don't particularly like your friend, but she's right on one point. I *am* used to people attempting to trade on my royal status. I just didn't imagine you would be one of those people.' Then he turned on his heel and crunched his way across the freshly cut grass of the quad, back towards the hall.

I stood there for a bit, with his tailcoat wrapped around my shoulders – until Kev came out to retrieve it.

'Sorry, but you know how it is. He's none too pleased.'

I knew if I said anything I would start crying, so I just passed him the coat. It felt like I was Cinderella and it was time to go back to my pots and pans.

SIXTEEN

Crying for Britain

fter Kevin retrieved Freddie's jacket, I ran crying into the loos where Star was trying to help Clemmie pull the zip of her top up. Apparently on their mercy run, Honey threw up on poor Clemmie, so they left Honey with a hose and told her to stay in the shadows until she sobered up. Then they had washed Clemmie's spewie top under the tap and dried it under the hand dryer.

Once I'd finished garbling out my sorry story, Star immediately offered to go and give His Royal Bloody Stuck-Up Highness a smack. She was furious. Clemmie was keener on getting back into the social and wrapping her lips around someone with the unlikely name of Razzle.

I felt ill again and with the smell of spew in the air I vomited. The others filed off back into the hall while Star arranged for us to go back early on the minibus.

I couldn't stop sobbing and feeling ashamed. I suppose

I shouldn't have let anyone else hear his messages, but then I hadn't really had any choice in the matter. Star had grabbed my phone, then Georgina and after that . . . oh, it was all such a mess.

When we got back, Sister Regina insisted I spend the night in the infirmary. She said she blamed herself for making me go in the first place and started crying as well.

I woke up late in the morning to find her still sleeping, slumped in an uncomfortable chair at the foot of my bed. As I watched her I replayed every horrendous moment of the night before in my head.

Star walked in with the newspapers. Every paper you can name had a photo of Freddie and me tongue-fencing in the bushes. The photograph showed my hair covered in leaves and the papers all had clever headlines. My favourite (not) was *The Prince and His Bit of Rough-and-Tumble.*

'I just can't believe the audacity of the guy!' Star ranted. 'A girl stinking of spew, whom he's virtually told you he despises, tells him that you've been trading on his royal status and he believes her? Now his own bloody security guy, or one of his other mates, sells a photo to the press! Talk about Prince Bloody Charming.'

Sister Regina, who had woken up and was reading one of the papers, shook her head. 'What a bounder. What a bounder. You are well out of it, luvvie.'

Star said, 'Well I've got a mind to bound right over to Eades and tell him exactly what I think of him.'

Georgina flew into the room next. 'This is so random, darling,' she cried out. 'I can't believe it – what a bastard!' Then, seeing my puffy eyes, she dispatched Sister Regina for cucumber slices. 'I've never seen such puffy eyes in my life, darling. Now that you are a national icon you have to look your best.'

Then she sat on the bed and gave me a cuddle.

'National icon?'

'Darling, you are the first girl that Freddie, heir to the British throne, has kissed! You will go down in history. This is huge, sweetie. *Huger* than huge.'

'Oh, yes,' I replied in my drollest droll voice, 'this is what my parents have invested their swimming pool, holiday and car fund money into – my place in history as Prince Freddie's bit of rough-and-tumble.' I couldn't believe that Georgina was so shallow, as if being made out to be an utter slapper was the loveliest thing in the world. All because Freddie was a prince!

'Oh, darling, don't dwell. No one believes what they read in those trashy papers. Believe me, you will be the envy of every girl in this country.'

My next visitor was Sister Constance. Her mood was a little more circumspect, to say the least. She had her hands tucked up inside the sleeves of her robe. 'Your parents will be arriving the day after tomorrow, Miss Kelly. I have given them permission to take you to their hotel for the weekend and filled out the necessary exeat form.'

'I don't understand, Sister.'

She gestured with her chin towards the fan of newspapers on the floor. 'It would seem that news of your liaison with His Royal Highness has crossed the Atlantic. Your parents, quite understandably, feel you may need them. I shall discuss the details with you after you've been signed out of the infirmary. Needless to say, both Eades and Saint Augustine's will mount a full and thorough investigation into how this sordid story manifested itself.'

'Thank you, Sister,' I replied in the most humble voice I could muster, which was pretty humble, quite frankly, after all I'd endured recently.

She made the sign of the cross, told me she would pray for my soul and swept out of the room imperiously.

'"News of your liaison has crossed the Atlantic,"' Star and Georgina mimicked once they were sure she was out of earshot.

I couldn't see anything funny about it, though. All I could think of was Freddie and what he must be feeling. Or rather what I hoped he must be feeling. Was he having second thoughts? Was he missing me?

Basically, was he even thinking of me?

At all . . . ?

He probably hated me. His own parents must be furious. I must be the most hated girl in Britain where the royal family was concerned.

I was so obsessed with Freddie, in fact, I hardly gave a thought to my parents' impending arrival and what that would mean . . .

SEVENTEEN

Wear Your Pain Like Lip-Gloss

*A*fter the Prince and His Bit of Rough-and-Tumble episode, the school swarmed with paparazzi. Sister Constance immediately doubled the number of security men and guard dogs patrolling the grounds. They could be seen everywhere – behind trees, the stone crosses along the driveway, next to sheds and bushes, talking in that strange language they use when they communicate on walkie-talkies – 'Ten-four,' 'That's a copy,' and that sort of thing.

The sight of terrified cameramen being chased by dogs, security men and nuns through the grounds became routine. Sister Hillary and Sister Veronica caught one photographer hiding in the chapel when he'd 'popped in for a quick prayer,' and wasted no time in pressing the fire bell, then whipping him with gladioli from the altar. He was finally rescued, cowering in the confessional, by security guards. Later that day, Sisters Veronica and Hillary regaled us with stories of the episode, embellishing their bravery and righteous fury with each telling, until the tale sounded very much like that bit in the Bible where Jesus chases the money-lenders from the temple.

The press were desperate to speak to someone in the school who actually knew me, but no one would say a word. Apart from anything else, we were collectively threatened with expulsion if we so much as made eye contact with the press.

Sister Constance broke her own rule when she had Mr Morton move the umpire's stand from the tennis court onto the playing fields, where she broadcast a scathing message to the press on a megaphone, suggesting they pray for mercy and forgiveness and describing them as emissaries for Satan and the servants of Beelzebub.

We were all in our classrooms at the time, but the teachers let us peer through the mullioned windows for a glimpse of our Mother Superior in all her superiorness. We were very proud of her, but we had no idea who Beelzebub was.

My parents' arrival had all the fanfare and status of a Hollywood premiere. Even though they drove up in a taxi, everyone had lined up in the driveway as if expecting royalty to climb out. Instead, Bob and Sarah clambered out in their trackie bums and hoodies, trying to look all young and hip and 'street.'

God, it was embarrassing. Why they couldn't just wear Laura Ashley and Savile Row suits like everyone else's parents, I'll never know.

I hadn't really given myself time to think about how I would feel about their arrival, which I suppose sounds very self-centred and un-daughterly. I know it was very sweet and parentally responsible of them to take that horrible flight across the world to be with me in my hour of need, but all I could think of was Freddie.

He hadn't called and he hadn't responded to my text messages. I'd sent him three. The first one asked for a chance to explain. The second asked if he'd received my first text. The third text was a repeat of the first. Tragic, I know.

Clemmie's brother, who was in a lower year at Eades, had said that although I was the talk of the school, Freddie was being very tight-lipped over the situation. When she'd told me this, all I could think of was how soft and loose his lips were when we'd kissed.

'He probably thinks you orchestrated the whole thing, darling,' Honey had remarked, sitting on my bed smoking a fag.

Star had grabbed the cigarette and flung it out of the window.

'What do you think you're doing?' Honey had shrieked.

'You'll set the fire alarm off and only get us all suspended, you idiot.'

Honey had sighed heavily. 'OK, *whatever*, Star!'

Honey had been hanging around in our room again as if nothing had happened.

As if her sister, Poppy, hadn't slapped Georgina across the face.

As if she hadn't mounted a campaign of Post-it note harassment against me.

As if she hadn't spiked my lunch with laxatives.

As if she wasn't the total psycho toff who had ruined my life.

Instead, it was all 'darling' this, and 'sweetie' that, and we were sort of playing along with it because, well, it was just so random and none of us really knew *how* to deal with it.

It was only Georgina and Star who hardly spoke to her, and when they did, they were polite, but left her in no doubt that they loathed her. I wondered how it made Honey feel that Georgina, after all their years of friendship, now hated her. And not just hated her, but was now friends with Star and me – the two girls they had had so much fun taking the piss out of over the past three years.

'So, as I was saying before Star went berserk,' Honey continued, staring pointedly at Star, 'Freddie is probably worried that you are still trying to trade on his royalty, darling. Princes do tend to get the teeniest bit worried about these things.'

Star snapped, 'Funny that, Honey, given that *you* were the one who told him that Calypso was doing just that.'

Honey raised her eyes towards the ceiling and stood with her hands on her hips, her puffy, pouty lips bursting with indignation. 'That is so untrue, darling. I was just mucking about. I thought that he might have a sense of humour. If being amusing is a crime now, fine, shoot me.'

I really would have liked to shoot her.

Honey was the first to introduce herself to my parents too, charging down the stairs, clutching her ghastly new pink rabbit, Duchess. '*Sooo* thrilled to meet you, Mr and Mrs Kelly,' she smarmed. 'My name's Honey O'Hare. I'm a very close friend of Calypso's. We're more like sisters, really.'

What? Why on earth was Honey sucking up to *my* parents, my 'nobody' parents – untitled, without so much as a helicopter or a pile in the country to make them worth wasting her breath on.

'Swell,' Bob said.

'Super,' agreed Sarah.

'Any friend of Calypso's is a friend of ours. Call us Bob and Sarah, Honey,' Bob told her vaguely, looking about the crowd for me.

I was standing on the steps, but Star pushed me forward so that I sort of fell into their arms and they cuddled me really hard. Then Dad picked me up and swung me around like I was five or something. He had tears in his eyes. 'Oh, Calypso,' he sobbed.

Could he make more of a spectacle of me? I wondered as I applied more lip-gloss.

Yes. He could.

Sister Constance swooped down in an attempt to restrain the atmosphere. She extended her hand stiffly, speaking in her most imperious voice. 'Mr and Mrs Kelly, welcome to England. Perhaps you'd like to come into my office. As I said, you are free to take your daughter for the weekend, although as you will appreciate her workload . . .'

Bob, being Bob, was having none of her imperiousness, though. 'This is just swell, Sister. Just swell. Sarah and I can't thank you enough.' With that, he grabbed her in a bear hug and gave her a little spin, which caused the entire school, teachers included, to smirk.

I just kept reapplying my lip-gloss.

'Quite,' was Sister's response.

She smoothed her habit down and rearranged the large wooden crucifix that hung around her neck, and without further lapses into the strange realm of my parents' Californian informality she bustled them through the doors and down the corridor into her office.

I waited for the onslaught. At least when I was just the class freak I was largely ignored. I would gladly swap those good old days of invisibility for this new hell of being the subject of an international news scoop and having my parents turn up and swing my nuns around.

'Your parents are so cool,' Clemmie cooed.

'Wow,' was all Star could say. And this from a girl whose father thought nothing of falling backwards off his chair at breakfast and spending the entire day on the floor with cereal all over his face.

'They certainly have a lot of energy, don't they? I mean, for parents, that is,' Georgina said.

'They do yoga,' I explained.

I didn't really know what else to say. I was running out of lip-gloss.

EIGHTEEN

Hollywood Hits Windsor

My parents had booked a room in a chintzy hotel near Heathrow. It was quite strange being on my own with them after everything that had happened this term. I suddenly realised how much I'd changed. I mean, *hello*, I'd pulled the Prince and become a media sensation.

We ordered dinner from the room service menu. I had the most enormous burger with chips and my parents didn't so much as mention the word 'carbs' or the dangers of eating gluten products. I kept waiting for them to start on me about being a slapper, and complain about how they'd had to drop everything and spend exorbitant amounts of money on flights across the Atlantic, etc, but all they did was ask me to take them step by step through the evening of the Eades social.

They wanted every detail.

Especially my dad, who kept asking questions like, So

where was Star when this was happening? Or where was this Honey girl when you were dancing, and how much do you trust Georgina? It was like an interview, but not a threatening one. I got the impression they were really keen for me to realise that I was the victim and not the criminal.

They didn't once tut or sigh but made sympathetic noises, and when I told them about Freddie accusing me of trading on his royalty I noticed a knowing look pass between them. At the end of the story my dad declared that I'd been framed, and Mom agreed. Dad said he was going to get to the bottom of it.

Later, we watched an in-house movie. Actually it was all really cool. It was weird, though, sharing a room with my folks. My parents were in the same bed together. I mean, they always sleep together, but not when I'm in the room, if you know what I mean. They had offered to get me my own room, but I would have felt too lonely. Actually it was kind of nice. Apart from when my mom started snoring. I swear I don't know how my father puts up with it.

Saturday was great. We went for a ride on the London Eye and Dad kept telling lame jokes the way he does when he thinks I'm down, but I didn't mind. On the Eye I even snuggled close to them and told them I was really pleased they'd come.

And I was.

On Saturday night my parents – or rather, Bob and Sarah, as everyone was now calling them on their insistence – took Clemmie, Arabella, Georgina, Star, Honey and me to dinner at Pizza Express in Windsor. I'd tried to convince them that I didn't want Honey there, but Sarah (even I had been reduced to calling my parents by their first names now) said, 'Nonsense, she's one of your closest friends, Calypso. It will be super.'

Honey brought the horrible pink Duchess in her new matching pink Prada bag and my mother made the most awful fuss of it, and asked me why I didn't have a rabbit.

I was gobsmacked. HELLO, *you* were the one who said being deprived of a pet was character building!

But I didn't get a chance to say it because Honey said, 'I know. Isn't it a shame, Sarah? I offered her my old rabbit, Claudine, but she refused.' Honey looked at Sarah sadly and sighed heavily.

I glared at her, as did the other girls, but my parents were completely taken in. So I said, 'You don't just give pets away because you're sick of their colour.'

Honey made her ridiculously puffy lips wobble as if she were about to cry. 'I just thought it would be really sweet if our rabbits could be as close as we are, darling,' she explained – only she was looking at Sarah when she said it.

My mother was such a softie. She reached out and took Honey's hand and my hand. 'Come on, you two. I suppose in a way, Calypso, Honey was just, well . . . maybe it's a bit like recycling?' she suggested, trying to smooth things over.

Surely, though, even *she* could see what an utter psycho toff Honey was for giving away her pet because it wasn't this season's colour?

'It's a pet,' I reminded my mother. 'Not an empty milk carton, Sarah!'

'Calypso. Don't be churlish,' Bob chastised.

'Oh, whatever,' I said churlishly.

Sarah explained to Honey that the whole tabloid fiasco had been really hard on me.

I couldn't believe my parents were being so taken in by Honey. I know I'd never told them about her horribleness, but wasn't it blatantly obvious in her every mannerism that she was evil incarnate?

'Swell,' Bob said, trying to change the subject. 'Let's order.' Then he called over a waiter and asked which pizzas were gluten- and carb-free, which made all the girls giggle. Apart from me. I was still feeling extremely churlish.

Star gave my hand a supportive squeeze under the table, which helped a bit, and then my father asked about her father's band and that cheered me up even more because it meant Honey was left out of the conversation entirely.

The pizzas (loaded to the rafters with carbs and gluten) arrived and we all tucked in. Arabella asked Sarah about her work and my mother was surprisingly funny, regaling us with stories of the latest melodramatic plot lines and the hissy-fits the stars were always throwing – especially the men.

I started to relax. I even started to look at my parents in a different light. I mean, it was quite sweet of them to drop everything and come all this way to see me in my hour of need, and they seemed to be making a surprisingly good impression on my friends. I was glad they'd come. It hadn't occurred to me that I wanted them to come, but now they were here I realised how much safer I felt. And their visit had helped to take my mind off Freddie . . . for a while.

My parents had been really kind about the Rough-and-Tumble photographs. Bob had told Sister Constance that we shouldn't be too hasty in blaming the paparazzi for the photograph. 'From what I understand, Sister, there were an awful lot of security guards patrolling the grounds that night, what with the Prince there and all. More often than not, you find these things turn out to be inside jobs.'

Inside jobs? Honestly, where does my father come up with these lines . . . oh yeah, I forgot, he's a Hollywood writer.

'By the way, Calypso,' Sarah suddenly said. 'Jay sends his love. Asked if you got his package.'

'Jay as in James?' Honey asked, all ears.

Sarah went, 'No, Jay as in Jay, my assistant. Why? Has Calypso mentioned him?' She looked at me questioningly.

I shook my head at her in a pleading, please-don't-go-there sort of way.

Sarah tilted her head, trying to grasp what was going on.

Honey screeched, '*Told* us about him, Sarah? She had his pictures pinned all over the board. She was so mad keen on him. Well, at least she was until she pulled Prince Freddie.'

So this was it. I was going to be exposed as even more tragic than Honey and the others always imagined. Just when I thought it couldn't get any worse.

I reapplied my lip-gloss.

I closed my eyes and resigned myself to my fate. Fine. Bring it on, I decided as I kept running the lip-gloss over and over my lips. Let's just have it all out . . .

Sarah laughed. Well, I couldn't blame her, she had no idea what she was about to do to me. No idea that she was about to turn me into an object of ridicule. I could already feel the slap of Post-it notes landing on my back.

Then she said, 'I was exactly the same at your age,' and giggled like a teenager.

I opened my eyes and looked up at her and she gave me a wink.

Oh, thank you, Sarah. Thank you for being weird, and Californian, and liberal, and understanding. I love you!

'One boy after another,' she went on, looking at me conspiratorially. 'Every one of them was The One, the love of my life. I used to write all their names on my pencil case.'

I have never loved my mother as much as I did at that moment. I wanted to run out and graffiti a bus stop shelter. *Sarah is the coolest mother in the world.*

'So tell us about what it was like at Saint Augustine's when you were there, Sarah,' Georgina urged.

So she did – only she made it all sound so funny and mad, and not a bit boring like she did on the plane when she first brought me out here nearly four years ago and promised me it would be 'super.'

I could tell that Honey was peeved that she was no

longer centre stage, because she'd started sending text messages on her phone.

Bob leaned towards her and said, 'Is this one of those third-generation phones, Honey?'

Honey looked up. 'Sorry, darling? What was that?'

'I just wondered if your phone there took photographs.'

'*Absolutely*, darling,' she said, beaming, thrilled to be in the spotlight again. 'Shall we take one of all of us? Star, you take it,' she ordered, handing her the phone.

Typical of Honey to want Star excluded from the photograph.

'Oh, no, I'm sure the guy that served us wouldn't mind,' Bob insisted. 'That way we can all be in it.' He summoned the waiter back.

After the waiter had taken a few shots, my father asked if he could have a look at the camera-phone and Honey eagerly swapped places with Sarah so she could show him all the phone's various features. Then Honey lost interest and left Bob to play around with it on his own.

'Hell of a lot of scandal these camera-phones are caus-ing in Los Angeles,' he remarked after a while. 'Now anyone can snap a photo of a star in a restaurant or at a premiere – a*nywhere*, really.' He smiled at Honey.

She smiled back, only it was a wobbly, weird smile.

I didn't understand what was going on at first, but then Bob casually passed the phone over to me, and there on the screen was the photo of Freddie and me, kissing in the bushes.

NINETEEN

Coventry

W ord that Honey was the culprit of the Rough-
and-Tumble photographs spread through Saint
Augustine's and Eades like spilled nail varnish.
I didn't even get time to miss my parents. I had been
sad to see them go, even though they had invited all my
friends to LA for a couple of weeks in the summer. I had
almost melted into the ground with embarrassment.

'We'd love to have you visit. Calypso gets a bit bored
during the vacation, don't you, sweetheart?' Bob had
declared.

'Thanks, Bob, that sounds really cool,' Georgina
replied. 'I'd love to come to LA, check out all the stars and
do the shopping malls. Wouldn't that be fab, darling?' she
trilled, grabbing my shoulders as if she really meant it.
Clemmie and Arabella jumped about excitedly.

'I'd definitely come,' Star agreed in a more subdued sort
of way . . . no doubt casting her mind back to all the

stories I'd told her of my life in Los Angeles – the unglamorous version.

She looked at me sympathetically while Georgina, Clemmie and Arabella danced about. I could just imagine what Georgina *et al.* would make of my tragic LA house, with its new furniture and lack of pool and helipads and horse. What would they say when they saw my bedroom with its tragic single bed? And then there was Jay, my fake boyfriend, to discover . . . It was all just too horrendous for words. Also, even though darling Bob hadn't realised it, I knew that from the girls' perspective, his invitation meant that he had actually offered to pay to fly my friends out – first class, of course. As Georgina and Honey always said, 'Never turn right, darling – only plebs do that!' (People who fly first class turn left when boarding a plane.)

My only hope was that they'd forget all about it before term ended.

Before Sarah and Bob went home they took me to a pet shop in Windsor and bought me a baby rabbit – a tiny black one, with the softest, biggest ears and the sweetest little golden eyes.

When Georgina saw it she kissed its little nose. 'Oh, darling, she's so sweet. What are you going to call her?'

'I thought, maybe, Dorothy Parker . . . ?' I replied.

'Oh, darling, I love it – and I'm sure Tobias will too!' She kissed little Dorothy on the nose again.

'That's brilliant,' I told her, 'because I was hoping we could share her . . . I mean, that she could be *our* rabbit. I mean, well, I can't exactly take her back to Los Angeles with me, can I?'

'Are you serious, darling?'

'Yaah!'

And then she wrapped Dorothy Parker and me in the biggest cuddle. 'I'm so glad we ended up sharing a room together this term.'

'Me too,' I agreed. And I was.

Star came round the corner and gave little Dorothy a pat. 'I still think you should have got Bob and Sarah to get you a rat. They are *soooo* intelligent. Also, that way I could have taken her home with me in the holidays.'

'I've asked Georgina to share her with me.'

Star nodded. 'I hope you're not planning on carrying her about in one of those sad LVT carrier bags,' she warned Georgina in a mocking way.

But I was secretly hoping she would.

'No,' Georgina agreed. 'But we should get something cool, though.'

'Or you could decorate one in art class so that it looks cool,' Star suggested.

'We are not having a black pet bag for a black rabbit,' Georgina insisted – to which we all laughed.

For a second, my thoughts flashed back to the first day of term, to our initial mutual dread of sharing a room with Georgina. But after everything we'd been through, it seemed like ages ago. Underneath all her grandeur and away from Honey, Georgina was actually really kind. I suppose Ms Topler was right – she was always babbling about there being 'more things in heaven and earth than dreamt of in your philosophy, Horatio.'

Or, as Sister Regina would say, 'Diddley-dee.'

Even the excitement of having my own pet was overshadowed by the school's reaction to Honey. Every dorm room – including Honey's – was burning with gossip.

Everyone in the entire school wanted her sent to Coventry. I'd first heard the term used by some girls in the Upper Sixth. There was a rumour that one of them had stolen another girl's boyfriend, and everyone had voted to send her to Coventry.

It was when no one looked at you or spoke to you at all: not in class, not in dorms, not walking down the corridor, not in canteen, not in sports and not even during that part of Mass where you shook people's hands as you offered them the sign of peace.

And at boarding school, where there was no respite, being sent to Coventry was a million times worse than having Post-it notes slammed on your back.

Even Poppy – her own sister – wasn't speaking to her. Which was how I came to find myself in the unlikely situation of being Honey's only ally. I use the term in the *loosest* sense.

I did actually feel genuinely sorry for her, though.

Her parents had been summoned and were informed that if Honey was given so much as a blue they would have to find alternate schooling for their daughter. As it was, she had been suspended for a week and gated for the rest of the term. A gating meant you couldn't go home on exeat weekends – sort of like boarding school in the old-fashioned days. Sort of like boarding school for me.

And then I received a letter from Freddie. It was a formal letter, written on palace paper, apologising in the grandest way for his inappropriate behaviour! I read it, and reread it, and my stomach turned with the formality of it all. The tone of it left me feeling worse about Freddie than I did before, so I didn't show it to anyone, not even Star. Just the same, I carried the letter around in my pocket.

We had other things to discuss. Star and I were in the fencing salle having a practice bout when I first explained to her why I thought it was too mean to send even the horrible Honey to Coventry.

Star said she sort of agreed too. 'I know Georgina and the others are cool with us now, but they did put us through absolute hell for ages!'

'I suppose,' I agreed as we lugged our gear back to the armoury.

'Don't you remember how evil they were to us?' Star said. 'I didn't really give a shit, personally, but I think you did . . . although you never said anything.'

'But that's what I'm saying. Even though she is the most horrible, meanest, nastiest, psycho toff at Saint Augustine's . . .'

'Honey will bounce back. She always does,' Star said.

'Maybe you're right, but still . . .'

'Well, I hope you're not suggesting that either of us should become a Honey friend?' she gasped.

'No!' I laughed. 'I just think that we shouldn't be part of the Coventry thing.'

'Mmmm. Not convinced. I think it might do her a bit of good, actually. Maybe she'll become all saintly and wonderful like us,' Star teased, nudging me in the hope of breaking my serious mood. 'And let's face it, she basically ruined your night with Freddie.'

While we were hanging our kits back in the armoury, I showed her the letter.

'Well, obviously someone at the palace wrote it for him.' She passed it back.

'But he signed it.'

'I told you I thought he was a jerk for believing all those evil things Honey said about you. Forget him.'

I shrugged. 'Yaah. Besides, I'm totally over him,' I replied brightly, even though I so totally wasn't.

After that we rounded up the rest of our writing salon and went along to Sister Constance's office to discuss the launch party for *Nun of Your Business*.

We had to wait for her to finish her conversation with Father Conway and it wasn't long before our talk turned to Honey and sending her to Coventry.

'I don't know why you're so bothered about it. Honey's always hated you!' Georgina reasoned.

Star gave me a meaningful look, as if to remind me that

it wasn't so long ago that Georgina had hated me too.

Clemmie and Arabella agreed. The irony of it all didn't escape me.

Clemmie added, 'It's true, she deserves Coventry.'

'No one deserves anything,' I snapped irritably, which made everyone shut up.

We sat in silence after that and my thoughts turned to Freddie and his royal apology for inappropriate behaviour. Did he mean kissing me? Did he think that kissing a common girl like me was inappropriate, was that what he was saying? He'd signed off, wishing me well. Wishing me well! What was I – a leper?

Star's fury with him over his behaviour the night of the social now seemed spot on. How could he have believed a girl like Honey over a girl he'd just shared his mouth with for ten minutes? Still, I couldn't help wanting to relive that kiss in my mind, and I did, over and over, and over again. Only I didn't share this with any of the others.

'So what do you think Sister will say?' Arabella asked.

'What, about sending Honey to Coventry?'

'No, about *Nun of Your Business!*'

'Piss off?' Georgina replied. 'Let's face it, darlings, after the fiasco of the Eades social, she's hardly going to allow us to use the hall and invite the Eades boys from our year.' I slumped down in my seat . . . I was the 'fiasco of the Eades social.'

'I suppose not,' Clemmie agreed dismally.

'On the other hand, it is for charity,' Star pointed out,

as Father Conway walked out of Sister's office.

'Oh well, here goes nothing,' Georgina whispered, smoothing her uniform as she knocked softly on the Gothic old oak door.

Sister's voice was as clear and neutral as ever. 'Enter.'

Sitting behind her desk, straight-backed, her arms resting in her lap, she looked imposing enough, but with Christ looming over her on his cross the effect was just plain scary.

'Good afternoon, Sister,' we trilled.

'Girls.' She nodded to indicate we could proceed.

I nudged Georgina. We'd elected her as our spokesperson earlier.

Georgina nudged me back. Obviously she'd decided to back out. So I nudged Star. One of us had to step forward and it wasn't going to be me. Or Star, apparently, who then nudged Clemmie.

'Stand still, girls. This is not the appropriate setting for a vaudevillian tumbling act,' she warned. 'You have something to say. Speak.'

So I spoke. 'Erm, well, you see the thing is, Sister. Well, you know we're hoping to have the launch for our, erm, magazine thingamy and that sort of thing. Well, we were thinking. That is, if you say it's OK with you, we'd quite like to hold it in the hall,' I stuttered.

'And invite loads of boys,' added Clemmie.

'Or not,' I added hastily. 'I mean, we appreciate that you might not feel that is appropriate.'

Sister Constance had a special fondness for the word

'appropriate,' so I was hoping the mere use of it might soften her.

'On the contrary. I feel it is extremely appropriate, if not imperative, that we open up the hall to as many paying guests as possible. I've discussed the matter with Mr Raymond, the Headmaster of Eades, and he feels as I do that this magazine launch party is the perfect opportunity to put last week's unpleasantness behind us.

'Quite separately, but no less important, is the cause for which we are raising money. I've suggested a ticket fee of twenty pounds. Initially Mr Raymond felt this was a little steep, but as I reminded him, all proceeds of the launch will be going to the Children of the World.'

Star interrupted, 'You're kidding, Sister?'

But we all knew Sister Constance wasn't much of a one for kidding.

Georgina said, 'I need a fag,' and started fanning herself.

Not even that could wipe the smug smile off Sister's face.

I remembered that when Bob and Sarah had dropped me off on their way to the airport, Bob had remarked, 'She's a swell gal, your Sister Constance.'

Thinking of that made me smile and realise something. I missed Bob.

Actually, Bob was a bit swell himself.

TWENTY

Moonwalking

That night the Lit Chick Salon (Clemmie, Arabella, Star, Georgina and I) decided to go for a moonwalk.

Moonwalking was a Saint Augustine's tradition that went back further than anyone remembered – even Sister Francis, who was a hundred and two years old, couldn't remember how far back the girls of Saint Augustine's had been moonwalking. But then I suppose the nuns weren't really meant to know about it, otherwise everyone would have been rusticated (suspended).

Now that the security men and the guard dog numbers had been cut back to normal, we'd decided that a party in the woods under the light of the full moon was the perfect way to celebrate our victory over Sister Constance – or was it her victory over us?

Armed with torches, blankets, fags, Febreze, tuck and, of course, Body Shop Specials, we snuck downstairs and the East End? I doubt it,' I said.

I watched another star shoot across the sky as Arabella offered me a crisp – well, actually, she tickled my nose with it until I opened my mouth and she shoved it in.

'Got any matches, Georgie?' Star asked.

Georgina took the cigarette from Star's mouth and stuck it in her own, where three other cigarettes were already arranged. 'We only brought three matches down with us,' she explained, speaking out the side of her mouth as she lit all four with the one match and distributed them.

'So Freddie's best friend's brother is Poppy's boyfriend,' I repeated, trying to get my head around what that might mean – if anything.

'Yup,' Georgina replied.

'So he must know if it's true or not?' I went on.

'Or he might have been convinced by Poppy that it *is* true.'

'As if anyone in their right mind would believe Honey or Poppy? According to Mummy, Lady O'Hare – and by the way, she's not married to a Lord anymore, so she shouldn't even have a title – will appear at the opening of an envelope! Do you know she was even on some sordid Sky television channel last week showing off their house in Knightsbridge? I mean, how tragic do you have to be to do that?'

'What was it like?' Clemmie asked, her blue saucer eyes popping with curiosity.

'Darling, what do you think it was like? A five-star

luxury hotel – absolutely so ghastly. No personal touches. Nothing eclectic, and all their furniture was bought new – well, it was riddled with antiques, of course, but all of it was bought this generation, if you know what I mean. Mummy was like, "*Hello*, do you not have any ancestors?"'

This is where not being part of the English class system really gets to me. 'Well, erm, actually, Georgina, all my parents' stuff is new too.' I didn't add that our house doesn't even look like a five-star hotel, although I suppose it is madly eclectic.

'Yes, but that's different, darling. You're not trying to be all pretentious and pretending that your great-great-great-grandfather was best mates with the King. It's just fake and false and, well, tacky. I love modernism. When I get to buy my first house it's going to be madly Space Odyssey. I hate old stuff. It's all dusty. I bet your parents' place in LA is like supercool. Is it in Malibu, darling?'

'No.'

'I think it's really cool that we might be coming over to see you,' she added.

I watched another star shooting across the sky and wished like mad that Georgina would forget about Bob's offer.

'Honey's always been pretentious,' Arabella sneered a little later.

I didn't really give a toss about how tacky or pretentious Honey was. All I could think of was that if Freddie's best friend's brother was going out with Honey's sister, he'd be getting a whole different angle on everything.

Star took a deep drag on her fag and said, 'I mean, the mere fact that his best friend's brother would go out with a girl like Poppy means he's tragic. And if he's tragic, his brother's probably equally tragic and *ipso facto*, so is Freddie. You can tell a lot about a person by their friends.'

Georgina took a slug of her vodka. 'Oh, don't *ipso* bloody *facto* me. I'm only going to fail Latin, darling, and Daddy says if I fail Latin he's going to choose all my subjects in Lower Sixth.'

'Oh, look, there's a shooting star!' Arabella pointed up at the sky. 'Let's all make a wish.'

'To *Nun of Your Business* being a huge success,' Star declared.

'For raising thousands and thousands of pounds for Children of the World,' Clemmie added.

The girls all held their cigarettes against one another in the air in a toast. Georgina, realising I was left out, handed me one of the last of the two precious matches and I held it against their embers, where it exploded in a whoosh.

'I told you this was going to be a great term,' Georgina reminded me, taking my hand in hers. I reached out and took Star's hand and all five of us held hands and looked up the sky, silent in our own thoughts.

'And anyway,' Georgina remarked later as we took another swig of vodka, 'you've still got Jay back in LA,' which made us all howl with laughter for some reason.

'Actually, I haven't,' I told her when the laughter stopped and we were all just lying there silently again.

'Darling, you didn't drop him when you pulled Freddie, did you?'

'I didn't have to,' I told her as a shiver went through me at what I was about to do. 'He was never really my boyfriend, see. I made him up.'

I felt Star's hand squeeze mine and that gave me the courage to say what I knew I had to say if I was going to be honest.

'But the photographs?' Clemmie asked.

'He's my mom's PA. You know Sarah . . . Jay is her gay PA.'

Georgina spat out her vodka. 'Your mum's gay PA?'

'Uh-huh. Look, I'm not particularly proud of it,' I told them, praying that Georgina wouldn't pull her hand away from mine. I could take it if Clemmie and Arabella did, but not Georgina.

Georgina laughed. 'Darling, you are the end.'

'Delusional, you mean?'

'Delusional women and the boys they fall for. Let's do a piece on it for the next edition of *Nun of Your Business*,' Clemmie suggested.

'Or not,' I told them.

That was when I realised that I'd just fessed up to my greatest shame and here we still were, still holding hands, and the moon was still full and the stars were still shooting in the sky, and even though I'd pulled my prince and even though he'd dumped me, I was going to be OK. And suddenly all the things Star had been saying to me, about friendship not being based on being an insider or an outsider, or pulling princes, but on moments like these, rang true.

People aren't always what they seem. All my time at Saint Augustine's I'd been so wrapped up in my preconceptions about Georgina and their kind. What was it Star had said, that I'd have to accept who I was before I could expect other people to accept me?

Arabella interrupted my epiphany. 'Anyhow, you'll see him tomorrow.'

'Who? Gay Jay?' Star giggled.

'No, darling – Freddie. You've got fencing at Eades, remember? You might even be up against him again!'

Star nudged me. 'Possibly even a bit of tongue-fencing, if you can lose the security guys.'

God, how could I have forgot about fencing? Especially when it meant I'd be face-to-face with Freddie again.

'Tongue-fencing? You are totally gross sometimes, Star,' Georgina declared happily as she lit another bundle of cigarettes.

TWENTY-ONE

En Garde,
Your Royal Highness

I was unusually quiet on the minibus ride to Eades. It was almost like I was having one of those out-of-body experiences. My head was whizzing about and my heart was doing funny fluttery things, and it wasn't funny in a nice way.

Georgina said it was despair poisoned by hope (she'd been getting very literary in her language since we started up the writing salon). She had a point in a way, I suppose – only I think it was more a case of love poisoned by pissed-offness.

Our moonwalk discussion about Freddie actually believing that I was trading on his royalty was now ringing true to me. I felt very confused about it all, because:

a) I was really pissed off with that wretched letter he'd sent me.

and

b) I really, really wanted to kiss him again.

I still remembered the kiss vividly. It was on some kind of loop in my brain. On and on it played, always accompanied by the tingly feeling I'd had as he'd handed me his jacket to hold while he held open the window in the library.

Followed by the warm feeling as he placed his jacket over my shoulders and guided me through the bushes as if I, me, Calypso Kelly, were the princess.

Followed by the way his mouth felt pressed on mine.

Followed by the crescendo as my heart went *whoosh* as he ran his hand up my safety-pinned back and supported my neck as he kissed me.

It had all been so lovely and then within minutes it had all gone so sordidly wrong with the 'trading on my royalty thing' and the Rough-and-Tumble photographs. And if anything, it was made even worse after his stupid formal letter begging for forgiveness.

None of it felt sorted.

Of course he was the first and only guy I saw when we entered the fencing salle at Eades. He was looking even more fit than I remembered. He was doing warm-ups on one of the pistes. His hair was all tussled . . . oh, no – I wanted to rough-and-tumble him again.

When he saw me he smiled, but I couldn't tell if it was an it's-all-OK smile or merely one of those false how-charming-am-I? smiles, which he'd no doubt been trained to do since birth.

Star, sensing my pain, whispered wickedly in my ear, 'Excuse *me*, but do you know who I think I am?' which did actually make me laugh.

Star, Portia and I were on the first team – which didn't mean much, as there was only one sabre team at Saint Augustine's. The thing was, Portia also did *épée*, so she was called to a bout almost as soon as she'd finished her stretches.

Star and I were sitting around on the benches watching the other three bouts going on around us when Star nudged me. 'I think that's Kevin's brother, Billy, over there, fencing Portia.'

'God, he's really going for her, isn't he?' I marvelled.

He was good. Some boys have a very different approach to their game when they fence girls – actually, make that *most* boys. They didn't like to hit you anywhere above or below the stomach. There was nothing worse than a guy letting you win – it was like being lied to, or being made to feel you weren't worth the trouble.

Star agreed with me, but Clemmie thought we were mean. She thought they just let us win because they were being nice. But then Clemmie thought it was mean to eat Jelly Babies because they looked like her little brother Sebastian.

But Billy was ruthless. He was throwing everything he had at Portia.

I liked that.

When my first bout was called, I guess I had imagined it would be against Freddie, but instead it was his captain Billy, who was not only one of the best sabreurs in the country, but was probably going to be on the Olympic team.

As I waited to be hooked up to the electrical point recorder, I looked him up and down. Suddenly I wasn't thinking about Freddie at all. I was thinking of winning . . . and of Billy.

He looked like Kevin in a sort of older, better-looking way – short, blond hair and eyes that seemed to be laughing at you even when he wasn't smiling. I figured he'd probably be tired, having just been fencing Portia.

The president, in this instance the Eades fencing master, called, 'On guard, ready, fence!' He wasn't as mad keen on French as Professor Sullivan.

Billy lunged at me first, which sort of shocked me, so I parried and riposted with a hit to the back of his neck. This didn't actually register as a point and wasn't really the done thing, but it really, really hurt. (I knew this from first-hand experience!)

Billy cried, 'Ow!' and the president called, 'Stop.'

We began again – only this time Billy waited for me to make the first attack, probably because he was still in pain and a bit unsure of what I might do. Like Professor Sullivan was always reminding us, fencing was a physical form of chess.

I decided to unnerve him further by not moving from the *en garde* line for ages. When I did move, I scored a straight hit to the torso. After that, the bout was mine, five hits to nil.

After the game was called, Billy took off his mask and shook my hand. 'You're everything I'd heard you were and more.' He was laughing as he said it.

I was going really red, but I took off my mask, revealing my fluffy horns in all their embarrassing glory.

We shook hands again. 'Billy,' he said. 'I think you know my brother, Kevin?'

'Calypso,' I said, smiling. A fuzzy warm feeling started tingling through my body. I don't know how much time passed before I realised we were still shaking hands and everyone around us who wasn't fencing was looking at us.

The best thing was, it wasn't just me that couldn't stop shaking hands and staring. He was staring at me too, not letting go, and smiling.

Eventually, we both got a grip. I even rescued a slight chink of dignity by pulling my hand away first.

'Calypso,' he repeated.

'Uh-huh.' Here we go, I thought . . . my name again.

'She who causes men to be diverted from their goals?' he teased, referring to Calypso in Homer's *Odyssey*, who held Odysseus captive on her island until the gods petitioned her to let him go.

Normally I would have started digging a verbal hole to bury myself in, but something about Billy made me feel . . . well . . . like *me*, really, and instead I teased him back. 'Some men need a good diversion.'

To which he replied, '*Touché*,' and bowed in this mad, regal sort of way.

That was when Freddie came up to us.

'Hey man, how's it going?' Billy said.

'I think I'm up against Portia next,' Freddie replied – only he was looking at me as he said it, and he was looking sad.

I surprised myself by acting really cool. 'Hi, Freddie. Portia's quite good, actually.'

Freddie said, 'Only not as good as you,' in a meaningful sort of way, which made me blush.

Billy said, 'If she is as good as Calypso, all I can say is, watch the back of your neck, man.'

Freddie looked confused, having not seen our bout.

'Anyway, I'd better get going,' Billy said. 'My next bout's with Star. But listen, Calypso, great to have the shit sabreured out of me by you.'

I must have grimaced with embarrassment because he winked.

'Kidding – the pleasure was all mine. Catch you later, I hope,' he added pointedly.

'What's up with you guys?' Freddie enquired, obviously jealous.

Even though one part of me wanted to kiss him, another part of me was still too humiliated by the way he'd treated me. Either way, something inside me just snapped and I let out a heavy sigh.

Then he said, 'We need to talk. That is . . . I have some explaining to do, I think.'

Suddenly all my pent-up confusion, my anger over his letter, and my longing for more of his kisses just sort of exploded out of me.

'I don't think we have anything to say to each other.'

Then I turned to leave, aware by now that *everyone* in the salle who was not in a bout was watching us.

'Wait, Calypso,' he said, grabbing my arm.

I looked at his hand gripping my elbow and my mind flashed back to the night of the social as he'd helped me climb out of the library window. I looked up into his ink-blue eyes and he let go, which was probably for the best because a part of me suddenly wanted to kiss him again and we know how that ended up last time, don't we?

'You don't understand, actually,' he said.

'Actually,' I said, moving into motor-mouth mode, 'I understand just perfectly . . . you and your wretched royalty and all the ghastly people like me you're so paranoid about trading on it!'

'It's not like that.'

But I wasn't to be swayed. 'Who do you think you are?' I demanded, my hands on my hips. 'I mean, apart from heir to the throne and master of the nation or whatever other fancy titles you have, and . . . well, erm, that sort of thing?'

He looked shocked, so I really went for it. 'And anyway, another thing – even if I *had* sold all your bloody messages for like a thousand pounds a listen, it still wouldn't have been worth all the trouble you've caused me! Well, would it?'

He shook his head. He tried to say something, but I

didn't give him a chance.

'To hell with your royal status. What about me? Do you think it's some sort of royal privilege for me to be labelled as the Prince's Rough-and-Tumble?'

He opened and closed his mouth for a bit so I told him he could shove his wretched royalty and elitist behaviour anywhere it would fit, as long as it wasn't anywhere near my life.

I think I said a lot of other things too, because I was quite red-faced and croaky by the time I finished.

'I think you were just called,' was all he said in the end.

'What?'

'You've got a bout – they just called your name.'

'Oh, right. OK then, well, goodbye.' I turned on my heel and walked towards the piste, trying to gather myself together in the manner befitting the Captain of the Saint Augustine sabreurs.

Then I heard him calling out my name again.

I turned around. 'Good luck!' he called and gave me a little wave.

'I don't need luck,' I replied haughtily, because I felt wrong-footed by his unexpected kindness. Still, I was sounding almost like Honey and I wished I could take it back.

I won all my bouts, but I was still shaking over my exchange with Freddie when we finally clambered into the minibus for the journey back to Saint Augustine's.

Everyone immediately started going on about me giving Freddie a Right Royal Dressing Down, but I felt sick inside and didn't rise to the bait. I hardly said a word. I couldn't quite believe the things I'd said. I had been like a mad, erupting volcano and I hadn't even given him a chance.

Should I have given him a chance?

I didn't ask any of my friends because I knew what they'd say. 'No way. You were brilliant, Calypso . . . blah, blah, blah.'

Thank God it was an exeat weekend and we all got straight off the minibus with only half an hour to get ready for the coach that took us to London.

Star had invited me to spend the weekend at her place in Chelsea. This time her parents were there. That is, her parents and their roadies and their rock-star friends and their hangers-on – and, of course, their drugs.

That night there was a big party with loads of models and It-Girls and really ancient rock stars, all of them acting like they thought they were sixteen or something. What is it with adults who can't grow up? They reminded me of Sarah and Bob.

Star and I wandered through the party, sipping on our Jack Daniels and Coke, which tasted ghastly, but Star insisted it was the only drink one could drink at a rock-star party.

I suppose it was quite cool, not the yucky drink, but seeing all these famous people being really happy to see Star and talking to us like we were real adults, even though we were about a hundred years younger than they were.

The best part was when Elsa, a really famous super-model-turned-writer, hung out with us in the cupboard under the stairs and we talked about school and friends and make-up. We told her about our magazine. She was really impressed and asked if she could come to the launch. She said she was writing a book, which made me worship her even more.

The party went on all through the night and when we went downstairs for breakfast the next morning there were loads of sleeping bodies everywhere. Mostly they were Tiger's roadies, but as Star said, even really famous people look totally gross when they are sleeping and there is no one to airbrush them.

They were sprawled on sofas and the floor, and Star and I were quite wicked and put Coco Pops in their mouths and then ran off and hid.

All in all it was a weekend free of worry. Feeding sleeping rock stars Coco Pops turned out to be the perfect antidote to all my dilemmas, but on the coach back to Saint Augustine's they all came flooding back. I discovered a text on my phone, which had been sent on Friday.

I hadn't even looked at my phone all weekend.

PLEASE DON'T H8 ME. I DON'T H8 U. ACTUALLY . . . QUITE THE OPPOSITE. CAN I CALL YOU TO XPLAIN? F

I immediately texted him back.

I DON'T HATE YOU. C X

Then I immediately regretted the *x*.

TWENTY-TWO

Nun of Your Business

A week later, on the morning of the launch party for *Nun of Your Business*, I woke up pre-gong, which put Miss Cribbe into a bit of a mood. Honey was back at school, no longer in Coventry, ensconced in her role as Queen B (that's B for Bitch), but in a weird sort of way, it was actually quite fun having her back. There was too much going on for me to be bothered holding a grudge.

Honey had had a complete makeover. She'd had ringlets put into her hair, which was now blonder than ever, and Rystaline injected into her smile lines (even though she didn't have any). She'd also had her navel pierced and as a punishment/reward her mother had given her a diamond navel ring for it. Duchess had a real Tiffany diamond collar, with a white gold bell, so she could drive the other pets bananas.

'It's barbaric. Hilda is terrified!' Star had complained.

'She's so stressed out by that bell, she's constantly on her wheel now. I'm scared she's going to have a heart attack if she keeps this up.'

On this occasion even I felt quite sorry for Hilda (and all the other pets in the pet shed – especially Dorothy Parker). I mean, imagine having a bell sounding every time the horrible Duchess moved! It would be like Miss Cribbe banging on her gong all the time.

'I'm actually quite bored with her anyway,' Honey yawned when Star complained about her rabbit's bell. 'I'm thinking that the diamond collar would look so much more stylish on a white rabbit. Perhaps I'll give Duchess to Poppy.'

None of us said anything. I guess the makeover hadn't been that complete.

We had far more important things on our minds – making sure everything was in place for the launch. All day long, girls kept coming up to us and saying, Is Jono (famous rock star) really coming to the launch? and stuff like that. No one could pay attention in classes that day.

The nuns had volunteered to supervise everything (i.e., to wander around the hall oppressively, making sure no one had an iota of a chance of pulling any of the boys).

We had a plan, though.

My plan went like this. After sending Freddie the x on my text, I decided to go for gold, i.e., march straight up to him, grab him by the hand, and lead him to the secret passage under the stage and, while Star and Georgina diverted any nuns nearby, we would nip in the secret door and tongue-fence like mad. All the complications between us – whether to '*x*' or not – had made me think that some things are better said with tongues than words.

It was Clemmie's idea, actually. All term it had been clear that she'd been heading this way, but since the Eades social she had officially gone Boy Crazy. All she could talk about was who she was going to pull at the launch – she had a list with five names on it:

Kevin.
Kevin.
Kevin.
Kevin.
Kevin.

Georgina had a list too. Her list had thirty-six names on it (all different) but only twenty-four of the names on the list attended Eades. But Georgina could pull boys effortlessly (eighteen was her record so far), whereas Clemmie was a bit more like me – single-minded (or as Georgina called us, dramatic).

Star was back on with Rupert, who'd had his braces taken off and was now a realistic pulling option. She was hoping to pull a few older, fit boys as well, just in case Rupert was as hopeless a kisser without braces as with.

Arabella was keeping her pulling list open, but she had sworn that she was determined to pull at least six boys before the night was out.

Thank goodness our nuns were so old and innocent.

The painting that the kids from the village in Africa had sent us was hanging above the stage, next to the DJ's station. The nuns had really gone to town with decorations. The main hall was lit with multicoloured flashing lights and the standard disco ball hanging in the centre.

Sisters Hillary and Veronica were manning the *Nun of Your Business* desk at the entrance. Everyone who had bought a ticket to the launch was given a free copy as they came in, but we were also selling a limited edition of two hundred copies signed by the editors, that is us, the five Lit Chick Salon girls (Arabella, Clemmie, Georgina, Star and me) for ten pounds each.

All the Eades boys were arriving by coaches, and I tried to loiter nonchalantly around the entrance, looking out for Freddie as coach after coach arrived. Our hall was already at capacity by the time Kevin ambled in, laughing and chatting away with a few of his mates. I sidled up to him very casually/desperately and said, 'Hiya.'

He looked genuinely pleased to see me. But then that's how Eades boys are brought up to look.

'Hey, Calypso. How's it going? I heard you trounced my bro at sabre last week. Well done.'

I giggled like . . . well, a schoolgirl, I suppose.

'So, erm, how's Freddie, then?' I asked, craning a look over his shoulder for my prince.

'Down with some stomach bug, unfortunately. He said to say hi.'

Clemmie skipped over and my window of interrogation had closed. So I stood there at the entrance, clinging to my pathetic message.

Freddie said to say hi.

What could I read into that? Answer: A LOT.

I mean, did he say, 'God, I'm gutted that this stomach bug has prevented me from resting my eyes on the beautiful, intoxicating sight of Calypso Kelly, but say hi for me, will you, Kev?' Or did he say, 'If you see what's-her-name, the fencer girl – Calypso, is it? – tell her hi.'

Or worse still, did he say nothing at all, and Kevin, not wanting to make me realise how irrelevant I truly was, had made up the 'hi' to save my feelings?

I watched as Kevin and Clementine disappeared through the secret stage door.

Sister Veronica was polishing her spectacles.

Sister Hillary was eating a scone.

Clemmie was hotly followed by Star with Rupert, and Georgina with an Eades Sixth Former.

'So, Calypso, can you talk to mere mortals, or do I need to petition Zeus?'

I spun around. 'What?'

'Billy. We met at . . .'

'I know. Hi, how's it going?' I got that funny wiggly feeling again. Maybe I was coming down with Freddie's stomach bug? Wouldn't that be romantic, sharing a gastric flu . . . or not! The thing was, my wiggly feeling didn't feel gastric, it felt sort of . . . nice, really.

'It's going fine. Cool magazine, by the way. I love the satires, especially the one on Honey.'

And then I remembered. 'Oh, that's right, you go out with Poppy, don't you?'

He looked embarrassed and did that funny I'm-going-to-look-at-my-feet-now thing that boys tend to do. 'No . . .'

'Oh, OK. It's just that, erm . . .'

He still looked embarrassed and he didn't take his eyes off his shoes. He sort of shuffled them a bit, shoving his hands in his pockets, and he looked so cute.

'We went out a few times over the Easter break,' he explained. 'You know, down the Kings Road – that sort of thing. Nothing major. But we're not like *going out*, going out.'

'Darling! I wondered where you'd got to.' It was Poppy, looking divine in a breathtakingly short, pink, wispy number with matching Jimmy Choo sling-backs. She threw her arm around Billy in a proprietorial sort of fashion. 'Quick, darling, this way. I've got some vodka in my bag.'

With that, she took him by the hand and led him towards the stage passage. He looked back at me like a man being led off to a firing squad.

With a wardrobe like hers, it was no wonder Poppy could pull a boy like Billy. I looked down at my carefully constructed outfit, bought the night before for a fiver from one of the Lower Sixth girls. It was last year's cut, last year's colour, and the shoes I was wearing were a label no one in England had ever heard of, which I'd bought in LA in the sale at Bloomingdale's. Honey had declared them

'Don't-Fuck-Me Shoes!' But then I didn't really give a toss what Honey said, did or thought any more.

Besides, it wasn't all doom and gloom. In fact, it was really cool, especially when Jono, famous for his views on world debt, arrived. He looked quite cute standing on the stage next to Sister Veronica – they were about the same height – especially when he put his arm around her and she started to giggle.

Hello, was Sister Veronica flirting?

He gave a stirring speech about why the rich countries of the world should cancel the debt of really poor ones, and everyone cheered.

He said it was really cool that we'd put so much effort into raising all this money. Then Star's dad, Tiger, got on stage with Elsa, the supermodel Star and I had chatted with at the party, which was just totally random and unscripted.

Tiger was wobbling a bit when he grabbed the mike off of Jono and asked us if we were having a 'rocking good time.'

Everyone screamed back, 'Yes!'

Then he said, 'That's cool, but just remember, if all the rich arsehole countries in the world cancelled world debt, ninety million girls in Africa could have an education.'

Everyone clapped and I looked over at Star to give her a supportive smile about her dad being dead embarrassing, but she didn't look in the least bit embarrassed. In fact, she looked proud. And once I thought about it, I could see why. It was a very good point.

Then Elsa took the mike and she very sweetly reminded everyone that the magazine wouldn't have got off the ground if it wasn't for Star, Calypso, Arabella, Clementine and Georgina and their friends, and everyone clapped.

Then the party really kicked in.

I ended up dancing with a few random boys, but I didn't even really look at their faces – apart from Rupert's (he must have got the thumbs-down after his no-braces kiss with Star).

It was a fantastic party, but the only thing I pulled that night was a good laugh when we arrived back at our dorms.

Misty had weed all over Honey's duvet.

You could hear her scream throughout Cleathorpes.

TWENTY-THREE

The Glory and the Embarrassment

The week after the launch no one could talk about anything other than the party – or rather, who'd pulled whom.

Even though I'd pulled a grand total of nil, I was still caught up in the excitement. Also, both Freddie and Billy had sent me text messages and voice mails afterwards – but to tell the truth, pulling boys was the last thing on my mind. I was more excited about the next meeting of the Lit Chick Writing Salon.

We'd decided to wait until Friday to discuss our strategy for the next issue of the magazine because we wanted to find out exactly how much money we'd raised altogether.

Sister Constance made the announcement at Thursday's assembly and it was unbelievable. With the twenty-pound tickets all sold out, and with roughly eight hundred boys from Eades and four hundred girls from

Saint Augustine's, we'd made loads of money. Also people like Tiger and Jono had made extra donations.

Sister Constance had stood on the hall stage flanked by two ancient statues of the Virgin Mary. There were enormous vases of lilies surrounding them. The other nuns were all gathered on the stage with her. The elderly ones (all those over ninety) were sitting on chairs. It was like a conceptual girl-power exhibit – in a nun-ish sort of way.

She announced how much we raised, unable to suppress a smile. It was much more than the Lower Sixth girls had managed the year before.

No one even clapped at first. I think we were all too shocked. After a moment's silence the nuns all clapped for us and Sister Constance congratulated Star, Clemmie, Arabella, Georgina and me. Suddenly everyone burst into applause and threw their ties in the air, as is the tradition at Saint Augustine's. (Any excuse to rid ourselves of the revolting bows. We would have thrown them in the air if we'd raised five quid, to be honest.)

When the deafening noise had died down a little, a girl from the Saint Augustine's Old Girls Society took the microphone and talked to us about how much that money would mean to the Children of the World charity.

It was one of the most fantastic days of my life . . . well, it was up until the point when Camilla (the Old Girl) asked Georgina, Star, Clementine, Arabella and me to come up onto the stage.

Talk about catastrophically random; no one had

even hinted that we might be called upon to embarrass ourselves in front of the entire school. We all immediately started applying lip-gloss as we made our way through the aisles. The whole school started stamping their feet (even the nuns – apart from Sister Constance, who never lets her austere demeanour drop for a moment) and demanding, 'Speech, speech, speech!'

Sister Constance took the microphone and asked for hush. Everyone fell silent immediately.

'Now, I'm sure you'd all like to hear from one of the girls responsible for raising all this money,' she said, handing the mike over to me.

The school responded in the affirmative. 'Erm, well thanks,' I mumbled. 'I mean yeah . . . brilliant. This is so random and totally unexpected,' I stuttered. My mouth went all dry and so I applied a dab more lip-gloss.

Here I was, on stage in front of the entire school, a sea of girls all looking up at me, expecting me to say something profound or at least comprehensible.

How could this happen? So I tried to pretend I was Nancy Mitford or Dorothy Parker (the writer, not the rabbit) and say something poignant and witty, something inspirational – and not to mention how our writing salon, from which the magazine had sprung, all started with a food fight in the canteen. I had quickly decided that wouldn't sound very inspirational.

I did one of those little cough thingamies that Oscar winners do in the hope that it would add some glamour to the occasion, and then I just let my subconscious do the rambling for me, figuring it couldn't do a worse job than my conscious self – which couldn't think of much apart from whether my hair was sticking up and if it was possible to apply lip-gloss while holding a microphone and speaking. I must have said something vaguely reasonable, though, because I heard the applause. Also no one teased me afterwards.

When it was over I went to the technology room and sent Sarah and Bob an e-mail about it. I thought about texting Freddie, but couldn't think of an excuse that wouldn't seem tragic, so I joined the celebratory dorm party.

TWENTY-FOUR

The Myth of the Midnight Dash

Georgina invited Clemmie, Star, Arabella and me (and Dorothy Parker, of course) to spend half-term break at her massive stucco house on Eton Square. We spent our mornings lying in the spring sun of her vast garden square, sipping on various health drinks dreamed up by her housekeeper, after which we would head off to Sloane Street and do a bit of shopping.

Sarah and Bob had finally upped my allowance to a reasonable level – not to the heady heights of Georgina, Star and the others, but at least I could afford to chip in for a pizza now. Sarah and Bob said it was because next school year I was going to be turning fifteen, but I suspect they also felt that after the Rough-and-Tumble episode, my character had been built up as much as it was ever going to be.

The best part, though, was in the evenings, when we

dressed up in all our finery (even Tobias put on his best suit) and set off for the Kings Road to pull boys.

The Kings Road Promenade. It was a tradition. A tradition that up until now I had never properly felt a part of. Girls and boys from boarding schools from all over England came in droves, like homing pigeons, to march up and down the Kings Road in Chelsea. American teenagers went to malls; we strolled up and down the road every evening, checking one another out and trying to pull.

The boys tried to look all cool and wasted, like they didn't give a toss, and the girls, having spent hours trying to make themselves look effortlessly stunning, pretended not to look at the boys while arguing the fitness and pullability rating of each.

Clemmie and Kevin were an official item now. Star and Georgina both found her fascination with him immature and teased her mercilessly about stuff like when were they going to set the date for their marriage, etc.

My pulling rate that half-term was pretty low, mainly because I had Freddie on my mind. Although I did kiss Hugo, this totally fit boy from Downside (a posh Catholic boarding school), who was writing a novel.

A novel! Imagine that. An actual book. And it sounded really cool and witty too. I could have listened to him talk about it all night, but I had kissing on my mind and we had an eleven o'clock curfew, so I just flung myself at him.

Shame he was such a crap kisser – well, compared to Freddie anyway.

I'd heard/read that Freddie was away with his family in Scotland so I didn't expect to hear from him ... well, I tried not to expect to hear from him – although I did see him on television one evening, looking all gorgeous and charming. He was standing outside one of the royal retreats with the Queen and King and his mother and father, but just the same, I was disappointed he hadn't called.

I bumped into Kevin on the Kings Road a few times and he said that I wasn't to worry, as it was game on with Freddie and me, as far as he knew. I didn't dare mention his brother – although Kevin did say Billy was studying. I know that as he was in Year Eleven he probably was – but I still couldn't help imagining him with Poppy.

On the last day of half-term, while we were sipping lattés on the Kings Road, Georgina brought up Bob's mad invitation to visit LA in the summer.

I stared into my milky drink.

'The thing is, darling, Star and I have asked our parents and we're coming.'

'Oh,' I said, trying not to make it sound like a groan of pain. It wasn't that I wouldn't have loved spending the summer with them; it was just that I knew Sarah and Bob could never afford the first-class travel and entertainment they'd expect. 'That is, are you sure? I mean LA's pretty dull in the summertime.'

Star pitched in. 'Well, my dad spoke to your dad last night and it's all arranged. My whole family's going and I've invited Georgina because she was only going to spend the summer with her family in the south of France –'

'Which would be boring beyond belief,' Georgina added. 'All we do is go out on the *bâteau* and lie in the sun and eat loads and loads of really fattening food. I'd much rather be on the Atkins diet with you in Malibu.'

'I don't live in Malibu!' I insisted, looking up from my drink for the first time to see Georgina and Star grinning at each other.

'Darling, don't be so mad. You really are the most awful snob,' Georgina declared. 'As if we mind where you live. Besides, Sarah told us she had a new PA, and he's not gay!'

Clemmie and Arabella admitted that they were madly jealous and wished they come to LA too, but that they were already booked to go on a safari in Kenya with Arabella's family.

So that was that. Georgina's parents sent us all back to school in the family Rolls Royce and then Georgina gave Miles, the chauffeur, a fifty-pound note to carry all our bags up to Cleathorpes and unpack for us so that we could race off and settle Dorothy Parker back in the pet shed.

It was a far cry from my inauspicious arrival at the start of term.

The second half of the term was crammed with study. Our teachers must have held a heinous meeting over the half-term break about not being cruel enough to us because they were really putting the pressure on us now. They said we needed to start adopting a more serious attitude to our work and went on and on about how important the next school year was going to be because we'd be starting our GCSEs and 'defining our futures.'

Yawn.

'Your lives depend on the grit and determination with which you apply yourself to your studies, girls!' they trilled every moment of the day.

But finally the day came when our last piece of work for the term was handed in and we were able to put into action the dream of every self-respecting Saint Augustine girl. The legendary midnight dash to London to Fabric, where Georgina's brother knew someone who knew someone who could get us all in.

We went to bed in our trackie bums and hoodies, our party dresses and shoes and make-up in our gym bags by our beds. Miss Cribbe turned our lights off at ten and we even let her give us big beardy kisses on our cheeks. In fact, we even let Misty lick us to keep Miss Cribbe sweet.

'Aren't you lovely little girlsies? Misty loves her wittle girlsie-whirlsies, doesn't she, Misty?'

Misty showed her love with a big smelly fart and Miss Cribbe bustled her out of the room as if nothing had happened.

Actually, none of us hated Misty nearly as much now since she'd weed on Honey's duvet.

As soon as the clock hit half-past ten, we all snuck downstairs and climbed out of the bursar's window. Honey (we had to include her or she would have told on us),

Clemmie and Arabella were already outside waiting for us.

We dashed into Puller's Woods and changed into our party gear, hiding our gym bags under leaves and fallen branches.

The plan – perfect in all its details – was to dash to the train station and catch the 23:23 to London (having successfully dodged guard dogs, security men and the electric barbed-wire fencing that surrounded the school grounds).

Once in London we would dance ourselves stupid at Fabric and pull older fit boys before catching the 6:03 back to the station.

It was the perfect plan. Next year we would regale the Year Ten girls with tales of *our* Midnight Raving.

When we got back from London, we'd dig our bags back out from their hiding places and change back into our trackie bums and hoodies and stick our clubbing gear back in our bags, hide them back under the leaves and jog off to breakfast. If anyone saw us dashing back to our rooms, we'd simply say we'd been for a run. How athletic and disciplined were we?

We'd then collect our gym bags from the woods at lunch, giving the smokers a chance for a quick fag.

Like I said, the perfect plan . . .

Unfortunately, the guard dogs discovered us just as we finished changing – which meant I only got as far as up an oak tree while a vicious, bloodthirsty Alsatian barked and bared its fearsome teeth at me from below.

The other girls, who didn't share my fear of dogs, tried to persuade me to leg it with them, but my dog didn't look like the type to let me escape with my legs.

Honey didn't even bother with me or anyone else. She just ran off back to the dorm and eventually the other girls followed, although they at least promised that they would come back and save me later.

I watched them disappear through the woods, hotly pursued by the dogs (not mine). I guess all our cross-country running hadn't been for nothing, as none of them was dragged down and mauled.

Half an hour later my dog was still growling and salivating at the thought of tearing me limb from limb. I started to cry, imagining myself being discovered by a security guy and reported to Sister Constance and being excluded from the trip to the village school in Gambia.

'Talk about random,' I whimpered to myself and then it happened.

A torch illuminated my face. The security guys had finally found me. I began to cry harder, not that I thought tears would in any way get me out of this . . .

'Calypso?'

I looked down. Instead of the burly, mean security guy I was expecting, there was Billy, standing at the foot of my tree and grinning from ear to ear. He had the dog by the collar.

'I've often dreamed of what you girls get up to at Saint Augustine's after lights out, but I have to admit this particular fantasy hasn't featured.'

'Oh, shut up,' I said. I couldn't help smiling, even though I tried my best to look cool, collected and unamused.

'Nice dress.'

'Thanks.'

The dog was whimpering and licking Billy's hand now.

'Do you usually dress up for midnight tree-climbing?' he asked.

'Always. A girl can never be too stylish.'

I couldn't believe I was being so fabulously collected. I mean, the quality of my repartee was phenomenal. Dorothy Parker – the writer, not the rabbit – would be proud.

'The grey knickers being the *pièce de résistance*, of course,' he added.

I was wearing my big grey knickers – well, they'd started off white, but Matron had managed to turn them grey in the wash along with all my bras and gym skirts. Unlike the other girls' parents, Sarah and Bob wouldn't allow me to wear sexy Calvin Klein knickers. 'Not at your age, sweetheart!' Bob had ruled, and at thirty pounds a pair I simply didn't have the resources – not even with my increased allowance.

'So, are you coming down, then?' he asked. 'Or do you usually wait for dawn to break?'

Ha, ha, very amusing. But see, here was the thing. Climbing up the tree had been a breeze; I'd been driven by pure adrenaline. But clambering down without looking graceless, destroying my dress and scratching myself to pieces was another matter.

'Shall I catch you?' he asked, sensing my hesitation.

I know it sounds like a nice offer, but if you'd seen the smirk on his face you would have wanted to slap it.

'Well . . . ?'

God, I so wanted to say no.

'It's fine – just sort of throw yourself backwards and fall and I'll be here to catch you. That way you won't scratch yourself.'

Yaah, right.

But I did it anyway. OK, so it wasn't my most graceful moment – plopping backwards out of a tree into the arms of a gorgeous boy who made me feel all wobbly inside. But it was nice. Especially the part where he held me in his arms for a bit, before placing me on the ground. (Note: He smelled delish.) The Alsatian even gave me a little lick.

For a minute I thought Billy was going to kiss me – or rather, that I was going to kiss him – but then I remembered Poppy and started brushing the bark off my dress dementedly.

'You're seeing Freddie, aren't you?' he went.

'Erm, well, I'm not actually sure.'

Billy laughed.

'You're seeing Poppy, though,' I reminded him.

'I so am not. That's what I've just been doing at Saint Augustine's. I told her in the break we weren't an item, but she kept texting me and pretending we were. I figured I'd better have a face-to-face with her.'

'Just now?'

He nodded. 'Yaah, just now. What, do you think I just escaped from Eades and struggled with the electric barbed-wire fencing for a stroll in the woods?'

'So it's all over with Poppy?' I pretended to be all casual and cool about it – and not turning bright red.

'Yes, but that's enough about me. Tell me about you and Freddie. What's the deal?'

I wished I had a simple answer. Even more important, I wished I knew what I wanted the simple answer to be.

Then suddenly Billy whispered, 'Shit, I've got to leg it – so do you. Here comes a security man. I'll text you.'

I didn't have time to ruminate on our encounter as I sprinted back to the dorm.

I told Georgina and Star about Billy in a whispered voice. It all sounded very nice and romantic, but how was he going to get my mobile number?

'Is it possible to fancy two boys at the same time?' I asked Star as we were lying in bed, too exhilarated by the evening's events to sleep.

'Absolutely, darling,' Georgina pitched in. 'In fact, it's normal.'

I wasn't so sure, though. The thing with Freddie was very troubling, what with all his security men and the paparazzi, but then, he is a prince, so maybe that's all part of the royal package?

On the other hand, Billy was sooo fit and hadn't given me the least bit of trouble. In fact, he'd saved me from a ferocious dog and a tree.

Then again, I couldn't stop thinking of the night I'd pulled Freddie and how lovely kissing him had been.

I could see I was going to have a lot on my mind over the summer holidays.

Calypso's fencing terms and English words

FENCING TERMS

attack *au fer*: an attack that is prepared by deflecting an opponent's blade

bout: a single fight, usually lasting around six minutes

compound attack: an attack incorporating two or more movements

corps-à-corps: literally body-to-body – physical contact between fencers during a bout (illegal in sabre)

disengagement: a way to continue attacking after being parried

en garde: the 'ready' position fencers take before play is called

épée: one of the three fencing weapons. It has a pointed blade, like foil but with the blade mounted on either a pistol or French grip. The blade is fluted and roughly triangular. The target is the whole body

flèche: a way of delivering an attack – the attacker leaps to make the attack and then passes the opponent at a run. French word for 'arrow'

flunge: an attack specific to sabre – a type of *flèche* attack in which the legs don't cross

foil: one of the three fencing weapons – usually the weapon on which you would learn. It has a pointed blade with a plastic bobble on the end. The target is the body, excluding arms, legs and head

lamé: jacket made of interwoven wire and fabric

parry: defensive move; a block. **Parry of quinte:** in sabre, a parry where the blade is held above the head to protect from head cuts

piste: fourteen-metre-long combat area on which a bout is fought

plastron: padded under-jacket to protect the torso (where most hits land)

point: the tip of a weapon's blade

pool: in competition, a fencing team is divided into equal groups, called *pools*

president: referee or arbiter of the bout

retire: retreat

riposte: an offensive action made immediately after a parry of the opponent's attack

sabre: one of the three fencing weapons – the only cutting weapon. It differs markedly in shape from foil and *épée* in that it is flatter and the point is folded back on itself to form a small loop. The hand is protected by a guard. Points are scored both by hits made with the point of the blade and cuts made with the blade, but most commonly by cuts. The entire weapon, including the guard, registers hits. The target is everything above the line formed by the crease where the legs join the trunk when a fencer is in the *en garde* position

salle: a fencing hall or club

salute: once formal, now a casual acknowledgement of one's opponent and referee at the start of a bout

seeding: the process of eliminating fencers from their pools, based on the results of their bouts

supermans: a fencing exercise – a holding stance used for warming up, so called because the fist is raised like Superman's before he flies

ENGLISH WORDS

a 15: a film you need to be 15 years or older to view (like PG-13 in America)

arse: *derrière*. To make an arse of yourself means to embarrass yourself

bin: where you put your rubbish (garbage can)

blag: to talk your way into/out of something, or to fake something

blue: blue paper given to write lines on, a minor punishment

bollocks: literally means testicles, but used to mean nonsense or ridiculous

bottle out: chicken out, lose your nerve. 'Bottle' is another word for nerve, so you can also lose your bottle

bursar: school's financial manager

champagne socialist: a rich person who claims to have left-wing politics while enjoying a luxurious lifestyle (i.e., champagne)

chubba: chubby, overweight person

Co-codamol: an over-the-counter medication to treat high temperatures or pain

common: slang for vulgar, of low social status. **Well common:** of very low status or trashy. (Note: You can be rich and still common)

cosh: a heavy stick or bludgeoning implement. To be under the cosh is to be under pressure

Coventry (to be sent to): to be ostracized

crisps: potato chips

cupboard: storage closet

cut: to ignore someone, to look right through them

delish: delicious

dressing down: telling off

en-suite: bathroom attached to bedroom

exeat: weekend for which pupils attending boarding school may go home, usually every three weeks

fag: cigarette

fairy bread: open sandwich made with sliced white bread, buttered, sprinkled with tiny, brightly coloured sugary freckles; usually served to very young children at parties

fancy: to find someone attractive

fit: cute, hot, attractive. Girls and boys use the term to describe the opposite sex. (Note: A girl would never refer to another girl as fit; she'd say *stunning*)

form/year: girls start boarding at age eleven (Year Seven) and the 'years' go up to Year Eleven (age fifteen/sixteen). The final two years are referred to as the Lower Sixth and Upper Sixth (age sixteen/seventeen and seventeen/eighteen)

frock up: dress up

GCSEs: General Certificate of Secondary Education. A standardized test most students take upon finishing secondary school. Comparable to the SAT.

ginga: (first '*g*' is hard, rhymes with *singer*) a derogatory term for a person with red hair

glandular fever: mononucleosis

Hon: as in The Honorable Georgina Smart-Arse – child of a life peer, baron or viscount

Horsey Girls: rich, spoiled and posh girls who own their own horses

house mistress: woman in charge of a boarding school house, sometimes referred to as a house mother

HRH: His (or Her) Royal Highness

It Girl: society girl with a large media profile

Jelly Babies: soft, brightly coloured candies shaped like babies

kit: equipment or outfit for sports, an event or activity

knickers: panties

Lady: (as in Lady Portia Doo-la-la-lee) daughter of a duke, marquis or earl; female life peers or wives of hereditary peers are also Ladies

leg it: make a run for it

Lower Sixth: see **form**

lycée: French school in which classes are taught in French

mad: eccentric, crazy or unreasonable – out there!

mental: see **mad**

mobile: cell phone

OTT: over the top; outrageous or extreme behaviour or style

PA: personal assistant

piss-take: tease, to make fun of someone, either maliciously or fondly

pleb: short for plebeian, a member of the lower social classes

prat: idiot, fool

pukka: authentic, proper

pull: to make out, score, kiss, etc.

queue: line. To queue is to wait in a line

quid: slang for pound (British currency)

readies: slang for folding money, actual notes

rinse: to totally decimate your opponent in sport or debate

rhyming slang: Cockney rhyming slang – the use of rhyming words rather than actual words. Originally a code language used by criminals in London's East End so that police and informants wouldn't understand. Now used as general slang

rusticated: suspended from school without being given schoolwork to carry on with – meaning that on return, the pupil is further disadvantaged by having to catch up

safe: OK (see **sorted**)

Sky (TV): cable

slack down: to disrespect someone, ignore their instructions

slapper: slut

Sloane: posh, snooty girl (named after Sloane Street and Square, an upscale area in London)

smart: sassy. Can also mean fashionably attired

social: interschool dance (girls and boys)

sorted: 'no problem'

sovereign ring: a large, flashy ring with a gold coin on it. Associated with common people and gangsters

spots: pimples, zits

squaddie: soldier

stick: a hard time. To give someone stick is to tease them

suspended: sent home from school with schoolwork (less harsh than a rustication)

swot: someone who studies very hard; egghead

term: three terms make up a school year. Winter term is before Christmas; spring term is between Christmas and Easter; summer term is between Easter and the summer holiday

ticked off: told off, reprimanded

toff: snobby aristocrat

torch: flashlight

trackie bums: sweatpants

trainers: sneakers

trousers: pants

tuck: snack foods you can bring to boarding school – junk food

tuck in: pig out

wardrobe: closet

year: see **form**

Acknowledgements

Enormous amounts of praise and gratitude must go to my gorgeous children for entertaining me with their stories of boarding school life, especially my eldest son, Zad, for being a brilliant but patient *sabreur*. Thanks also to the Old Girls and Old Boys of Saint Mary's Ascot, Eton, Benenden, and other boarding schools around England where clearly a good time was had by all! Also, to Eric Hewitson for his map of Saint Augustine's; my inspirational agent, Laura Dail, for her vision; Victoria Arms at Bloomsbury USA for knowing the real deal about English girls boarding schools; and the team at Piccadilly – Brenda, Yasemin, et al. – for being fab.